Krissi was born in Yorkshire and now lives in Dorset on the Isle of Purbeck with her husband, Bob. After spending the last 20 years in the world of estate agency, she is now retired. So with the family grown up, she is free to spend her time indulging in her love of walking, gardening, volunteering and, at last, her passion for writing.

For my husband, Bob, with love.

Krissi Morris

TORN BETWEEN TWO

AUSTIN MACAULEY PUBLISHERS™

LONDON • CAMBRIDGE • NEW YORK • SHARJAH

A CIP catalogue record for this title is available from the British Library.

ISBN 9781788238472 (Paperback)
ISBN 9781788238489 (Hardback)
ISBN 9781788238496 (E-Book)
www.austinmacauley.com

First Published (2018)
Austin Macauley Publishers Ltd™
25 Canada Square
Canary Wharf
London
E14 5LQ

Acknowledgements

Writing for me, like many, began as a hobby; writing short stories that soon became an obsession, turning into this—my first novel. I'm very fortunate to have some lovely friends—Sybil Voysey, Brenda Walker, Anne Wright and Jenny Pearson—and I thank them all so much for their encouragement. Special thanks go to Clair Bossons, who read my novel checking for errors and inconsistencies.

Chapter 1

'Alright, Mother, but please, no surprises.' Alistair let out a sigh, snapped his phone shut and resigned to another boring weekend down in sleepy Dorset. He threw his bag onto the backseat of his wonderful but 'unsuitable' car, according to his mother, pulled out into the traffic, turned up the radio and gave himself up to the journey.

Dusk had fallen and the last rays of sunshine were disappearing as he turned into the top of the lane that led to his parents' home. He could just make out the lights below, a smile creeping across his face at the thought of his mother having cooked all day, assuming he only ate convenience food in London, while his father tried to read the paper in front of the fire. The big old farmhouse had been built in the early eighteenth century and Alistair and his brother were both born here. Thoughts of his brother crept into his mind as they always did when he came back home, pushing them away, he pulled over and stopped. He took off his glasses, squeezing his eyes shut, pinching the bridge of his nose; he exhaled deeply wondering how he had let himself get into this position yet again. It had been a long day. He stared at the roof line of the old house with its twisted brick chimneys stark against the darkening skies, birds screeching overhead and swirling through the air diving for the trees. He let out the clutch and started down the hill once more.

A loud thud brought his mind back from his reverie as something or someone landed on the bonnet of his car; he slammed on the brakes and jumped out as a horse reared and galloped away.

'What the bloody hell...?' He stared at the retreating horse and heard a moan; the beam of his headlights silhouetted someone on the ground. 'Oh...shit!' Grabbing his mobile he called his father, who could be with him in less than two minutes. 'Dad...Dad, I've knocked someone off their horse. I'm just at the top of the lane, please hurry.'

'I'm on my way. Don't try to move them and, Alistair...call an ambulance,' said George.

Alistair knelt down and he could see a trickle of blood making its way down the face of a young woman. His hand shaking as he pushed a wisp of her hair, sticky with blood, out of her eyes and whispered, 'Help is on the way, please don't move.'

She moaned again opening her eyes, trying to push up onto one elbow as she let out a yelp.

'What...what happened? Who are you?' She looked at Alistair as she screwed up her face and twisted herself around scanning the lane.

'Alistair Warren, please don't move. Help is on the way, I am so sorry, I just didn't see you. Are you alright?'

'No, I'm not alright. My arm, I think it's broken. Where's my horse?' She struggled to sit up and Alistair reached out his hand tentatively wanting to help but afraid of making things worse.

'I...I don't know, but I'll go and find him. Please don't move anymore, my dad is just coming and an ambulance is on its way.'

'I need to find Falcon, he will be frightened. I can get him and go to the hospital later.'

'Oh no, you can't. Look, here's my dad now, let him take care of you and I promise I will find Falcon,' Alistair stood up and glanced down the lane, his heart thudding in his chest. He rubbed his hands up and down his jeans, peering into the gloom.

Minutes later, the ambulance arrived and was soon heading up the lane, its blue light flashing.

'Is she going to be alright, Dad?' Alistair hung his head, 'In this light, I just didn't see her.' He lifted his hands and plunged them deep into his pockets, hunching his shoulders, despair on his face.

'She'll be alright. Let's get you home. I have a bottle of whisky tucked away; you look like you could do with one.' The horse had wandered back on his own and George retrieved him. 'Look, don't worry, go and let your mother know what has happened, she will be worried. I will get the horse home, and go see Lucy's parents.'

Alistair climbed back into his car. He shook his head pushing his hair back, glancing at his watch; he picked up his phone twisting it over and over before opening it and sending Molly a text. He released the brake and crawled down the lane. Glancing up at the stars and mumbled, 'What a mess!' He parked his car and dragged his bag into the house.

'Alistair, darling, are you alright? I have been so worried,' cried Alice rushing to bring him into her embrace.

'Mother, please…' Alistair fought to pull his mother's arms from around his neck. 'I'm fine, don't fuss. I just need a drink.' He pulled out a chair taking off his glasses and dropping them onto the table.

'I'll put the kettle on. I'm sorry, Alistair, but I am just so pleased to see you and I wasn't sure if you had been hurt too.' Alice turned and clattered in the cupboard pulling out mugs and teabags as George bustled into the kitchen straightening his waistcoat, grinning at them both, he announced, 'Lucy is going to be fine, bruises and a broken wrist, lucky you were driving so

11

slowly, Alistair, I suggest you go and see her tomorrow and apologise.' He pulled out a chair and sat at the table sipping his tea, 'argh, I think I can find something stronger than that. Give me a minute and I'll go and find it.'

Leaning back in his seat, Alistair let out a sigh of relief; he had not been able to think of anything else but this girl, not even his mother's cooking or the thought of Molly had helped. He rubbed his forehead, relishing the glass of whisky from his father. After dinner they retired to the snug but Alistair wasn't in the mood tonight for chit chat.

'I'm sorry, Mum, but I am going to get an early night, I'm all done in.' He grabbed his phone and headed for the stairs.

The next morning, after a fitful night's sleep, Alistair was grateful to see the dawn creeping in through the curtains. He could hear his mother downstairs as he clambered out of bed. He pushed up the window, breathing in the reviving fresh air. The only sounds he could hear were the stream as it flowed swiftly down towards the sea and the chorus of birds, nothing like the noise of the Thames as it teemed with boats back and forth.

'You're up and about early darling,' said Alice waving a frying pan, '…breakfast?'

'No thanks, Mum, I'm going to take some flowers to Lucy Hamilton and try to apologise. Will she be in Dorchester or Poole, do you think?' He planted a kiss on her cheek by way of apology.

'Your father has already telephoned and Lucy has been discharged, no concussion, I expect she will be home by now, coffee?' Alistair sat at the kitchen table staring out of the window, his phone buzzed and he picked it up. He licked his lips as a smile played at the corners of his mouth at the sight of a text from Molly. Alice made coffee and toast pushing it in front of him, saying, 'She has just moved back home with her parents at Honeysuckle Cottage…you know, by the village

12

shop. I don't know why, I shall have to find out. You could go and see her, her mum will be in the shop…lovely family.'

Alistair couldn't help smiling, his mother's legendary matchmaking at work again already, but this time, he didn't mind. Lucy was one person, he thought that he would like to get to know better. He sipped his coffee for a moment.

'And I suppose you know all about her career, her father's job and…boyfriends?' He added feeling a bit guilty about the boyfriend question but he had to know.

'Why, of course. Her father spends every spare minute at the steam railway down in Swanage, loves being covered in oil and grease. I don't know what it is with you men. Your father is always tinkering in the shed when he is not in his study, never happier than when he is getting dirty,' she laughed.

'And Lucy, what does she do?' he lathered his toast with marmalade spilling some onto the table.

'Oh well, Lucy is a midwife, boyfriends…I am not so sure about.' Alistair caught her looking at him from the corner of her eye, coffee pot poised.

He grinned, 'Mother, how do you know so much about people?'

'Oh, that's not difficult in a small village. Now go and see Lucy and don't forget those flowers.'

Alistair decided to drive into Trentmouth preferring to get a proper bunch of flowers rather than the measly looking efforts from the local garage. Hesitating by the gate to Honeysuckle Cottage, he took a deep breath and stood for a few moments surveying it, his hand on the latch. It was built of local Purbeck stone with a thatch roof that had seen better days and *it just had to be covered in Wisteria, didn't it*? He thought. It stood for everything he had tried to get away from, but not today. He lifted the heavy metal door knocker, it slipped from his fingers banging louder than he wished.

'Bloody hell,' he muttered.

'Come in, the door's open,' came the response to his knock. The click of the latch made his nerves jangle, adrenaline surged around his body. *This is quite ridiculous*, he thought, *I am only dropping off some flowers*.

'Umm, hello,' he called poking his head around the door. 'Alistair Warren, I've come to see Lucy.' He glanced around the cosy cottage. Lucy was sitting by the inglenook fire, book open on her lap, her wrist in plaster. 'I'm so sorry,' blurted Alistair. He walked across the room holding out the flowers. 'I'm so sorry,' he said again, 'I have brought these and I…I want to apologise.' He found himself staring; she was captivating with her penetrating deep chocolate coloured eyes and long dark hair.

'Better put them in water then,' she snapped. 'You will find a vase under the sink in the kitchen.' She sounded as if she hadn't even heard his apology. He retreated to find a vase, feeling like a naughty schoolboy; at least this gave him chance to regain his composure. *What did I expect?* He thought, *I suppose I have brought her world to a standstill.*

'Can I make you a cup of tea?' he called as he fumbled with the flowers.

'Yes, please,' her voice softer now making him even more nervous, seeing her in the kitchen beside him. 'I will do the flowers, you make the tea,' said Lucy. They settled back by the fire and Alistair tried to apologise yet again, explaining how he had been distracted by the lights in the valley; Lucy sat observing him without showing any signs of accepting his apology. He groaned inside.

'I know all about you…' Lucy hesitated, placing her cup of tea down on the table and picking up a biscuit. She glanced sideways at him, 'Your mother is always talking to my mum in the shop, telling her how well you are doing in the city. Still single…?'

He looked at her feeling heat spreading up his throat, swallowing hard, he said, 'Well, I'm due back in London tomorrow, but I do ride, so if you would like me to exercise your horse over the next couple of days, I would be only too pleased. It's the least I can do. And yes, I am still single.' Alistair stood up to leave, 'I think I'd better go.'

'No thanks, about the horse, I mean. Molly Craven, the vet, is taking care of him. Goodbye.' Having been dismissed like a contestant on a game show, Alistair left stunned by what had just happened and...she knows Molly. The thought of her knowing Molly chased around in his brain. This was not good news and he wondered how much Molly had told her. He climbed into his car, his head buzzing, gripped the steering wheel and stared ahead. Bad enough, she thought him a reckless driver but what else must she be thinking? He drove back home distracted, turning the conversation with Lucy over and over in his head. He leapt up the steps two at a time and burst into the kitchen.

'Mother, what have you been saying about me? I feel like someone to be pitied,' he broke off, red faced, as he spat the words in her direction.

'What are you talking about, darling? I have only ever wanted the best for you,' she cried.

'No, Mother, you wanted me to become a doctor and follow Dad into general practice. You never thought about what I might want; will you please stop meddling in my life and leave me alone.' Silence engulfed the room. It had finally been said and it hung in the air. Alice put the wooden spoon, she was using, down and pulled out a handkerchief.

She sniffed, 'I'm sorry but I really do not know what you are talking about, Alistair. What have I said that's so wrong?' She stared at him twisting her handkerchief. George bustled into the kitchen, newspaper in hand, and stared at them both.

'Now come on you two, what is this all about? Alistair, apologise to your mother.'

'No, Dad. I'm going home. I've had enough for one weekend.' His father raised his eyebrows, open mouthed. He turned to look at Alice.

'Oh, George,' she wailed as she dashed across the kitchen, burying her face on his shoulder.

'It's alright, my dear. I know you meant well, but you must let him work things out for himself,' he hugged her close.

'Dad…' Alistair tried to speak, 'Mum is always trying to partner me off with some girl or another, every time I visit. I don't want a wife and children. I'm happy as I am,' he hung his head.

'I know, Son, but your mother and I…well, we always hoped for grandchildren, your happiness is more important. Just visit once in a while, eh?' He lifted Alice's chin and looked into her puffy eyes. 'That's right, my love? Isn't it?' Alice nodded turning to look at Alistair.

'I'm sorry, I didn't realise,' she let out another sob.

'I'm sorry too, Mother, I didn't mean to shout but I have to leave. Would it be alright if I came again next weekend or I could stay in a hotel if you'd rather?'

George dropped his arms and Alice took a step towards her son. 'Of course, you can. We love having you stay whenever you can make it,' she added reaching up to kiss his cheek and Alistair placed an arm around her frail body with a gentle hug.

'Alright, Son, you go. I'll look after your mother,' George walked across to his wife and enfolded her in his embrace. Alistair picked up his bag and turned to walk away.

'Sorry,' he muttered.

He set off back to London, his thoughts darting between Lucy, his mother and a side of his father that he had not seen before. It was unnerving, he tried to make sense of it all; such a scene of tender domesticity, he had not expected. And

Lucy…true, he had startled her horse and caused her broken wrist but frosty! He could not fathom this reaction. His head was all over the place, not understanding what had happened this weekend. His life was a mess and he hadn't even seen Molly. He resolved that despite everything, he would be back in Trentmouth to try and straighten things out, not only with Lucy but also with his mother. *Molly,* he thought, *how I miss you.*

Chapter 2

'Coo-ee, Lucy, only me,' Molly bounced in. 'I've given Falcon a good workout and he's back in the field, no worse for his fright yesterday.' She closed the door and turned to see Lucy dabbing at her eyes. 'Lucy, what on earth is wrong?'

'Oh nothing, it's just that Alistair Warren came this morning with a bunch of flowers thinking that would put everything right,' she sniffed and pulled out another tissue. At the mention of Alistair, Molly stiffened. She sat down next to Lucy and put an arm around her shoulders.

'Oh Luce, come on, it's not that bad. Is that what this is really about? Or is there more to it? Come on, you can tell me.'

'I suppose that I'm just…well, a bit down,' she said at last. 'You know everything just seems to be going wrong and I…miss Lionel.'

'Right…well, let me see if there is a cup of tea left in the pot and we can talk about it.' Molly pushed herself up off the couch, tired this morning having attended a call out in the night to a cow having difficulty with a breach birth, then Falcon to attend to as well as morning surgery. 'Where does your mum keep the biscuits? Oh, here they are,' she rattled the tin, piled up the tray and turned to see Lucy forcing a smile onto her face. She put the tray down and picked up the poker raking out the ash and putting more logs onto the fire, making it flare up and spit sparks. She poured the tea and Lucy picked up a bourbon, crunching into it.

'I have never eaten so many biscuits. I will be putting on weight,' she laughed. 'Come on, Molly, you never did tell me the whole story about exactly what happened that night at the Warrens?' Molly detected a slight grin.

'Not a lot to tell. Alistair was in the snug with his dad, and he stared at me in surprise when I walked in. Mrs Warren, Alice, greeted me in the hallway and I could hear Alistair saying to his father "Not another of mother's offerings, when will she leave me alone." Mrs Warren either didn't hear him or pretended not to.' Molly paused her eyes glazed over for a moment as she shuddered.

'That much I know, it's what happened. Next, I want to know.' Lucy leaned over and rubbed the back of Molly's hand. Molly gulped her tea and dipped into the biscuit tin.

'Well, as you can imagine, I had no intention from then on to be anything but polite and try to escape as soon as possible...more tea? I could do with one.'

'Yes, please. That can't be it?' Lucy flopped back adjusting her cushion.

'Not quite. Alistair sat quiet all evening, the atmosphere felt like treacle. I tried to ask him about his job in London, did he go to the theatre, you know, that sort of thing. I had to say something, I just couldn't sit there but he didn't ask me a single question; he made it quite clear that he wasn't happy about the whole arrangement. Anyway, Mrs Warren asked me about my job, and I told her about my finals. She feigned surprise as she already knew all about me including my shoe size!' They both giggled. 'I said that I had become a vegetarian and she apologised that the main course was lamb!' They both fell about laughing.

'...But you're not vegetarian, Molly. Why did you say that?'

'For a bit of fun. It was getting rather tiresome and I thought that might stir things up a bit,' she smiled. 'He could

19

have the pick of any girl he wanted, but he either plays the field without his mother knowing or maybe he really isn't interested in women at all. Maybe he's gay? Who knows? Anyway, why the sudden interest in Alistair Warren?'

'Just curious...I don't think he's gay. According to my Mum, he will be back here next weekend and will want to come and see me,' Lucy pulled at the fringe on the edge of the cushion.

'Guilty conscience if you ask me. You should sue him, get some compensation; he can afford it,' smiled Molly.

'No, I couldn't do that. I just wanted to know more about him, that's all.'

'Hmm, well, to my knowledge, he has never taken a single girl out from around here. Perhaps, we are not good enough for him; I mean we are all country girls in wellies most of the time. When do we get the chance to wine and dine or fly to Paris for the weekend,' laughed Molly.

'More's the pity,' Lucy let out a sigh, 'I could do with a weekend in Paris.'

'Yes...but not with Alistair Warren,' Molly snorted. Lucy didn't reply.

'He must be feeling guilty. He only makes the village every few months or so and then under protest. I would keep out of his way if I were you,' Lucy's eyebrows shot up.

'He doesn't need to visit me. I will soon be back on my feet. I haven't the time to be sitting around. I need a job,' she declared with sudden urgency. 'I must find my own place and leave Mum and Dad alone. It was only meant as a bolt hole for a bit.'

'I wouldn't worry about it. I don't know where I'd be without my parents. I was shocked and then grateful when they decided to live in Spain, selling all the land and leaving me in the farmhouse. There's even a little holiday cottage that I look after in lieu of rent.'

'I am grateful to them and Mum is enjoying fussing me, but I have been away for so long and forgotten how claustrophobic their life is,' Lucy continued to pick at the fringe unravelling it.

'So, come on then, if you are up to it, I want to know all about Lionel. Isn't he the love of your life?' Molly claimed the last custard cream and tucked her feet up under her, mug of tea poised.

'Yes, you could say that. When we met, I thought that he was divine, older than me but that didn't matter. He was charming, his dark green eyes felt as if he could just know everything about you by looking at you. Oh, and his voice...' Lucy shuddered, '...his voice, deep and smooth like melting dark chocolate on your tongue.' A tear had squeezed its way into the corner of Lucy's eye, and Molly watched as it tumbled out. Lucy rubbed at it and sniffed, 'I spent that first day in a dream world. Sounds stupid, I know. Nothing bothered me, even changing dressings or emptying a bedpan.' She took a deep breath. 'So, you see, when I found him with someone else in our bed...' tears flowed and Molly grabbed the tissues and waited for the torrent to subside.

'You don't have to tell me if you don't want to,' she said. 'I didn't realise. Your mum told everyone that you had bought a house together and well...she thought that there would be a wedding.'

'Ha, not a chance, but then that suited me too; my career was going well and I had plans you know. It's just that I fell for him big time and never expected...so here I am. You could say that I ran away, I did runaway, it's over.' Lucy looked down at her hands and then at Molly. 'There you have it, my story.'

'So, where is Dr Lionel Maddox now?' she asked.

'Still in our house...our house, listen at me, it used to be our house. All the details haven't been finalised yet but he is going to buy my share, then I will be free of him and I can start again. I think that I will stay in Dorset and build my career here

21

if I can get a job.' Lucy turned and stared out of the window, her eyes fixed on somewhere else.

'Hey, come back,' Molly snapped her fingers. 'You've gone, left me. Come on, say it out loud, you can tell me,' she coaxed.

'Sorry, I'm always saying sorry these days. I thought that we were forever. I know you never met him, he always said that he didn't have time to visit my parents, now I know why. Mum and Dad came to us one year but before they arrived, Lionel said he had a conference that he had forgotten to tell me about, and yet again, they didn't get to meet him. I think that they thought that I had made him up,' she laughed.

'That's better,' cried Molly. 'Time for a cup of tea, I think; unless I can persuade you to have a glass of wine.'

'Oh, a glass of wine is a much better idea, make mine a large red one.'

They both laughed and Molly went off to find a corkscrew.

The next morning, Molly couldn't help going over and over the story from Lucy the night before. She leaned on the kitchen sink watching the hens scratching and pecking about the yard and downed a glass of water and two headache tablets, suffering after drinking too much wine with Lucy. Her conversation with Alistair rattling around her head, making her feel nauseous; she rewound the whole sorry tale, it seemed to be on a loop in her brain.

'Sorry, I didn't get to see you this weekend,' he had begun, 'bit of a mess. I expect Lucy told you all about it?'

'Yes, but I missed you. Couldn't you find even five minutes to come and see me?'

'I wanted to…had a row with mother and left sooner than I expected,' he paused.

'Oh dear, Lucy said you were coming back again this weekend. Not like you, two weekends in a row…but I need to talk to you so why don't we have dinner. I'll cook here for us.'

'Maybe, I'm not sure yet. No promises.'

Molly made a dash to the outside loo and threw up, her head aching. She collapsed into the armchair that resided by the Aga and Rex crawled out of his bed and padded across the kitchen, flopping by her feet. He pushed his wet nose against her leg; Molly reached down and ruffled his fur.

'Hey boy, I'm alright. No need for you to worry.' Rex looked up, picking up his ears and turning his head on one side, Molly smiled. She began to feel better and clutching her tea wandered down to the allotment, sitting on the bench with Rex beside her. Pretending to be vegetarian, she had to continue her lie saying that working with animals, she had seen a different side to the piece of meat on her plate and somehow couldn't face a lamb chop, a bacon sandwich or a bit of steak anymore. She laughed at herself feeling quite virtuous, eating an omelette instead of a rack of lamb. Although on reflection, having seen some of the conditions the animals are kept in at abattoirs, she was appalled and was now a fully signed up member of the Vegetarian Society, much to her parents' disgust.

Molly admired her vegetable plot, doing her best to keep it organic. Green shoots were appearing and she would soon be planting runner beans and her next crop of potatoes. She had become an expert in growing tomatoes, beetroot, carrots and salads as well as fruit. Hugh Fearnley-Whittingstall had a lot to answer for with his series on vegetables. She couldn't quite give up fish though, loving salmon, prawns and seabass. She sat turning her phone over and over and then with a sigh, she pressed the number for Stella.

'Hi, Sis, what are you up to?' she tried to sound up beat.

'Hi, Molly, I'm very busy but I have a minute. What's up?'

'Oh, nothing much, I just thought that I would catch up. How's the chocolate wedding cake coming along?'

'Great, bit of a fiddle, but that's not why you rang, come on out with it,' Stella sounded exasperated.

'It's Alistair.'

'What's he done now? You should dump him, he's been messing you about for far too long.'

'That's easy for you to say but I do love him and well, I'm sure you're right; if I can't trust him, what's the point?'

'Hey, come on you, this isn't like the Molly I know. Look, after this wedding on Saturday, I'm free and the girls miss their auntie. Why don't you come over for a night or two and we can have a proper catch up, send out for a pizza and down a couple of bottles of red. What do you say?'

'Okay, sounds good, you talked me into it. See you Friday.'

'Great. Love you, bye.'

Molly felt better and pulled out a few weeds; she looked up at the watery spring sunshine, trying to absorb what little warmth she could. Her thoughts turning again to Alistair; after the almost disastrous evening at the Warren's, Molly had not expected to hear from him or them again, but then a chance meeting with Alistair whilst she was out horse riding changed everything. She had seen him first and had decided to dismount and admire the view, she knew that he couldn't help but see her.

'Hello, Molly, what a glorious day,' he looked awkward and embarrassed.

'Yes, it is, you staying on a few extra days?' she had glanced at him over her shoulder as she pulled off her riding hat letting her long curly red hair fall about her shoulders. She watched his face as she allowed her hair to fly in the breeze and then she pulled it to one side.

'Well...' he had stuttered, 'I don't get down here too often and I enjoy riding...look, I'm sorry about the other week, you know at my parents' place.'

'Don't worry about it. I had fun anyway,' she tossed her hair again, raking her fingers through it.

'I just wanted you to know that I admire the way you stood by your principles, over the meat thing, that's all.'

Thinking back now, she couldn't quite remember how it happened but they went from near strangers to intimate lovers; their bodies entwined amid the cowslips and bluebells, ecstatic and soporific from love making, rolling in the grass. Alistair became a regular visitor to Trentmouth but always wanting to meet out horse riding, even though she had her home...and bed. Several months later, Molly had the opportunity of going up to London on a two-day course staying in a hotel, not far from his office. Alistair joined her at a charming vegetarian restaurant that he had discovered and over a candlelit dinner, they chatted about farming and banking; two more different lifestyles were hard to imagine. Molly wanted a more permanent relationship but Alistair was adamant about secrecy. Her eyes stung at the thought of losing him, she took a deep breath attempting to stop the moisture slipping onto her face; she brushed the embarrassing thing aside and picked up her gloves. *I must get back to work,* she thought closing the gate on her allotment.

Chapter 3

The events of the weekend plagued Alistair and not seeing Molly left him feeling uptight. He had found their relationship a fun diversion at first from his stressful life, and the last thing he had ever wanted was marriage; it had never been on his agenda. He had no time for all that commitment, despite his mother's craving for grandchildren. It wasn't down to him to fulfil their life for them. Now it was Molly applying pressure to him, wanting to tell his mother about them, but Alistair knew that once his mother had any idea, she would expect a wedding. What on earth should he do?

Alistair drove back to London with his head buzzing; he ran scenario after scenario through his mind. He wanted to see Lucy but how could he redeem himself? How could he extricate himself from Molly? Did he want to? Would Molly tell Lucy?

He was so wrapped up in himself and keeping their affair secret that he had forgotten that she had a life! A real life; one that didn't include him, his choice, and now, he was beginning to realise that he was missing out. Love…stupid nonsense invented by Hollywood, although he had to admit that he couldn't get these two women out of his mind; Molly and Lucy, they invaded his every thought. He was playing chess with his life! If he did this, would that happen? Or worse, could he see himself without either of them? And then there was his mother…what a mess!

The next morning, Alistair sat staring at his computer screen, his head aching.

'Hey, mate! What's wrong with you?' A voice broke into his silence. Alistair considered ignoring Bertie but he knew that wouldn't work for long. To buy time, he tried to deflect him.

'Oh, nothing much. I might go to the theatre tonight.' He continued to stare at the screen.

'You expect me to believe that. There's only one thing that would stop you working and that's a woman,' he smirked.

'Two,' he let out a sigh regretting his answer. Alistair glanced over at Bertie, who was grinning at him.

'Bloody hell, tell me more.' Bertie swung round to give Alistair his full attention. 'Come on, you can't stop now. I want to know who, what, when and why you didn't tell me before.' Alistair gave a brief update to Bertie who blew a low whistle. 'You lucky devil.'

'It's a bloody mess and I do not want mother to know either; she will have me married off so quick,' he half laughed.

'I don't know how you are going to keep it away from her. Both girls in the same village, I've got to hand it to you; you know how to get yourself into trouble, if you ask me.'

'Which I didn't,' Alistair snorted.

'If you ask me,' Bertie repeated, 'you should just enjoy yourself. Relax, have some fun and then stay away from Trentmouth or wherever it is you come from.'

'Easy for you to say. Believe it or not, I like Lucy and yes, Molly too, but I never intended more than fun with Molly, and now she is getting clingy and dropping hints about moving in together and telling mother.' Alistair thought of his mother, she doted on him and he didn't want to hurt her and Molly…they had a good thing going. Lucy, on the other hand, was getting under his skin. He tried to get back into commodities but today, they were not exciting him. He pushed his chair back and wandered over to the coffee machine. He downed an espresso in one and poured another; he rubbed his eyes pushing his glasses up on top of his head.

What an idiot. Why can't I just be honest and tell Molly that it's over? Is that what you really want to do? The voice in his head asked. 'What am I going to do?' he sighed out loud.

'Take the afternoon off.' Alistair spun round grinning at the sight of Bertie, he wasn't going mad.

'I might. I'm certainly going to take a long lunch.'

'Come on, I'll come with you.' Bertie grabbed his jacket and Alistair gave in. Over lunch, Alistair filled in the blanks, leaving Bertie with even more admiration.

'So, what are you going to do then? You are one lucky bloke.' He threw his napkin down onto the table, downed his wine and began to fiddle with the empty glass.

'Shall I come with you at the weekend?' He exhaled, looking up at Alistair.

'Hmm,' his first thought was an outright no, but on reflection, it wasn't such a bad idea; Bertie could be a good diversion, his mother would be delighted. 'Okay,' said Alistair. 'Why not, I've been meaning to take you down to the coast for a while,' he lied.

'Great. We will go in my car; I've been waiting to take the old girl on a decent run,' grinned Bertie. Alistair agreed and they made plans for Friday. Returning to the office, Alistair put both, Molly and Lucy, out of his mind and telephoned his mother.

'Of course, you can bring Bertie, dear. It will be good to meet him at last,' said Alice. 'What does he like to eat?'

'Anything you make, he will eat, Mother,' Alistair smiled to himself.

'Good as I am busy making lemon drizzle cake, banana bread and how about some fruit scones?'

'You don't need to go to all that trouble, Mother,' but Alistair knew that she would.

'You know I like cooking and it gives me an excuse,' she giggled. 'I was wondering about inviting Lucy, what do you think, Alistair? By way of an apology, of course, I mean.'

'No, Mother,' he said frostily. 'Let's just keep it simple and you can get to know Bertie. Where's Dad?'

'He's in the snug, keeping out of my way I expect. I will pass the phone to him and we will see you on Saturday.'

'Alistair, my boy, I hear you are coming at the weekend after all. Wonderful!'

Alistair missed talking to his dad, *if only Mother wasn't so overbearing*, he thought. He could picture him sitting in his study, a newspaper on his lap, his glasses pushed into his thinning hair, banished out of the way of Alice. He chuckled at that thought.

'Coffee...?' Alistair heard his mother say in the background.

'Yes, please,' his father called. 'I was wondering if you fancy a walk after lunch? It's such a lovely day.'

'No thanks, Dad. It's a bit far from London...but thanks for asking.'

'Sorry, Son. I have been trying to encourage your mother to go out a bit more. She works so hard and it isn't necessary, there are only the two of us.'

'Okay, Dad. Got to go, see you at the weekend. Bye.'

It was a beautiful day as Alistair and Bertie set off down to Dorset. The window wound right down, resting his elbow and humming to himself. Alistair was quiet. Bertie gave him a sideways glance.

'You've never told me much about your home town and family,' he quizzed. 'What's this place like?'

'Not much to tell, really. I was glad to leave the place to be honest. It's a sleepy little back water, the place people go to retire. It's all green fields, nothing happens there.' Alistair knew

29

that this was not entirely true but he had no intention of filling in any more blanks, at least not today.

'Doesn't sound very sleepy to me, there are at least two gorgeous girls in Trentmouth and you found them both,' he grinned.

'Mm, don't remind me. I still don't know how I am going to sort this one out.' Alistair looked out of the window and let his mind return to the 'two gorgeous girls' as Bertie put it.

'I am looking forward to meeting Molly and Lucy. I might be able to take one of them off your hands. You know help a mate in need and all that.'

Alistair threw his colleague a sharp look.

'I don't think so, old boy. That is not why I brought you down here; I don't expect you to do anything except entertain my parents.' He snapped, feeling suddenly unnerved, how dare he presume that he could take care of his problem so easily?

'Sorry,' said Bertie, 'I was just having a bit of fun. I didn't mean to rattle you; you've really got it bad, haven't you? Maybe you should forget them both, is it worth it?'

'No, I'm the one who should be sorry. I shouldn't have reacted like that. It's just such an awkward situation; I was happy with Molly till I knocked Lucy off her horse and now...' he trailed off leaving his thoughts unsaid. 'We're nearly there, take the next left, Bertie and we will head down to the coast a different way. I want to show you something before we get to Trentmouth.'

They turned down the spur road that led to Bournemouth and Alistair regaled Bertie with stories of funny, and sometimes risky, times spent boating in Poole harbour. They drove through Lilliput and on down to Sandbanks.

'Which one of these is your family pile then?' asked Bertie.

'No such luck, mate. These places are worth millions, we live on the Isle of Purbeck.'

30

'You live on an island?' Bertie gasped turning to look at Alistair as they drove onto the ferry, 'Now I am impressed.' Their light-hearted banter helped Alistair relax as they finally made their way through Corfe Castle and into

Trentmouth village.

'This is a nice place, why did you never tell me about it before? Why are you living in London when you could live here?'

'Questions, questions…I don't know, to be honest, it seemed the right thing to do at the time.'

'There's a shop, do you mind if we stop? I need to get something.'

'Be my guest.'

Bertie pulled over and went into the shop. Alistair gazed at Honeysuckle Cottage and wondered if he might see Lucy or Molly but it all looked quiet. Bertie emerged with a large bunch of flowers.

'For your mother,' he said as he got back into the car. Alistair was touched by his friend's thoughtfulness. He couldn't remember the last time he had taken flowers to his mum. *I should have thought of it myself, especially after how things were left on my last visit at home,* he thought.

'Come on, we had better get going, my mother will have been baking all day and she will want to fatten up a skinny rake like you.' They drove on out to the edge of the village and down the familiar lane. Alistair could see smoke rising up above the house and felt contented to be here again so soon; perhaps, he would move back to Dorset but not too close to his mother.

Later that evening, the boys joined George as he retired to the snug with a bottle of brandy and Alice promised to join them after she had cleared up the kitchen.

'What a wonderful place you have here, Dr Warren,' said Bertie accepting a brandy.

'Oh please, call me George, I'm retired now. We have lived here a long time and you forget how good things are. Anyway, what plans have you two for tomorrow?' asked George, 'I expect you will want to show Bertie around the area, there is so much to see.' And before Alistair could reply, he said, 'What sort of things are you interested in, Bertie? If you like, we can walk along the river or visit Corfe Castle or Swanage for fish and chips on the quay?'

'I...I don't really know,' said Bertie glancing over his shoulder at Alistair.

'Sorry, Dad, I haven't given it much thought. Bertie had never heard of the Isle of Purbeck till today. We'll think of something.' There was a thump and they all turned to see Alice struggling in through the door with a tray of coffee and what looked like homemade Florentines. Bertie jumped up and held the door, George cleared the coffee table and they all sat by the roaring log burner. Alistair watched the scene unfold before him, stretching out his legs, feeling more comfortable than in a long time; he pushed back in his seat, watching his parents and began to see a different side to Bertie.

The next morning, Alistair found himself having been persuaded to take a walk into the village, but before they left, Alistair had to make a call. He turned his mobile over in his hand hesitating, he had never felt so nervous. What was he going to say to Lucy? Till now, he had the perfect speech lined up, the words seemed inadequate. Here goes, he thought.

'Hello, Lucy, Alistair Warren,' he hesitated and in that unending moment of silence, Alistair wished he had never phoned.

'Oh. Hello, Alistair.' She was making him do all the work, but at least, she didn't put the phone down on him.

'I wondered how you were, you know...after the accident.'

'I'm coping.'

Alistair groaned inside. *It's hopeless*, he thought, *she is determined to make me suffer*.

'Sorry, sorry. I just didn't see you,' he stammered.

'I know…you said.' Lucy was short and snappy but Alistair decided that he had come this far so in he plunged.

'I wondered if you might like to go for a drink tonight at the Kings Arms.' Another silence and Alistair held his breath and waited.

'Oh…alright, I don't see why not. See you at eight and I'll bring Molly,' the phone clicked. He dragged his hair off his face dropping his shoulders. He punched the air, then it hit him like a sledge hammer, she was going to bring Molly. He was still sitting turning his phone over in his hand as Bertie stuck his head around the door.

'Come on, mate, everyone is waiting.'

'Sorry, I was thinking, I forgot we were going out for a walk…of all the things we could do.'

'Give it a go, it's only a walk. I like George and Alice, they are good company, come on.'

Alistair pushed himself up, euphoria disappearing, slipped on his jacket and followed Bertie. They set off across the fields towards Wareham. It was still a bit cold on these early April mornings, but the sky was clear and Alistair began to relax, letting the sun warm him. He still didn't know what to do about the coming evening; he and Molly were a secret but that didn't stop his imagination creating a whole new list of 'what ifs'. It was Alice who broke the silence. She wasn't used to Alistair being so quiet and just going for a walk was a whole new experience for them all.

'Is everything alright, dear?'

'Yes, just thinking. Bertie and I are going out tonight after dinner, down to the Kings Arms in Stoborough, to have a drink with Lucy and her friend, Molly.'

33

Everyone tried to speak at once but Bertie managed to get in first.

'Wow, when did that happen? I don't know how you did it, mate, but I am looking forward to this.' Bertie was jubilant. George and Alice gave each other a puzzled look but Alistair jumped in before any more questions could be asked, relaying his conversation with Lucy, leaving out some crucial bits.

'That's nice dear,' said Alice. 'Do you remember Molly? She had dinner with us once and she is a vegetarian, you know. You must give her our regards and Lucy too, of course.' Alice beamed at George and Alistair watched them squeeze hands.

'Spill,' said Bertie as soon as they were alone.

'Nothing to spill. I telephoned Lucy, asked her out for a drink and she said yes and she would bring Molly, safety in numbers, I presume.'

'She doesn't know about me then?' he quizzed.

'I didn't get the chance to tell her; she just put the phone down.' His mobile buzzed, it was Molly.

'Hey, what are you playing at?' demanded Molly. Alistair excused himself to Bertie.

'That's a nice welcome,' he snorted.

'Well, you should have warned me, I was taken aback when Lucy invited me to join the two of you for a drink. I didn't even know you were here this weekend.'

'Sorry about that, it was a sudden decision and I am still trying to apologise to Lucy. You're alright with it, aren't you?' he paused.

'I suppose so, it will be a bit awkward though the three of us, when I will be wishing that I could rip your clothes off.'

'I won't be able to see you this weekend. I'm afraid, not on our own anyway.'

'What! You can't come all the way down here and not see me, why can't you?' said Molly softening the tone of her voice.

'I've brought a friend with me, a work colleague.'

'What work colleague, male or female?' Alistair flinched, lifting her claws.

'His name is Bertie. You will meet him tonight. If I can get away, I will. You know that.'

'Sorry darling, I just panicked. I wasn't expecting you and when Lucy said...' she trailed off, then said, 'anyway, I'm looking forward to meeting Bertie, it'll be fun.'

'Good. I'll see you later,' he closed his mobile.

Alistair flopped down in the chair opposite Bertie, who was dozing in the conservatory after the huge lunch that Alice had made.

'You okay?' asked Bertie opening one eye.

'Look,' he said taking a moment, 'Molly has promised to be good tonight and I don't want you to give any indication that you know anything at all. We are just four people having a drink, that's it.'

'Hey, this is me you're talking to, I know the score,' he paused. 'How do you feel about me chatting them both up?' He grinned.

'Be my guest. It won't do you any good but you can try.'

'I am looking forward to it. I have a lot of questions. What did you say about me by the way?'

'I didn't, just a friend from London.' Bertie stretched and yawned, looking soporific. They sat chatting for a while until the door opened and in came Alice carrying a tray of tea and scones.

'Mrs W, I can't eat another thing,' Bertie patted his stomach.

'Course, you can, it's not very much.' She handed him a napkin and Bertie gave in.

'Fancy a run later?' he asked Alistair.

'Not likely, but you carry on. I've got some work that I want to catch up on.' They finished their tea and Bertie disappeared to change and Alistair pulled out his laptop.

'On your own, Dear?' said Alice collecting the tray. Alistair looked up at his mother; he knew that tone and resigned himself to an interrogation.

'Bertie loves running. He's trying to get the weight off that you are putting on him,' he teased. Alice grinned.

'I just want to make sure that our guest is happy and Bertie looks very thin to me,' she straightened her skirt and Alistair sat waiting. 'I came to ask about this evening.'

'What about it? We are meeting Lucy and Molly at 8.00 o'clock, is that a problem?' he asked.

'No dear, not at all. I just wondered what time you would like your evening meal,' she enquired.

'Mum,' he said as he looked at her sideways, 'you don't have to do this. After that huge lunch, we will burst,' he shot her a smile.

'I see Molly sometimes in the village, she is very nice, don't you think?' she peered at him over her glasses.

So that's it, thought Alistair.

'I can't really remember. Lucy is very nice too, don't you think?' He smiled. His mother disappeared into the kitchen and Alistair stretched out, hands behind his head. He felt very comfortable this weekend; was it Bertie taking the pressure off? He wasn't sure but, nevertheless, it was not going to become a habit.

Alistair and Bertie seated themselves in a quiet corner of the Kings Arms at quarter to eight, early enough to get a stiff drink in but not too early.

'So, come on then. I am totally at a loss here, mate, as to what to say to these two girls,' Bertie shuffled in his chair, glancing at the door.

'Don't worry about it, just be yourself and don't forget that you know nothing, nothing at all. You're a friend from London visiting for the weekend. Don't make it complicated.'

36

'It's already complicated,' joked Bertie. He jumped as another customer entered the bar.

'Anyway, here they are.' Bertie turned towards the door, his mouth dropped open.

'You dark horse,' he gulped. 'You didn't tell me that they were the most stunning girls on the planet. No wonder you can't make your mind up.'

'Put your tongue back in, you're dribbling,' teased Alistair. Bertie jumped to his feet and knocked his chair over, banging into the table, promptly spilling his drink. He grabbed the glass, his hands shaking. Alistair watched as the two women walked across the bar. They glanced at each other and back at the men.

'Lucy hi…Molly.' Kissing each in turn on the cheek, he did his best to sound calm and natural. 'This is Bertie, a friend and work colleague.' Bertie shook hands with them both, he managed a strangled grunt. Alistair smirked.

'What would you girls like to drink?' asked the very proper and polite Alistair.

'Red wine please,' they both chorused.

'Bertie…?' He was amused at his mate's face. He looked like he'd been slapped with a wet kipper.

'Hmm, same again,' he managed to say. 'I'll come and help you.' Bertie jumped up and followed. Propping up the bar, Bertie stared at the two girls. Molly had the most gorgeous long legs and shiny red and gold hair falling over her shoulders.

'You didn't tell me how ravishing they are,' he stuttered.

'You didn't ask,' Alistair grinned.

'But I don't know what to say, you have the best problem in the world. Not one but two heavenly angels to pick from!'

'It's not like that. It's a question of…well, I'm not sure what it's a question of…' he hesitated.

'Lust, mate, pure and simple.'

'Could be,' he trailed, 'hope you both like Merlot,' said Alistair placing the bottle on to the table.

'So,' said Molly giving her full attention to Bertie, 'tell me all about yourself. I want to know everything.'

Alistair, thankful for this diversion, turned to Lucy. He knew that Bertie wouldn't let him down, even though Molly could be very persuasive.

'I am so very sorry, Lucy,' he said for the thousandth time.

'I get it,' she said a little clipped, 'but thanks for the drink, it wasn't necessary.' Lucy did not smile. He looked at Molly. *Yes, she is stunning, vivacious and very capable,* he thought. He toyed with his glass watching her with Bertie. She could eat him alive and spit him out; he grinned at the idea of her making mincemeat out of him. The evening passed with a promise to go for a walk on Sunday morning before the two men had to go back to London. Much later, on the way back to the Warren's, Bertie fired a million questions at Alistair.

'Are you mad, mate?' He asked. 'Are you out of your tiny brain or what? Molly is totally gorgeous. I wouldn't ever let her go; in fact, I would get her down the aisle so fast, make her mine forever and ever.'

'Steady on,' said Alistair, 'marriage is a bit far, isn't it? Who volunteers to get married? All that commitment and children…no, not me. Play the field you know, have some fun.'

'You're not having much fun though, are you? Keeping Molly a secret. Who wouldn't like her?'

Alistair had to admit that he wasn't having much fun; maybe he should just get over it.

'It's not that simple,' he began.

'Come off it, this is me. You're afraid, that's all.' Relieved at not having to give a further explanation, Alistair admitted that he was afraid of making a mistake, not marriage itself. *That will put him off,* thought Alistair. But Bertie pressed on.

'Lucy has amazing eyes, you just want to dive in and swim,' He stared into space for a moment, '…feisty too.'

'Shut up, Bertie,' glowered Alistair. Bertie shoved his hands deep into his pockets, hunching his shoulders.

The next morning, over breakfast, they all sat chatting.

'What did you think of the two girls?' Alice asked Bertie with a smile.

'Mrs W,' he said, 'they are gorgeous.'

Alistair glared, firing a warning shot as he kicked him under the table. Alice beamed.

'I talk to Molly quite a bit, what an amazing woman. She's a vet, you know and it made her turn vegetarian.' Bertie cut up his bacon holding it aloft for a second, then shovelled it into his mouth before saying, 'She has told me all about her work and family, and she has an allotment...respect.'

'Thank you, Bertie, mother doesn't want to hear you dribbling on and on about Molly,' said Alistair.

'No, no, that's fine, Bertie. I do want to hear all about it. Molly has given me some lovely recipes,' she said with a grin.

Alistair nearly choked. *What else had she been saying? This is terrible,* he thought. He scratched his head pushing his glasses up and rubbing his eyes.

'Lucy is very pretty too. Quiet, she thinks a lot but doesn't say much. I'm hoping to have a chat with her this morning; they are taking us to Tyneham for a walk,' Bertie held up his hands as Alice offered more food. 'No, please, I can't manage anymore. It was great, thanks.' He rubbed his extended stomach.

'Oh, that will be nice. We haven't been there for years, have we darling?' she said turning to George.

'Let the young people go on their own, Alice,' he smiled at her, 'they don't want us hanging around them. We can go another day, on our own.' Alice looked down and wiped her hands on her apron.

'I will make lunch for you all when you get back; make sure that you bring Molly and Lucy with you. It will be fun.' Alice looked pleased with herself.

'You really don't have to do that,' Alistair groaned. 'Don't put yourself to any more trouble and anyway, they may have other plans for lunch.'

'Nonsense,' said Alice as she stood to clear the table. 'I will call Molly now.' For the second time that morning, Alistair nearly choked, but he knew when to give in and gave a wan smile instead.

'Let your mother do this, Alistair,' said his father. 'She enjoys cooking so much and it would make her happy.' Alistair opened his mouth to protest, but thought better of it remembering how he had left home the last time he had visited; he didn't want to hurt his mother again.

'Sounds alright to me,' broke in Bertie. Alistair looked up, having almost forgotten him.

'Yeah, I suppose so, but we do have to get back straight after lunch,' he chided.

Alice breezed back in to the room.

'That's settled then, Molly is delighted to be asked for lunch. It will be ready at one o'clock Alistair, so please be on time.' He smiled at her, feeling a sudden rush of pride and decided that he would bring the flowers next time. A split second later, Alistair realised that his mother had Molly's number.

Chapter 4

Molly picked up Lucy in her Land Rover and they headed out to Tyneham. The village had been taken over by the army during the Second World War and all the residents moved to Sandford near Wareham. They were promised that the village would be given back to them after the war, but this had never happened and now the cottages had fallen into ruin. Some were overgrown and it seemed strange to look at the remains of peoples' lives. The church, still intact, and the school room were fascinating to visit, giving a potted history of the place with black and white photographs and old school books to look at.

The girls arrived first and parked overlooking the duck pond and the original phone box still in place. It was eerily quiet and still. Molly looked up at the sky, the sun was making a brave effort glinting through the clouds. She turned to Lucy,

'We didn't get much chance to talk last night. C'mon, tell me what you think of Bertie?'

'He's cute in a geeky sort of way,' they giggled, 'I want to try and chat to him today; I should be more sociable after all, it's not his fault that Alistair Warren is such an oaf. Oh, and thanks for coming last night, things could have been awkward.' Lucy lifted her broken arm and cradled it glancing at Molly who was grinning unashamedly. 'What's that look all about? Anybody would think that you are trying to partner me off with Bertie, is that it?'

'I remember my last visit to the house when Alice tried to partner me with Alistair, I was truly awful. I will be on my best behaviour today. Invited to lunch, that is a new one, but you will see for yourself later.'

'Right, I suppose so. I'm not so sure about having lunch, what with my wrist and everything, but it is nice of her to invite us. I've always wanted to see the house.'

'The boys are here. Look, we need to talk later. I've something to tell you,' exclaimed Molly pushing open the door. 'Here goes.' She climbed out of the Land Rover and greeted the men. Lucy struggled out and Alistair dashed to help her. This gallantry did not escape Molly and she began to think that she needed to take urgent action.

'Sorry Luce…' she said. 'I forgot about your wrist, are you okay?'

'Fine, I can manage. It's not that bad, I'm fine,' she said smiling at Molly as she grabbed a tissue from her pocket and sniffed. They headed past the duck pond towards the first cottage.

'You're very quiet,' said Bertie. 'Are you always this quiet?'

'Sorry, I was miles away. I need to get back to work. I wondered if I should go back to my old job or try to find one here, in Dorset.'

'Oh, you must stay here, in Dorset,' quipped Molly.

'With your skills, I would think that you could get a job in any hospital.' Bertie tried to sound encouraging. Lucy tipped her head on one side.

'It's not that simple, with all the cut backs. They might want me and need me but they are restricted with budgets and targets,' she explained.

'That's ridiculous if you ask me. So, what about all these women having babies, what happens to them? I have to admit that my knowledge of babies is less than nil…but just the

42

same.' Lucy began to explain the complexities of midwifery services as they all wandered up to the church admiring the architecture and reading all the various plaques on the walls. Bertie even bought a guide book. They sat down in a pew admiring the carvings; a trunk of a fossilised tree had Bertie and Alistair fascinated leaving the girls alone to talk.

'You seem to be getting along with Bertie, alright,' quizzed Molly.

'Oh, we were just talking about jobs; getting a midwifery post isn't as simple as it sounds. Actually, he is quite nice but he isn't Lionel,' she glanced around the little church and shuddered.

'You've got to move on. You said you wanted to or are you still in love with Lionel?' Molly rubbed her hands together and blew into them in an effort to warm them a little.

'I don't know anymore. It's just that I thought we were good together despite everything. I know that sounds pathetic but...' Lucy looked over her shoulder to see where the boys were and turned back to Molly. '...but I am more interested in what you wanted to tell me.' She leaned in close to Molly.

'I can't tell you now, maybe later. So, come on, Lucy. Bertie is a nice guy, he might be just what you need to get over Lionel.'

'I don't know about that. I'm not ready for another relationship just yet. Come to think about it, you're a good one to give out advice, no boyfriend to speak of; so, what about you and Bertie? You were getting on very well last night, I seem to remember,' she smirked.

Molly, turned to look around the church, seeing that the boys were far enough away, said, 'Look, I'll fill you in later, but well, Alistair and I have been seeing each other but no one knows. So, can you keep it to yourself? Please?' she pleaded.

'I had no idea,' stammered Lucy, 'I thought that you hated him, what changed?'

'It's a long story, all I can say is that he's been really nice this weekend, very attentive to us, both, actually, and his mother is lovely. I see her sometimes and give her recipes. She's interested in vegetarian food and likes to try them out on poor George. So, lunch could be quite interesting, don't you think?'

'I suppose so,' said Lucy staring at Molly, looking stunned by this revelation with her eyebrows scrunched together. The boys wandered back to the girls both chatting, Alistair pointing at something high up in the belfry.

'Fancy walking down to the sea?' asked Alistair. 'It's a bit cold and damp in here,' he sniffed, pulling his jacket tightly around himself.

'Why not?' said Molly as she flashed him a warm smile. The girls followed them out of the church and began to walk down the footpath that led to the sea. It was a crisp morning with a salty breeze blowing off the sea. Lucy breathed deeply.

'Are you alright?' Bertie asked.

'I'm sorry,' said Lucy. 'Things on my mind, you know how it is.'

'Like what?' Molly raised her eyebrows.

'I was just thinking that I love snow-boarding and the beaches are perfect in Dorset. I might try sand-boarding when my wrist is better, what do you think?'

'Great, why not. Never tried it, but I'm willing to have a go at anything,' said Molly. Bertie and Lucy stopped by the waters' edge and Molly saw the opportunity to get Alistair alone. They walked unsteadily over the rocky beach, the cold wind hitting them as it blew off the sea, the waves were crashing onto the shore, rolling and sucking the pebbles back and forth. Molly glanced at Bertie and Lucy and watched as Bertie picked up some pebbles and was skimming them on the waves. Lucy transfixed, her shoulders hunched with her hands covering her ears and jiggling from one foot to the other.

'What are you playing at?' Alistair asked Molly. She shot her head round to face him.

'What are you talking about?' she stammered taking a step backwards, 'I...I am pleased to have you to myself for a while, if that's what you mean. I've missed you and I've something to tell you.'

'Look, you know how it is, we have to be careful. I don't want anyone suspecting anything,' his voice torn away by the wind, Molly was horrified.

'Why do we have to keep everything secret? Your mother likes me and...' Molly had to quicken her step to keep up with his long strides.

'That's another thing,' Alistair interrupted. 'What's this about you giving mother recipes, been having cosy little chats, have you? Molly, please, I have asked you to keep our relationship a secret; that's how I want it to stay.' He stopped to face her. 'I've been thinking, we should cool it, have a break for a while.'

Molly stared at him. 'What! Why? Where has this come from?' she stared at him, her eyes searching his face. 'I can't believe you're saying this and anyway, I have something to tell you, something important.'

Alistair quickly glanced down the beach, Molly followed his gaze just as Bertie turned and waved to them. 'We can't talk now. Let's go back and join the others. I'll call you tonight. What did you want to tell me anyway?'

'It will keep.' Molly pushed her fists deep into her pockets, frozen to the spot, staring at his retreating figure. She could see Lucy watching Bertie, trying to rescue something from the surf and decided to run back along the beach as if nothing were amiss. 'Come on, slow coach,' she called behind her. Alistair shook his head and ran after her.

'What's all this?' joked Bertie, 'Running at your age!' Alistair, out of breath, stood hands on knees gasping.

'He needs to get some weight off; it's all that sitting at a desk in dirty old London,' said Molly.

Alistair took a few deep breaths.

'You are always saying we should join a gym,' he gasped again. 'Well, maybe you're right. I could do with toning up a bit.'

Bertie's eyes flew open wide. He stared at Alistair who threw him a wink. Molly saw this code pass between them and moved over to Lucy to link arms.

'Yes, alright. I'll look into it tomorrow, especially after the food your mother has given us this weekend. Speaking of food, shouldn't we get back; Alice did say one o'clock sharp if I remember right.'

'I'm starting to feel cold,' Lucy drew her coat tightly around herself, 'we should go.' Alistair and Bertie both leapt to remove their jackets for Lucy but Alistair got there first. Bertie bowed in submission. Molly dropped her shoulders and released her arm giving Bertie a wan smile. They drove back to the Warrens in subdued mood.

'There you are,' said Alice, 'I was beginning to think that you had forgotten.'

'Never Mrs W,' Bertie beamed at her, 'it smells delicious. I can't wait.'

Alice fussed around her guests, 'Alistair, take the girls' coats and get them a drink, they look frozen.'

'Hello Mrs Warren,' said Lucy putting her hand out.

'Oh, call me Alice please, and Molly, how nice to see you again. I've made that recipe you gave me last week; I hope that it will be alright.' Molly tried to look at Alistair but he turned and disappeared with the coats.

'Oh, I am pleased. Just trying to help, I know you're interested in organic food, too.' She followed Alice to the kitchen, with Bertie at her heels, leaving Lucy standing in the hallway with George.

Molly excused herself and followed them into the snug.

'Come and join me in the study both of you,' he said. Molly admired this sweet mannered man, he was nothing like his son. He poked the fire and added another log. 'How is your wrist now?' His voice calm and soothing,

'It's much better, thank you. I have been trying to find a job in midwifery but nothing yet. I may have to resort to a couple of part time jobs, not what I really want but under the circumstances...'

'There you are,' it was Alistair. 'What circumstances?' he asked. He looked like his father but he has his mother's colouring, mused Molly.

'Hi,' Lucy threw him a smile. 'Nothing really, we were just talking about my job search.'

'Oh, right. I came to see if you had warmed up yet and what you would like to drink.' He returned her smile. George steepled his fingers and hummed to himself.

'I'm fine, thanks. It's so nice to have a real fire, don't you think?' she spread her fingers out in front of the fire. '...And yes, I would love a glass of red wine, please.'

'Great, I will see what I can find,' Alistair headed for the door.

'Oh, Alistair,' called George. 'I think that I'll have one too and don't forget Molly.' Alistair turned, red faced,

'Sorry. How about a Merlot? Do you have something Australian in your wine cellar dad?' George nodded and turned his attention to Lucy.

'You were saying my dear about a job. Have you decided to stay in sleepy old Dorset?' He smiled kindly.

'Probably,' she sighed, 'at least for now. I have been offered a job at a garden centre and another as a care assistant, better than nothing, I suppose.'

47

'Well, in my experience, a qualified midwife has always been in demand but I do understand, my dear. Have you contacted Dorchester yet?'

'Yes,' said Lucy, 'I thought that I would try Poole too and further afield if necessary, then I can look for somewhere to live. I know that mum and dad would be happy for me to stay with them and I don't mind in the short term, especially until my wrist is better, but I do want to get back to my own space.'

'Ah, yes. I can understand that but I thought that you and Dr Lionel Maddox were together?'

Lucy and Molly shot a look at each other.

'Do you know him? H...how did you know about us?' George smiled and indicated for her to carry on. 'I, well yes, we were together but I left him a few weeks ago.' Her face flushed pink and she pulled at her hair.

'I do know of him actually, and I am sorry to hear of your break up.'

'Err, well...' she stammered just as Alistair walked in with their drinks.

'What have you all been talking about?' enquired Alistair. 'You look flustered. I hope you haven't been interrogating Lucy, Dad.'

'Lucy is thinking of making Dorset her permanent home,' announced George.

'Oh, I've only just begun to think about it, nothing is decided yet,' she quickly added accepting a glass of wine from him. 'Ooh...that's lovely.'

'What? Here in Trentmouth?' he interjected. 'With your boyfriend?'

In the deathly silence, Molly could see the heat flooding up Lucy's neck and Alistair's mouth drop open as he looked from one to the other, all eyes on him.

'Sorry,' he said, 'none of my business. I didn't mean to pry, I should take my big foot out of my mouth,' he slapped his

48

forehead. 'I seem to be always apologising to you, not a good way of starting any new relationship...I mean friendship.' Alistair let out a groan and a smile played at the corner of Molly's mouth.

'Don't apologise, you weren't to know. We have broken up, my decision,' she took a gulp of her wine. 'I have just been talking to Dr Warren about midwifery posts in Dorset.'

'Oh, right.'

'Lucy, I'm retired now, a long time ago in fact, please call me George.'

'Thank you, Dr Warren,' they all laughed just as Alice popped her head around the door.

'Molly dear, do you think you could give me a hand? Lunch is ready if you would all sit at the table please.' Molly followed her to the kitchen.

'Wow, you have been busy.' Alice grinned and passed the soup tureen to Molly.

'Parsnip and apple soup, a lentil and bean casserole, finishing with a chocolate and pear sponge drenched in cream. I wanted to make sure that the boys had a good meal before they go back to London.'

'You've excelled yourself, Alice. You must let me have your recipe.' They piled the table with food.

'Mrs W,' said Bertie pushing his empty plate away, 'if you were my mum, I would be home every weekend. That was fantastic.' They all laughed including Bertie, but Alistair shuffled in his seat and said nothing.

'Let's retire to the conservatory, there is more room in there for coffee,' exclaimed George. The boys insisted on helping Alice to clear away the dishes. Molly came back with a tray of coffee.

'Is this your handiwork?' Lucy asked George as she surveyed the garden.

'Goodness gracious, no. Alice is in charge of the garden. I mow the lawn but that's about it.'

'It's beautiful, I love those red and yellow tulips interspersed with bluebells. I will have to have a garden when I move.' Molly stood by her side to admire the garden.

'You can help me in my garden if you like; there's always plenty to do, and I've been thinking that you could come and live at the farm with me; If you like, get away from your parents. It would be fun.' Lucy stared at Molly for a second.

'I'd love that. Thanks.'

The others bustled in to join them, sitting chatting, trying to ease expanding waistlines. Alistair looked at his watch.

'Sorry, Mum, but it is time for us to go, we don't want to get caught up in the traffic if we leave it any later.'

'That's alright dear,' said Alice, 'what about the girls?'

'Don't worry about us, Alice. I have my Land Rover, I'll take Lucy home,' smiled Molly.

George and Alice waved them all goodbye with a promise to visit again very soon. Alistair turned to wave just as George put his arm around Alice, hugging her to him, laying a gentle kiss on her lips.

Chapter 5

Alistair pressed the number for Molly and waited.

'Darling,' she gasped, 'are you alright? I have been so worried,' she trailed off.

'I'm fine, Molly. It's just that these last few weeks, I have been in a bit of turmoil and I want some space.'

'Turmoil…? I don't understand. I can help you whatever it is, you seem distracted. I love you,' she went quiet and Alistair knew that this was not going to be easy to explain. 'Are you still there? Alistair, I…I said I love you.' Alistair looked down at his feet, crossing and uncrossing his legs.

'I'm still here,' he heard her sigh. 'Look, Molly, I've always made it clear that marriage is not for me. I don't want any of that commitment; I am happy the way things are but…' he paused and Molly jumped in.

'But, we are great together, you said it yourself.'

'Yes, we are but you very nearly told mother at the weekend, don't deny it, please. You seem to be getting very involved in their lives,' he paused but Molly said nothing. 'That's why I want to cool it, Molly.'

'We had a great time this weekend. We make a good foursome and even George and Alice looked happy.'

Alistair, if he had to be honest, knew it had been a long time since he had such a good weekend, even admitting that his mother and father looked happy too, but then it didn't take much to bring a smile to his mother's face.

'That's true but it was a one off. I'm just not the settling down type. What did you want to tell me by the way?'

'Nothing, it doesn't matter now, it will keep. I miss you. I will be up in London next week perhaps, we can get together then? I prefer to tell you face to face.'

'I don't know about that, maybe. Why can't you tell me now? What's the big deal here?' He waited. He had things to do. *Women*, he thought.

'Alright…I'm pregnant.' Alistair coughed and spluttered.

'You are what? I don't believe you, you're just saying this to get me to commit,' he choked.

'Believe what you like, but I'm pregnant and I'm going to have this baby with or without you.'

'I don't want anything to do with it, it's your problem, not mine.' He found himself shouting, his head reeling, he took another gulp of whisky.

'Fine.' He heard her say and the phone clicked dead, the dial tone ringing in his ears. Alistair closed his phone, rubbed his eyes, he poured another drink. He flopped onto the couch chasing around the millions of thoughts—all vying for his attention—and Bertie; he never stopped talking about everything the whole way back. He was like a bloody Cape Canaveral moon launch, he mused. *He is a good mate, maybe I'll call him.* He swallowed his drink and stared into the bottom of the glass. He pressed Bertie's number, it transferred to voice mail, switching it off, he tapped his phone on his chin.

'She must be lying,' he told the bottle of whisky as he poured another drink letting his thoughts take him back over that weekend. 'What a mess! Perhaps, I should stay away from them all for a while, see what happens.' He splashed the last drop into his glass and gulped it down, falling asleep where he was, too tired to move.

Alistair groaned. His head hurt. He groaned again, *what is that noise?* He grabbed a cushion and squashed it against his

52

face in an attempt to escape. He flashed his eyes wide open and shot bolt upright realising that his mobile was bleeping. He fumbled around on the floor, found his phone and flipped it open.

'Bertie, what do you want at this time in the morning?' He yawned and stretched trying to focus his eyes on his watch.

'Are you alright, mate? It's nearly lunchtime.'

'What!' He leapt to his feet, 'Why didn't you ring me earlier?'

'I did, several times. I was about to come over there. Are you sure that you are okay?' Alistair moaned, his head throbbing, remembering his call with Molly last night.

'I'll be there as soon as I can.' He had slept on the sofa again. He rubbed the back of his neck twisting his head around. He picked up the empty whisky bottle and headed for the bathroom, trying to put all thoughts of Molly and Lucy aside. *Molly*, he thought. He had to get to the office, fast.

'You look awful,' said Bertie.

'Thanks, do you have anything for my pounding head?' Alistair grimaced.

'Not for self-inflicted injuries. No, you need another glass of whatever you were drinking last night,' he said grinning as Alistair dashed for the men's room. 'Here, one very strong black coffee.' Bertie held out a mug in front of him.

'Thanks. Sorry about earlier. One of those nights, you know.' Alistair took a sip letting the sticky sweetness trickle down his throat.

'Yes, I do.' He raised an eyebrow. 'Molly or Lucy?'

'Molly. I phoned her.'

'Want to tell me about it?'

'No, actually yes. As you said, it's lunchtime anyway and my head hurts too much to concentrate on work.'

'Don't worry about the office, I've dealt with everything. What you need is a greasy all-day breakfast and I know just the place.'

Alistair attempted a smile meekly following Bertie without too much fight left in him. The café turned out not to be his usual haunt and Alistair slid onto a corner bench seat still holding his head. They cooked up a mean breakfast; he had to admit that he did feel better.

'Thanks for that suggestion. Come here often, do you?' Alistair smirked.

'Now and again.' Bertie grinned in return. 'Now, come on, what happened last night that put you on such a bender?'

'I'm no nearer solving my problem than before. Molly wants us to carry on as if nothing has happened; Lucy is still in love with her ex according to Molly; my parents think that I have had a Damascus Road experience and you?'

'Oh, I think that you are bloody mad, mate. If only I had half your troubles, I would be the happiest man in the world,' a smile cracking his face in two.

'Come on…'

'You know what Alistair, I would give anything to swop with you. My parents are both gone and my sister lives in Oz. I haven't seen her for ten years. I can't remember the last time I got laid and apart from my old Jag and F1, that's it.'

Alistair looked stunned. *I know nothing about Bertie,* he thought, *when did I become a self-centred, narcissistic bastard?*

'Mate, I didn't know.'

'Yeah, well you do now.' Bertie plunged his hands into his pockets and shrugged his shoulders. They walked back to the office in silence.

Alistair, still reeling the revelations from Bertie and his own stupidity with Molly, chastised himself, *why did he want their affair kept secret? Why can't I just be honest? Where have I been in my own life? What the hell am I going to do now?* He

54

spent the afternoon on autopilot, leaving most of the work to Bertie. He stood by the water cooler shaking his head. He had not been a good mate to Bertie; he had worked with him for ten years. That's another mystery, he thought, putting up with me for ten years but he still couldn't bring himself to tell him about the pregnancy.

'What are you doing tonight, Bertie?' he muttered as he scrunched the plastic cup and threw it in the bin.

'Err, not much. Why?'

'Let me buy you dinner, to say thank you for lunchtime, you rescued me.'

'No problem, just don't make it a habit.' He paused, 'You don't think it's a bit weird though? Me going to dinner with my boss,' he grinned, relieved that Alistair appeared to be back to normal, 'but thanks, I really fancy a curry.'

Curry. Curry was the one thing that Alistair did not like.

'Weird? No weirder than you coming to visit my folks with me,' they both chortled, 'I know a vegetarian restaurant not far from here, and they do a very good curry, I understand.'

'Great. Veggie hey, sounds good to me.'

Later that night, Alistair sat down with a glass of red wine, no whisky left but some decisions to make. He had his future all worked out, organised, in full control, Molly in Dorset and freedom in London. He swirled the red wine around and around, tempted to pour another. His life had taken a turn he wasn't expecting, he paced up and down. He had a successful business, but other than that, what did he actually have? He was nearly 40, his family life had been strained for the last 30 years since his brother died...he loved his parents but they were like strangers to him, his fault, he knew. Giving in, he poured another glass of red wine. What did he really want? He felt numb to think that this was it, his life. He looked at his watch, *toys, that's all I have, an expensive car, an expensive watch, a very expensive rented flat with a view of the Thames*, he sighed.

It's not too late to phone mother, he thought and pressed his keypad.

'Hello, Mother,' Alistair tried to sound as natural as possible, but phoning his mother was not something he did very often.

'Hello dear,' Alistair raised his eyes, *I suppose she will always call me dear; it's time I just ignore it, stop letting it bother me.* He forced a smile onto his face.

'How's Dad?' He almost didn't know what to say. This is silly, she's my mother, just be normal, whatever that is. He listened for a few minutes to what they had been doing; her garden and the weather. At least she didn't mention Molly or Lucy.

'I've been thinking.'

'Thinking about what, Alistair?'

'Well, it's been on my mind for a while that maybe I should buy a cottage or a flat or something down in Purbeck. I can't keep staying with you, it's not fair.'

'Well, if that is what you really want to do, Alistair. You know your father and I love to have you stay with us, don't you?'

'I know, Mother, but I can't afford to buy in London, and I just thought that it would be an investment for the future, a better place for my savings, that's all.' He tried to sound matter-of-fact so that his mother wouldn't read too much into it. 'Do you think that you could pick up some details for me from the estate agents in Wareham? I only need two bedrooms, something with a small garden and not too expensive.'

'Yes dear, of course, we will. Does this mean you might be coming down again soon?'

'If that's not too much trouble, I mean if you are busy, I can leave it for another week or two.'

'No dear, we would love to have you and bring Bertie, he's such a nice boy.' Alistair couldn't help himself but smile.

'I'm not sure what he is doing, but I will ask him. See you on Friday.'

Friday arrived and he found himself heading for Dorset with Bertie rambling on by his side. Alistair, half listening, and still thinking about Molly; he had expected to have her on the phone every other minute but instead he had heard nothing. He found it a little disconcerting, perhaps she meant it about the baby. Whatever the situation, it felt strange for her not being on the end of the phone in most nights, or in his bed.

'What do you think?' Bertie asked breaking into his daydreams.

'What? Oh, sorry, mate. I didn't quite catch that. I was miles away. What do I think about what?'

'About the business. You know, relocating down here. It would make a lot of sense.'

'Hang on a minute. Where did that come from?'

'Haven't you been listening at all?' Bertie frowned. 'Come on, what's bothering you this time?'

'To be honest, it's Molly, but that's not the point. You were saying about relocating to Dorset. Have you been speaking to my mother?' Bertie let out a laugh.

'Mrs W? No, not at all. Lovely though she is, I just thought that it made sense. What with you looking to buy a bolthole and everything.'

'Everything, what do you mean by that?' Alistair raised his eyebrows glancing at Bertie.

'You know, a little love nest for you and the delectable...' he hesitated.

'Ye...es, carry on.'

'Well, a little love nest, away from your parents' inquisitive eyes. I mean, I guess you have never taken a girl back to your parents' house, have you?'

Alistair was quiet. He let the question, both of them, go unanswered. He thought of Molly's big iron bed in her old

57

farmhouse, but then what if he didn't see Molly anymore, what then? His mother had collected a number of details for him, appointments made; he had a busy weekend coming up, but relocating the business down to Dorchester was another matter altogether. It had occurred to him of course, but he had always resisted, wanting to keep his parents at arms' length, live his life in London, after all that's where all the money is. He needed to see and be seen, he did the circuit, knew all the right people, even becoming friends with a junior assistant to a minor politician.

'I'll take that as a "no" then, shall I?' Bertie gave a snort as he flashed a look in Alistair's direction.

'What are you laughing about? Cut me in on the joke.'

'Oh, it's nothing, honest. I was just thinking about seeing F1 live, instead of on the box, follow it around the globe, you know, chill out for a bit.'

'Why now, what's different? You've never mentioned it before?' asked Alistair suddenly giving Bertie his full attention.

'Oh, you know, first buying a property down in Dorset and then maybe relocating the business. You won't want me down there, so I thought that I should plan the rest of my life double quick.'

'Whoa, slow down, where did all that come from? To begin with, my buying a property is purely for financial reasons, it's a retreat; secondly, I have never mentioned moving the business to Dorchester or anywhere else, and come to think of it, if I did move out of the city, why wouldn't I offer you the opportunity to move as well? Where would I find someone else daft enough to work for me?'

'Well, put like that I suppose I would need to work somewhere; there's only so long that I could be a beach bum in Oz. I've always wanted to be a babe magnet on a beach somewhere.' They both began to laugh uncontrollably.

58

They drove through the New Forest and down towards the south coast.

'I'm getting hungry. I wonder what Mrs W has made for us? Just the thought of her cooking is making my mouth water. My mum wasn't much into baking, she had to work and then she was ill.' Alistair saw that he had wandered off into his own thoughts and jumped in.

'You are always hungry. So, come on, what's on your mind old chap? You disappeared on me.'

'I was just thinking that it's no good going over the past. My life now is pretty good. I play snooker and go clubbing with my mates, and now, I've been invited down to Dorset again and best of all, I might even see Molly and Lucy again.' Empty road ahead, they sped on enjoying one of the warmest springs on record. 'Are we likely to see the stunning redhead or the gorgeous Lucy this weekend?'

'Mm, that's what you call them is it?' Amused by the thought of gorgeous Lucy, she was that, alright and the stunning redhead Molly, 'yes, she is stunning, he sighed. 'Would you like to?' he asked teasing Bertie

'Too right, what excuse have you thought of?' At this, Alistair just laughed out loud; the one thing he didn't need was an excuse to see either of them, but then he couldn't just walk up and knock on the door, could he?

'I asked mother to invite them both to dinner tonight.'

Bertie swerved off the road and hit the grass verge grinding to a halt; he turned half round in his seat and stared at Alistair.

'You didn't? What, tonight? You didn't tell me. You don't hang around, do you? Bloody hell, that's a shocker.' He regained control of the car and pulled back onto the road.

Home, thought Alistair, *the word had been alien to him for a very long time. There must be something wrong with me!*

'Well, the truth is that I haven't asked Mother, but I'm sure she wouldn't mind. I'll give her a call. We are almost in Brockenhurst, we could stop for a coffee, and I'll call her then.'

'Alright mate, good idea. What about the girls? Don't you think that you should ask them first? What if they have made other plans?'

'Yes, I suppose that's true, I'll give Molly a call.'

Bertie wandered off around the town as Alistair made his calls. A few minutes later, they headed into a café bar.

'Well, what did they say?' asked Bertie. 'I was wondering if I had brought anything suitable to wear; my best 'pulling' shirt is in the wash, not that it has worked recently.' He grimaced and they both smirked.

'The girls had planned a pizza and a film but Molly said that they would cancel and Mother began to flap as usual. I tried to tell her to keep it simple, but I don't think that she was listening. I told her, I can always pick up fish and chips in Wareham but she wouldn't hear of it.'

'Your mother is amazing, you are a lucky chap. I don't know many women, correction, any women who would do that, cook for their son, his mate and two girlfriends.'

'Hey, hang on a minute, since when did they become our two girlfriends?' grinned Alistair.

'Well, you know what I mean. I wish they were though, our two girlfriends I mean.' Bertie slumped back in his seat, and Alistair stared at his coffee thinking the same thing.

'Come on,' he said eventually, 'we had better get going. We are still a good hour away from Trentmouth.' As they walked back towards the car, Bertie veered off into a florist.

'I will just pop in here a minute, won't be long.'

'No, you don't.' Alistair grabbed his arm, 'I am buying my mother the biggest, most obscenely large bunch of flowers she has ever seen. I'm not having you show me up again.' Bertie followed him in to the shop and as Alistair was busy buying up all the flowers he could for Alice, Bertie bought two small bunches of freesias.

'Let me buy some wine,' pleaded Bertie, 'as you have cornered the flower market.'

'Alright, good idea. Everyone seems to like red, especially Australian.'

'Funny you should say that. My sister is only a couple of hours from the Barossa Valley and she has recommended one or two very good reds to me before. I will see if I can get them for tonight.'

'Excellent, you do that and I will put these flowers in the car.'

They set off again towards Trentmouth, winding their way through Bournemouth and down to the ferry at Sandbanks.

'This place is incredible, just look at these properties. Why don't you buy one of these, Alistair?'

'When we make our first million, no sorry, make that ten million, I can probably just about buy one on Purbeck; Sandbanks will have to wait till next year.' They both chuckled as Bertie drove onto the ferry.

'I could never get bored of doing this,' Bertie said at last. 'Look at those yachts, it's another world down here. You think that it all happens in London, even the sun is shining. This is the life.' Bertie leaned over the hand rail on the ferry watching the gulls circling overhead. Alistair watched the boats and made no reply.

Chapter 6

The next day, Molly promised to pick Lucy up and take her shopping; she needed to cheer herself up and maybe some retail therapy might help.

'Hey, you're looking much better,' said Molly, anxious to keep Lucy on side and their friendship intact.

'Yes, thanks, I am. The fresh air did me good yesterday and I haven't been down to Tyneham in years. They are a lovely family, the Warrens. Aren't they?' Lucy strapped herself in.

'Yes, Alice is a good friend. I have spent many an afternoon talking to her, especially when I deliver some veg or other.' Molly pulled out into the traffic.

'Oh yes, I forgot. How did you pull that off?'

'Easy really. I bumped into her in your mums' shop one day and she was full of apology again about the evening that I went up there saying that she didn't know much about vegetarian food. So, I offered to lend her a cookery book and it sort of went from there.'

'She's a very good cook, lucky them.' Lucy wistfully looked out of the window. 'I never really learned to cook. My mother mainly uses up near the sell by date food from the shop and living with Lionel, we were both so busy that the main staple was frozen meals or restaurant nights out. So proper home cooked food has become a rarity.' She fell quiet, staring out of the window.

'Penny for them, you have disappeared somewhere,' Molly brought her back.

'Just thinking of Lionel, wondering where he is.'

'You still love him, don't you? Have you rung him at all? Told him about your accident? I'm sure that he would want to know,' Molly encouraged.

'No, it's best to leave things as they are.' She let out a sigh.

'Who are you trying to convince? I think that you should go and see him, tell him how you feel; if you don't try, you could lose him forever.' Molly wished that she could take her own advice but for the moment, her priority lay in reuniting Lucy with Lionel.

'I don't know anymore. One day, I think I still love him and the next, I can't believe he had an affair, several in fact. I'm all upside down.' Molly had to admit that if Alistair had an affair, she would not take him back, but then they weren't officially a couple anyway and for all she knew, Alistair could be seeing someone else in London. Her attitude to her friend softened,

'Let's stop for coffee. They have opened a new tearoom at the garden centre and I can pick up my seed potatoes.' Over coffee, she suddenly felt quite sorry for Lucy, split up with Lionel, back home with parents and now a broken wrist, Molly felt guilty. She reached across and squeezed her arm, 'you need cheering up, why don't we see what's on at the Rex in Wareham? It will be a laugh. Come on, what do you say?'

'Why not. That's something I haven't done for years. Is it still gas lit and does it still have that funny ticket kiosk?'

'Yes,' said Molly, 'that's a date then. We can eat first, maybe go to the Granary and sit overlooking the river. I'll check out timings and let you know later. Have you thought anymore about moving in to mine?' She asked.

'I have been giving it some thought. I really don't know what to do. I need to get my life sorted out, that I do know.' She sipped her coffee. 'You know what, it would be fun. Maybe that's just what I need. Yes. Yes, I will.'

Molly flipped open her mobile and saw two missed calls from Alistair. She was tempted to ignore him but changed her mind and listened to his message. She quickly sent him a text and turned her attention back to Lucy.

'Great. I've so much to tell you but that can all wait till later. We've been invited to dinner at the Warrens' with Alistair and Bertie. We need to go shopping.'

'Oh!' exclaimed Lucy. 'Poor Alice.'

They finished their coffee and set off again. This time, to Dorchester for a wander in and out of the little side streets searching for something different to the mega store offerings. They found a tiny shop up an ally way with its window displaying some gorgeous underwear. They went in and spent far too much money.

'Shall we go back to the farm and I can show you round? Then we can have that chat.' Molly shivered and pulled her coat around her, a chilly wind blowing up the street catching dust and rubbish swirling it into the air.

'Yes, why not. I am starting to get cold and it will be dusk soon.' She looked up at the darkening sky. 'Maybe we should have bought thermal underwear instead.' They both giggled and set off arm in arm loaded with booty to the car park. Back at the farm, Molly added logs to the Aga and put the old battered kettle onto the hob. Rex fussed them both sniffing bags and shoes excitedly. Lucy sat at the scrubbed pine table and pulled the paper over at the open jobs page.

'You're not thinking of giving up your practise, are you?' Lucy looked up at Molly eyes wide.

'Never, but I thought that you might want to take a look.' Molly took down two mugs and put teabags into her chipped blue Poole pottery teapot. Lucy flicked through the local paper and Molly joined her opening a cake tin to reveal a cherry cake with coconut icing.

'Better not,' said Lucy peering into the tin. 'There's nothing jobs wise but listen to this, "A very nice two bedroomed flat at Poundbury. The project set up by the Duchy of Cornwall, the dream of the Prince of Wales; to create a diverse mix of properties in a new community." Sounds interesting. If I could get a job at the hospital in Dorchester, I could even walk to work. The exercise will do me good,' she grinned.

'Good idea. You have certainly cheered up.' Molly sipped her tea looking at Lucy over the top of her mug.

'You know what? I've had enough moping around; it's time to get my act together, move on. I will call the hospital first thing in the morning. The sooner I get my life back on track the better.' She took a gulp of tea. 'Speaking of which, what is happening tonight? I don't know what to wear and you still haven't told me your news.'

'Oh, that can wait. Let me take you home. We can sort out what you are going to wear. Come on.' She pushed her chair back, collected the mugs swishing them under the tap and dumping them on the side. She grabbed her keys, Rex bounded out of his basket following them out to the Land Rover, he leapt into the back. They headed towards the village chatting about their day.

'I've got nothing to wear,' wailed Lucy staring into her wardrobe.

'No, neither have I. What are we going to do?'

'Well, it's too late to go back to the shops. Why couldn't Alistair have given us more warning?'

'I don't know. He's just one of those people who does things on the spur of the moment and expects everyone else to fall into place,' sighed Molly. Lucy looked sideways at her friend.

'How do you know that? Have you developed sixth sense or is there something more that I don't know?'

65

'Alice tells me all sorts of things; talking of Alice, I'll give her a call, find out what sort of evening she's planning.'

'Good idea. I'll go and open a bottle of wine.' Lucy went downstairs to find the glasses and left Molly talking to Alice.

'I'm so glad you rang dear, I just do not know what to make. I have been searching through Hugh's book for inspiration and I haven't much time. Typical of Alistair to spring things on me like this. I don't mean you, my dear, it will be lovely to have you and Lucy over, I do miss female company.'

'Well, let me see if I can help. What were you planning to make for the boys?'

'I have four salmon fillets but that won't stretch to six people.'

'Yes, it will and I do eat fish, so no problem there. Have you any pasta and cream?'

'Err, yes. But how will that help?'

'All you need to do is poach the salmon, flake it into small pieces, cook the pasta, add the cream and some basil. I will pick up some focaccia, strawberries and goats cheese. You make a large bowl of salad and we can have cheese, crackers and fruit for dessert. How does that sound?' Alice was delighted.

'My dear, that sounds marvellous. See you at seven?'

Lucy came back wielding a bottle of red and looked hopefully at Molly, who nodded saying, 'Will do. Oh, and is it a casual sort of evening or should we be thinking more formal?'

'Casual tonight, Molly dear. The boys will probably be tired from travelling and I haven't time to cook and dress up. Is that alright with you?'

'Great, suits us fine. See you later, Alice.' She flipped her phone shut with a satisfied grin.

'Well, casual it is.'

'Thank goodness, that helps a lot. Actually, no it doesn't, is that casual as in jeans or my black trousers? What do you

66

think?' They both started to laugh at the utter absurdity of it all and opened the wine. Lucy put on her black trousers and then one top after another.

'Nothing seems right. I don't know what to wear; it is all very strange to me.' Lucy leaned over to top up her glass. Molly placed her hand over it shaking her head.

'I'm driving, better not. And I think it's strange too. I wonder what this is all about.' She drained her glass. 'Let's stop worrying and have some fun.'

They both fell into fits of giggles.

'It's not as if it is any sort of date, we are all just good friends.' Lucy took another slug of wine.

'Sounds like you would rather if it was more than friends and here's me still thinking that you are in love with Lionel and wouldn't look at another man.'

'I've been thinking about what you said; you know that I ought to move on. To be honest, if Lionel still loved me or ever loved me, wouldn't he have followed me? Try to get me back or something?'

'Who knows?' she sighed, 'who knows what men think, I certainly don't. Anyway, I'm happy for you that you want to move on. I think there is a lot more to Bertie. He has been very quiet, maybe it's because Alistair is his boss, but I think he's good looking even though a bit skinny.'

'He's not really skinny, he works out a lot and I like him too. He doesn't seem the type that would have one girlfriend and then have sex with lots of others at the same time. But I was wrong about Lionel. I think that sometimes, I would be better off on my own, forget men altogether.'

'My sentiments entirely, are they really worth it? All this effort and they don't seem to even notice.' Molly began to feel a bit melancholy, letting her thoughts drift to the last time she had found herself in bed with Alistair. At that time, she had thought that her life just couldn't get any better; she had even

67

practised writing her name as Molly Warren. She snorted at the foolishness of it. Lucy looked up.

'What are you thinking?'

'I think I have had too much red wine, remembering times past, or should I say boyfriends past, what an idiot I am!'

'I am so sorry, Molly.' She put her arm around her friend's shoulder, 'I didn't mean to upset you.'

'No, no, please don't. Actually, I have been meaning to tell you something and I suppose now is as good a time as any.' She paused looking round the room swallowing hard. She turned and looked into the concerned eyes of her friend, 'I…I think I'm pregnant.' Molly hung her head waiting for a response.

'Are you sure?' Lucy grabbed her hand and rubbed it. 'I mean…have you done a test? Been to see the doctor?' Molly let out a sigh and swung her legs off the bed.

'Yes, I'm sure. I have done a test but that's all. Anyway, I am beginning to think like you about men, who needs them? Let's drink to "no more men",' she raised her glass draining the last dregs.

'I'm sorry, Molly, but I can't take it in. I mean you have just split up with Alistair. Does he know? About the baby, I mean.' Lucy curled her legs up under her, crossing and uncrossing her arms.

'He does know and of all the things that I hoped he would say,' she paused grabbing a tissue as for the first time tears started to well within her, her throat tightened with the pain of the reality of her situation. Lucy placed a comforting arm around her friend's shoulders. 'He…he said that he wanted nothing to do with it. Getting married and having children was my problem, not something he had ever wanted in his life.' Lucy's mouth dropped open as she stared at Molly. Steve Wright's cheery voice babbled out from the radio into the strangled silence flooding the room.

'Turn that off, will you?' said Molly. Lucy leaned over, pressing the button on her pink 'Roberts' radio.

'Shall we cancel tonight? I mean it will be a bit difficult now after this,' Lucy grabbed her drink and took a deep gulp. 'It's funny though, don't you think? That being invited yet again up to the Warrens is odd, especially with what's happened between you and Alistair and…and everything else.'

'I suppose so but then Alistair is still feeling guilty about knocking you off your horse. He's really working hard to make amends.'

'That is rather sweet of him, I suppose. I quite like being made a fuss of, it makes a change from…' she hesitated, 'well, you know.' Lucy left her words hanging in the air and Molly did not have any inclination to pick them up for her. They both fell quiet once more.

'You know what, I'm fed up with this,' Lucy said at last. 'I'm sorry to ask you for help again, Molly. Until my wrist is better, I can't drive, but how do you fancy house hunting with me tomorrow? It's time for me to get my life back on track, any track. I want to make some decisions in my life, be my own boss, no more knights in shining armour for me. Who needs them?' she grinned.

'Wow, where did that come from? I have surgery in the morning but after we close at one o'clock, I'm all yours. Where do you want to go?' Molly smiled pushing her tissue into her pocket.

'Great, Poundbury. I fancy having a look around to see what it's like and find out how close it is to Dorchester hospital.'

'Okay, why not? It'll be fun.'

'So, you want to buy a place in Dorset, do you? I have to say it would be great to have you around for good. There is so much that we could do together. Even in these times, it's still difficult to go anywhere on your own, for a woman anyway; the

69

last thing I want to do is end up joining the WI.' They both burst out laughing.

'Now that is sad. But I have it on good authority that you make excellent jam and pickles.' Molly picked up a cushion and threw it at Lucy.

'I'm not an old maid yet. Why is a single woman called an old maid and yet a single man carries the title of bachelor like a trophy. It's just not fair.'

'You're right. It's time for us, single women, to make a stand. We can do anything we want to and be proud of it. That calls for another toast to "single women".' Lucy raised her glass.

'Single women,' echoed Molly raising her empty glass. She glanced at her watch.

'I'd better go, I promised to pick up some things for Alice. I'll pick you up about ten to seven. See you later.'

Molly felt much better now having told Lucy about the baby. She took Rex for a walk, called in at the farm shop and drank a coffee as she stared into her wardrobe. She pulled on her jeans but they wouldn't do up. Molly sighed as she pulled them off again and put on her looser trousers, patting her stomach, she smiled at herself in the mirror looking from side to side. Satisfied, she set off to collect Lucy from Honeysuckle Cottage; she rapped on the door and let herself in.

'Lucy, are you ready? It's nearly seven,' she leapt up the stairs pushing open her bedroom door. The walls were covered in posters of boy bands hiding the faded wallpaper. It was quite dark with just a chink of light coming through the tiny window. Molly gasped a surprise as she saw Lucy, sprawled across her single wrought iron bed, sobbing.

'Lucy, you look terrible, what's happened?' Molly dashed in to sit by her friend. Lucy looked up and blinked her eyes, staring at Molly momentarily before her face scrunched and twisted as the tears fell.

'I phoned Lionel. It's too complicated, don't let me spoil your evening. You go, I'll see you tomorrow.'

'Not on your life. If we are late, it doesn't matter. Anyway, aren't we supposed to be late? Come on, I'll go and make you a strong coffee; you go into the bathroom and put your face on. Then you can tell me all about it.' Molly watched as Lucy meekly followed her instructions walking towards the bathroom, her shoulders down. Molly went to the kitchen wondering what on earth had happened. She could go on her own, of course, but not this time. Lucy drank her coffee as she dressed.

'My head hurts and my stomach hurts,' she moaned looking up at Molly. 'I feel awful. Honestly, you go without me.' She flopped down onto her bed like a rag doll. 'They will wonder why we are not there.'

'Don't worry. I telephoned when you were in the bathroom. Alice can leave the pasta till we arrive; she was more concerned about you.'

'What did you tell them? Please tell me, you didn't tell them about Lionel?' she wailed.

'No, of course not. I said that you had a migraine and that you had just woken up feeling a lot better. So now you can tell me all about it.' Molly patted the bed beside her and Lucy sat down.

'Well, I decided to telephone Lionel. I suppose I wanted to know why? I know the answer really but I thought that if I spoke to him, it would help me decide one way or the other. So, I used the excuse to ask about the house and when I heard his voice, I wanted to run to him, forgive him, but he was horrible,' her hands flew to her face and she sniffed rubbing her eyes. 'He accused me of wanting to be rid of him and I blurted out that I loved him. I could feel him grinning at me. He said that he could call his solicitor cancel everything and I could go "home".' She blew her nose, picked up her coffee drinking a few sips before taking in a deep breath and continuing, 'I told him that I missed him and took it that he wanted me back too and well, I stupidly thought that things would be different. I am such an idiot, Molly. He just said that we could go back to the way things were but that's all.' Molly saw the look of incredulity on her face and she felt sad for Lucy.

'I'm so sorry, Lucy,' she couldn't think of anything else to say.

'He said that "if I loved him". Can you imagine that? If I loved him that I would go back and I feel like he was laughing at me. He just trampled on my feelings, squashed them as if they were meaningless…worthless.'

'What on earth did you say to him?' asked Molly.

'I told him that I didn't love him anymore and that it was over.' She raised her shoulders and arms in resignation.

'Good for you, no wonder you had such a bad head. How do you feel now?' Molly gently stroked her arm like a wounded animal.

'Better. You are good to me, thanks,' she grinned.

'No problem, now put a smile on that face.' Molly picked up her bag and car keys.

'I'm hungry. In fact, now I think about it, I'm starving,' Lucy declared as she picked up her jacket.

'That's better.' They hugged each other and set off out of the village towards the Warrens' place and began to chat about the evening to come.

'You sound a lot better, are you alright now?' asked Molly.

'Yes, I'm really sorry to have made so much fuss. I am starting to get it into my head that it really is over. He was so cold. He wanted me back but I didn't have a say in anything about the future and if I'm honest, it's obvious that we don't have a future, not together anyway. I'm glad, really, to have spoken to him, at least now I know where we stand,' she paused. 'Nowhere,' she concluded.

Molly let out a sigh, questioning to herself; wasn't Lionel only saying out loud to Lucy what Alistair had been hinting at with her all this time? Men surely were not all the same? She wondered if she should back off completely.

'You know what?'

'What?'

'I think you are right. I wasn't sure before but this "conversation", we'll call it that you have had with Lionel, has made me see a lot of sense.'

'What do you mean? That sounds a bit weird to me.'

'I know. Off the wall, I agree, but there are lots of wonderful men out there who do want a proper two-way relationship. You and I are going to hit the town, go out clubbing, well maybe not clubbing, but we are going to have a great time. Do you fancy a weekend away somewhere or something? It's time we took ourselves out of Trentmouth; see the world a bit, have some fun. Men! Who needs them?'

'You're right. Why are we doing this to ourselves? Waiting for a man, how pathetic is that? Who says they get to make all the choices? It's time we made some of our own and yes, what a good idea. We can look online later and see where we fancy going.'

'Good, that's settled then and we will start tomorrow with your house hunting. I'm really looking forward to it, it will be fun. Come on,' she said turning up the drive to the house. 'Here goes. Oh, and lets' keep our secret to ourselves, for tonight anyway.'

'Agreed,' Lucy put her hand in the air for a 'high five'. 'Stuff Lionel, let's lighten up, relax and be "us" for once.'

It was a relief, she thought as she climbed out of the Land Rover to be greeted by Alice and George, what good hosts they are, how kind of them!

Chapter 7

'How are you, my dear?' asked Alice looking most concerned.

'I'm much better. Thank you, Mrs Warren.'

'Good, and please call me Alice, none of this Mrs Warren, nonsense. We're all good friends,' she beamed. Lucy stole a look at Molly and they both just smiled. Alistair watched the exchange. *I wonder what they have told each other,* he thought, *from that look I guess that Lucy knows everything.*

'Let me take your coats,' he fussed as he helped them both. Molly gave nothing away.

'Come on in and sit by the fire,' said George, 'it's turning quite chilly.' The girls followed him into his study where Bertie was hovering by the wood burner. Bertie gave them both a hug and a peck on the cheek.

'Are you alright now, Lucy? Only Mrs W said you had a migraine,' asked Bertie jiggling his hands in his pockets and shuffling his feet.

'Do you know, Bertie?' she grinned, 'It has completely gone, it was such a pain.' The two girls just smirked and Alistair wondered if he was missing some joke or other.

'Good. Can I get you both a drink?' Alistair cleared his throat for no apparent reason feeling decidedly awkward.

'G&T please,' said Molly.

'And I'll have the same,' echoed Lucy.

'Is that wise?' Alistair looked at Molly in surprise.

'Why? Is there a problem?' Molly was staring at him in defiance.

'No. Sorry.' *What am I doing?* Alistair chastised himself, *pull yourself together.* Bertie, having slipped out of the room, came back bearing a bunch of freesias for each of the girls.

'Oh, Bertie, how sweet,' they both exclaimed together and then laughed saying, 'snap!'

This time, both girls gave Bertie a kiss on the cheek, he looked petrified with red hot heat spreading up his throat and flooding his face. Alistair stood staring, open–mouthed. *why didn't I think of that?* he thought.

'Two G&T's coming up,' he stuttered.

'Ooh, thank you. I am ready for a drink,' said Lucy. She smiled at Alistair, he half smiled back. *I don't get it,* he thought, *she's smiling at me for the very first time and I am suspicious. It must be something to do with Molly.* He scratched his head, knitting his eyebrows together, he pushed his hair back.

'A sweet sherry for me dear,' said Alice.

'Oh, sorry, Mum. I was just thinking. Coming up…Dad?'

'Yes, Son. Thanks.' Alistair could feel his parents' eyes on him, but he was far too baffled to worry about them.

'Isn't this lovely, my dear?' He rubbed her hand and squeezed it. Alistair watched as his mother returned the gesture, glancing across at the flowers on the side table; all her favourites, he knew. She squeezed Georges' hand once more. Alistair felt a profound feeling of loss somehow, almost despondent, he couldn't quite put his finger on it. *Why?* He thought.

'I must check on dinner. I won't be a moment.' Alice stood to slip out of the room. Molly followed her into the kitchen as George quickly took charge of Lucy.

'Tell me, Lucy, have you made any progress with your desire to possibly stay down here in Dorset?' Lucy sat beside him in a conspiratorial manner, Alistair watching.

'Yes, I have made up my mind to find a permanent job and make it my home.'

75

'Jolly good. And if I can help at all, you must not be afraid to ask. I still might be able to pull a few strings, you know.'

'That's very kind and I appreciate it. If I have any problems, I will let you know. Thanks, all the same.'

'That is good news,' said Alistair causing Bertie to swizzle round giving his full attention to the conversation.

'Is it? Why do you say that Alistair?' Lucy questioned.

'Oh well, I just mean that…' he cleared his throat. 'I just meant that it will be a new start for you after…' he bumbled on, 'well, you know what I mean.'

'I think', said George, rescuing his son, 'that he means "it will be nice to have you around".'

'Yes, thank you, Father. That's all I meant.'

Alistair sounded relieved and Lucy threw a warm smile in Bertie's direction, just as Alice came in saying, 'Dinner is ready, please come into the dining room.'

They all got up and followed her. George had lit a fire in the dining room earlier and it was lovely and cheery.

'I think that I will look for a place with a chimney. A real fire is so welcoming,' said Lucy, stretching her fingers as she stood by the fire. Bertie watched her and Alistair watched them both. *Bloody hell*, he thought.

'You won't get a chimney in a flat up at Poundbury though,' grinned George.

'Poundbury, is that where you are thinking of buying?' asked Alistair as he joined her by the fire.

'If I can get a job in Dorchester hospital, I can walk from Poundbury. That's all,' she replied.

'I might look there myself. Mother has collected a lot of details for me, and I am going to look at them tomorrow, but I have been thinking of spreading the search area and I might look Dorchester way too. Would you like me to give you a lift?'

'No, that's alright. Molly and I have already made plans for tomorrow and anyway, what about Bertie?' She looked across at Bertie who was looking most surprised. *Not again,* he thought, *I can't seem to get anything right tonight. At least she seems to have made up her mind about this Lionel chap. It sounds as though that's over, some good news at least.*

'Sorry, of course, I wasn't thinking,'

Lucy turned her attention to Bertie talking to him about his home and interests. Alistair took his chance to speak to Molly. She had perched on the window seat and had been peering into the garden, watching the setting sun. She turned to look at him and he felt stirrings within himself. He couldn't go near her without wanting her. He groaned inwardly. Molly just smiled.

'Does this mean that you will be visiting our little backwater more often?' she teased.

'I have been meaning to buy a property down here for some time, but I have always been too busy with work and one thing or another, but I thought that I would take advantage of the downturn in the market and maybe pick up a bargain,' he said in an off-hand manner.

'I don't blame you, even if it is rather calculating and dare. I say "cold" on your part.' Alistair shrugged.

'Not really,' he took a large gulp of his red wine, 'it's just coincidental that I now have time to properly look around and prices have dropped, that's all. Anyway, where are you two heading tomorrow? Anywhere in particular?'

'I am just the taxi driver,' she said getting up and joining the others.

'Did you say F1? I adore F1. Most men only want to talk about football. So, come on, what do you think of Lewis Hamilton's chances?' Bertie grinned.

'I could talk for hours about F1,' he turned from one girl to the other. 'Do you really want to know all about it?'

'I'd love to go to Monte Carlo and see the race live. Have you ever been, Bertie?' she asked.

'No, but who wouldn't? I think that I might go to Oz next year though and see the race in Melbourne. I might have a better chance of that than Monaco, although one day I would love to.'

'Why the Melbourne race? Or is it that you just fancy visiting Oz?' Molly pushed.

'My sister lives in Adelaide actually, and I haven't seen her for ten years or my two nieces, so I thought two birds with one stone and all that, if Alistair can spare me for a month?' He looked at his boss who had been listening silently to their conversation. All eyes were on him.

'Well, we will have to discuss it nearer the time, but I suppose I'll manage,' he said at last.

'Great, thanks. I've always fancied visiting Sydney; take in the opera house and maybe climb over the harbour bridge. You know all the usual tourist stuff.'

'Sounds to me like you have it all planned, Bertie. Don't mind me,' said Alistair. Molly shot him a look which Alistair could not ignore without drawing any attention.

'Only joking, I'm sure it will be wonderful.' The attention returned to Bertie.

'If everyone has finished, I will serve coffee in the snug.' Alice stood up and began to clear the table.

'I'll help you,' said Molly.

'No, my dear.' It was George who spoke, 'You have done enough to help already and you are a guest. I will help Alice and…Alistair you can entertain our guests and pour everyone a whisky or a brandy. Oh, and I think that we have a bottle of port too, there's a good chap.'

Alistair didn't argue. They wandered into the snug and George followed his wife into the kitchen; he grabbed her arm and pulling her to him, he kissed her.

'I do love you,' she said snuggling into his arms. They stood enjoying the moment.

'And I love you too,' he said. Alistair watched for a moment feeling an emptiness deep inside, he thought that he would never feel. *I am a bloody fool, but it's too late now.* His arms dropped and he hung his head for a moment, then striding forward into the room.

'Molly…can I have a word?' he asked.

Chapter 8

Early the next morning, Molly prepared her bags ready for her day out around the local farms. It was part of her job to check for TB, not something she especially liked doing, as it could spell disaster for a farmer if all his animals had to be destroyed. She heaved her bag into the car and stood staring for a minute across the fields. *What am I going to do?* She thought, *but whatever it is, I can do it, I have to.* She turned to close the car door heaving a sigh and her eye caught someone running along the public footpath, which crossed very near the farmhouse. As she watched, she realised that it was Bertie, she waved and called out to him.

'Hey, Bertie, where are you going so early?' He stopped and ambled over.

'Hi, Molly, best time of day this is. The mist is still hanging over the river and two swans were weaving in and out of the boats rounding up a bunch of cygnets,' he smiled. 'I wish I had my camera but anyway, I'm sure that you are not interested in my ramblings.' He looked at his feet and shrugged his shoulders before stretching his arms. Molly watched his antics for a moment.

'Have you got time for a coffee? I have a few minutes before I have to leave.'

'Sure, I'd love one,' his face erupting into a huge grin. He followed her down the path and around to the kitchen door.

'What are you grinning at? You look very pleased with yourself.'

'Oh, nothing really. It's a beautiful day,' he said, still grinning, '…honest.'

Hmm, thought Molly, *a likely story*.

'Come on, you can tell me,' she coaxed.

'Well, if you must know, how lucky I am and how bloody stupid Alistair is,' the truth slipped out with ease. He hung his head for a moment and gulped.

'So, you know then?' The smile had disappeared from her face and she looked him straight in the eye. Bertie searched her face and Molly could see that he clearly didn't want to lie to her.

'Yes,' he said simply. Such a small, simple word but the truth within it was incalculable, thought Molly, what a good man he is! Bertie looked away from her and for a moment silence enveloped the kitchen; he pulled himself up straight lifting his eyes to look at her face.

'Don't worry,' a hint of a smile teasing the corners of her lips, 'I'm glad you know.'

'You are?' Bertie flopped down onto the nearest chair, a mug of coffee being pushed into his hand.

'Here, drink this. It's a bit early for anything stronger. You look as though you need it.'

'You have no idea,' he managed to say.

'I have to go to work soon,' she declared looking at her watch as she sat at the kitchen table next to Bertie.

'Okay, but first, it's your turn to tell me what you are thinking.' He took a deep gulp of his coffee.

'Sorry, but I saw you as another "geeky" guy and well, you have an honesty that makes a refreshing change…and a vulnerability that I can't quite figure out.' She had caught him off guard, she knew that but she felt pleased that he knew, it made things easier. 'Look Bertie,' she said after a moment's pause. He looked up at her expectantly. 'I appreciate that this is probably a difficult situation for you and it is for me too, but

81

can you please not let Alistair know that we have had this conversation.'

Letting out a sigh, he said, 'No problem, Molly. I had been wondering how to tell Alistair how stupid I am. You know what he can be like. I mean, he was adamant about it being a secret.'

'Stop talking,' she teased. 'I know all about Alistair and his secrets. Has he told you that we are over? He wanted a break, time to think things through. You know all that sort of rubbish?' She looked at him expectantly but Bertie made no reply. 'Anyway, now you and I have a secret. This conversation never happened. Fancy a scone?' Molly pushed her chair back and collected a tin from the shelf. Rex, who had been snuggled up in his basket, sat up, his ears raised in expectation as he slathered his lips.

'Come here, boy,' Bertie called as he patted his thigh. The dog lolloped out of his bed and nuzzled his nose into Bertie's hand. 'Good boy, what's your name then?' Bertie ruffled his ears and the dog just looked up at him with big 'love me' eyes. He felt his collar and twisted the identity disc so that he could read it. 'Rex,' he said out loud. 'Hello Rex, you're a good boy, aren't you? Not much of a guard dog, I have to say.' He ruffled him some more and Rex gave a little woof of appreciation.

It was a typical old farmhouse kitchen, everything you would expect from a property that must be a couple of hundred years old. The kitchen range pervaded the room with its warmth and although it was clearly old, covered in chips and knocks. It heated the house and could tell many a story of the scenes it must have witnessed. Bertie leaned back in his chair, hands behind his head.

'This place is wonderful, so different from Alice's kitchen,' he said looking around at the Welsh dresser against one wall, full of blue and white china; there were envelopes sticking out from behind jugs and faded photographs propped up by teacups, their edges all curled up. Rex gave him another nudge, his tail thumping on the stone flagged floor.

'You have a friend now, Bertie. He wants to go for a walk, don't you, Rex?' Rex bounded over to Molly as if he hadn't seen her in a long time, his tail wagging furiously. She patted his head and Rex wandered back to his bed, flopping down as though exhausted from the experience.

'I have to finish getting ready for work. You drink your coffee, there's no hurry. I'll be back in a minute.'

'Thanks for the coffee but I must go too. They will be thinking that I'm lost or something.' He gave a laugh and added, 'I understand. By the way, our secret is safe.'

'Look, I don't know what you guys are doing later, but I will make sure that Lucy and I are in the Kings Arms at eight tonight. If you happen to come in, that would be great; we can maybe even talk, but if not, don't worry about it. We can catch up some other time. Here's my card, now you have my telephone number, in case you ever need it, of course.'

Bertie took the card and pushed it into his pocket.

'Thanks,' he mumbled. He looked up at her and she leant forward, kissed him on the cheek and he hugged her. Molly picked up her bag. *There's a lot more to this guy*, she thought, *he doesn't know about the baby though.* She smiled and headed for the door.

'Come on, I'll give you a lift.' She hesitated and turning to Bertie said, 'I'm glad that we've had this conversation; I've been wondering about you, but you're alright.' She turned and opened the kitchen door, Rex raised an ear but he knew it wasn't time for his walk and settled down once more.

A taxi pulled up in the farmyard and Molly stopped and stared as two people got out.

'Mum...Dad? What are you two doing here?'

'Well, that's a nice welcome. Put the kettle on and we'll tell you all about it.' Beamed her Mother with her arms outstretched. Molly hugged them both as Bertie stood watching.

'I can't. I'm late already. I have to go. I'll see you later.' *No time for explanations*, she thought, *what on earth is going on*?

'And who is this? So early in the morning,' her mother asked looking at Bertie and ignoring Molly's obvious need to leave.

'Bertie, he's a friend.' Molly couldn't hide her exasperation and confusion. She picked up her bag once more and opened the car. The wheels spun as she reversed out of the yard and into the lane, spitting stones and dust into the air. She dropped Bertie off by the gate at the bottom of the lane that led to the Warren's place and sped off with a million thoughts chasing themselves around her head, but she had to put them to one side. Checking her watch, right now, she had visits to make.

Chapter 9

Alistair was gazing out of the window in the snug when Molly dropped Bertie off. He watched as Bertie half jogged then jumped in the air clicking his heels together as he made his way down the drive. He rubbed his cheek and then stood patting his chin, his hand clenched up into a fist. Alistair watched him for a few more minutes as his antics had him baffled. He opened the French window and called out,

'Are you alright, Bertie?'

'I am definitely alright, couldn't be better,' he called back with a stupid grin.

'Are you sure?'

'Quite sure. I haven't missed breakfast, have I?' he lolloped back towards the house.

'No, but you had better hurry up,' Alistair closed the door. *Hmmm,* he thought, *my questions will keep...for now.*

Bertie dashed in running up the stairs three steps at a time.

'I will be as quick as possible, must have a shower,' he called down to Alistair, who was standing hands on hips staring up the stairs after him. 'Mustn't keep Mrs W waiting, must I? The smell of bacon and eggs is magical. What a lucky bloke you are, Alistair.'

Alistair shook his head mystified. He could hear Bertie singing...singing no less.

'Mrs W,' he said later when they were all seated enjoying breakfast, 'you are the best cook in the world.'

'Well, thank you, my dear. You are happy today. What has happened to put such a smile on your face?'

Alistair looked up at his mother; she never ceased to amaze him, turning to Bertie, he said, 'Yes, come on, we all want to know, you are way too happy for someone who has just been out for a jog. What gives old boy?'

Bertie crammed another bite of toast and marmalade into his mouth, he tried to think but all that came to mind was the kitchen up at the farm, Molly, their secret and her daft dog, Rex.

'It's a lovely day,' he managed to say.

'And?' pushed Alistair.

'I ran along the river, it is so peaceful first thing, there were a family of swans busy with cygnets. I'm just happy to be alive,' he concluded raising his arms in the air, still clutching his knife and fork.

'I think that there is more to it than that. I've never seen you like this before,' Alistair felt suspicious wanting to probe further.

'Leave the poor lad alone,' said George.

'Yes,' said Alice, 'he is entitled to be happy you know.' Alistair returned to his breakfast.

'Changing the subject, I have been looking at a street map and I have worked out a route for taking in these properties.' He shuffled a bunch of brochures and placed them onto the table. 'We can probably see about six this morning, get a bite to eat in The Horse with the Red Umbrella in Dorchester and see the rest this afternoon.'

'The Horse with the Red Umbrella, you've got to be kidding me? That's what I love about Dorset. You think you have seen it all and up jumps another surprise,' Bertie smirked. The Warrens exchanged a look.

'Oh, you're not coming back here for lunch?' Alice said looking at Alistair with her shoulders stooped, a crest fallen look on her face.

'No, Mother. We can see more if we eat on the go but we will be back by six. Bertie and I are cooking tonight, no arguing.' Alice opened her mouth to speak and closed it again, '…maybe later, we might go down to the local for a drink.'

'Good idea,' Bertie broke in as he straightened himself, fork in mid-air. 'I mean, sounds a good plan to me. I've always wanted to visit Dorchester and don't worry about dinner, Mrs W, I love cooking.'

Alistair turned to look at Bertie, this was getting to be a day full of surprises.

'That's settled then. Come on, Bertie, let's go. We have a lot to see today.' The men stood up to leave the table and George stretched out his hand to squeeze Alice's.

'I thought that we might take a trip out today, dear. We haven't visited Kingston Lacy for a long time. What do you think?'

'That would be lovely, dear.' Brightening, she called after Alistair, 'Have a good day you two.'

The boys set off on their search for a property but not without Alistair first launching into his questions for Bertie.

'Right, you might fool them old chap but not me. I want to know what has put such a smile on your ugly face and what is all this about you wanting to visit Dorchester?' Bertie squirmed, twisting his hands around the steering wheel. 'Come on, fess up, Bertie. I know you remember.' Alistair was becoming impatient; he wanted the truth.

'To be honest, I just couldn't help myself this morning. I was running along the tow path and everything in the world just felt great.' He shrugged and glanced at Alistair.

'A likely story but do carry on, convince me.' Alistair stared out of the car window; he too felt a new desire for Dorset. He had always been happy to escape it in the past but recently, the urge to come back had grown. His thoughts wandered to Molly, *she doesn't need me and I wouldn't be good for her, anyway.* Bertie broke into his daydream.

'Well, it's obvious really. You have talked almost about nothing else except Molly, Lucy, your mother, now you are thinking of buying a property down here. I was beginning to think that you might be looking for office space too and if that was the case, maybe I should be thinking of a move to Dorset unless, of course, you have other plans or don't want me to transfer with you.' He paused for breath.

'That explains a lot.' Alistair sat pondering what Bertie had said, rubbing his chin, leaving Bertie to drive on in silence. 'Take the next left, we are nearly at our first property. Number 12, there on the right, pull up over there.' He pointed and they looked at the outside of a modern mid-terrace house with a child bike propped up against the wall, pink and purple tassels attached to the handlebars blowing in the breeze. 'Hmm, not bad. Small garden but that's what I want. I won't be spending too much time here, it's only a bolt hole,' confirmed Alistair, more to himself than Bertie. Bertie nodded.

'…Where next?'

'Let's stop for a coffee. All this work is making me thirsty.' Alistair directed the way down some narrow country lanes and as they drove down the hill towards Kimmeridge, Bertie pulled over to admire the view.

'What an amazing place! Just look at all those thatched cottages, it's not like anywhere I have ever been. What's that place over there?' He pointed to a tower on the top on the hill.

'That's Clavell Tower, it has been restored and turned into a holiday let.' They both surveyed the scene for a moment before Alistair said, 'Anyway, come on, I need a coffee and we need to talk.' Alistair sat on a bench outside the café and lifted his face to the mid-morning sun; he closed his eyes pushing his glasses up on top of his head. It felt good. Bertie returned carrying two large steaming lattes. He put them down onto the rough wooden table looking at Alistair.

'Before you start, I'm sorry. I shouldn't presume anything and...'

'Hold on a minute, you don't know what I am going to say, so just be quiet. There's a good chap and let me try this coffee.' He took a sip letting the soothing shot of caffeine take over. 'Firstly, if you must know, I have no plans at the present time to relocate the business to Dorset.' Bertie visibly relaxed. 'I want to buy a place for two reasons, one is that it is a good, sound investment as you know and secondly, should I want to invite someone back for a...well. Let's just say I can't take someone to my parents' home now, can I?' he paused.

'You had me worried for a bit there, Alistair. It's not that I would mind relocating, far from it actually, but I hadn't taken it very seriously until now. I'm glad we've cleared that up.' Bertie picked up his cup and Alistair watched him, curiosity getting the best of him.

'You must tell me why? But come on, it will keep, time to go. We have two more to see and then we can drive over to Dorchester. Did you know that Thomas Hardy came from round here? If we have time, we can drive up to his cottage in the woods and maybe even see Max Gate.'

'No, I didn't know, you are full of surprises, do tell me more. I know nothing of Dorset, I am ashamed to say. Geography and stuff wasn't really my thing, preferred computers and racing cars.' They chatted on about the attractions of Dorset and Alistair spent the rest of the day showing off to his friend; he surprised himself at his own knowledge regaling tales of the 'Red Signpost', which he promised to drive past later if possible, the Tolpuddle Martyrs and even 'Hanging Judge Jefferies'. Bertie took it all on board telling Alistair that he was truly fascinated by this amazing county. After lunch, they drove up to the village of Poundbury, which is not a village at all, really, just a development on the edge of Dorchester. They drove around looking at all the different styles of property before finally arriving at the one that Alistair could afford. Tiny hardly came close to describing it with almost no outside space and no garage. Alistair looked at it beginning to think that he would not be buying a bolthole after all. They were about to drive off when the front door opened and out came Molly and Lucy. They watched them walk along the footpath towards Molly's Land Rover; the girls were laughing at something and had not seen the boys. Bertie made to open the car door but Alistair grabbed his arm.

'No, leave it,' he let go of Bertie and continued to watch them.

'But why? What's wrong?' Bertie turned to look at him. Alistair sat still, just watching. 'What's wrong, mate? You look as if you have seen a ghost.'

'I'm alright. Let's go back to Trentmouth.' Bertie did as requested and drove out of Poundbury in the opposite direction to Molly. They drove for a few miles in complete silence; eventually, as they neared Wareham, Alistair spoke, 'Sorry about that, mate. I need a drink. Don't go home, there is a wine bar open in town, we'll go there. It's just that seeing the two of them together like that and Molly was so happy...' he broke off staring up at the sky. 'I don't know what came over me. We should have spoken to them, but I have been a bit short with Molly lately and well, the whole thing is such a mess...' Bertie followed the signs into a car park and stopped.

'I can't say that I am surprised,' said Bertie turning to look at him. 'You have messed Molly about saying you want a break but then still seeing her, what do you expect? She's not going to sit around while you make up your mind, is she?'

'I suppose but...oh, I don't know. Just seeing the two of them together...look let's get that drink. I don't know what I'm talking about.' Alistair opened the car door. They crossed the road and headed for the wine bar.

'Huh! I don't know about that but I know something's wrong.'

'Okay, you win. Come on then, here we are.' He pushed open the door to a warm, comfortable looking bar, busy with a crowd of people chatting. Alistair walked straight to the rear of the place where he knew there were some sofas. He motioned towards Bertie to sit down.

'I suppose I owe you some sort of explanation,' Alistair fiddled with a drinks coaster and tossed it down.

'You suppose right. Come on then, out with it.' Bertie sounded a tad annoyed and Alistair wasn't surprised. He owed him an explanation, although he wasn't used to being the one on the receiving end, however, justified Bertie might be.

'They did look like they were having fun and I didn't want to spoil it,' he blurted sheepishly.

'Right, that's the excuse. Now, I want the truth.' Bertie began drumming his fingers on the table, taking a sip of his wine, watching Alistair.

'Alright, you got me,' he grinned. 'I am pathetic I know, but to be honest, I found myself feeling on the outside.' He looked down at his drink wondering if this would pacify him.

'Hmm, that does sound pathetic; not like you at all. Do you know what I think?' he continued without giving Alistair chance to speak. 'I think that you panicked because for once, you are not in control.' He looked Alistair straight in the eye and paused. Alistair shuffled in his seat; Bertie watched him squirm. *He knows me far too well,* thought Alistair, *but I have to admit that I much prefer working on the success of my business rather than playing happy families. I suppose I do like to control everything, even my parents.* He sighed looking around the wine bar. There were two mums with pushchairs chatting and drinking coffee, a group of lads laughing loudly

91

discussing football and Bertie was watching him, arms folded waiting for him to say something.

Alistair stared at him for a moment thinking that how frightening it was that Bertie had pinpointed the problem at his first attempt. *I have always made things happen my way before,* he thought, *now it feels like I have stepped into mid-air and am in freefall...and no safety net.* He shuffled around in his seat and still Bertie sat watching him, it was unbearable. He picked up his drink and swirled it around. *Courage,* he thought, *takes a lot of finding and I am not about to confide in my parents.*

'You know me too well,' he finally managed to admit. 'So what do you think I should or should not do?' Alistair tried to off load on to Bertie and at the same time, save him any further explanations.

'Not for me to say. I'm listening to you,' his mouth twitching at the corners, he almost smiled the smile of smugness. Alistair glared at him.

'I think that you're enjoying this, Bertie.' Alistair floundered. Bertie raised his eyebrows saying nothing and leaving Alistair back at square one. He looked over to the bar and caught the attention of one of the girls, indicating two more glasses of wine. He turned back to see Bertie still staring at him, waiting expectantly. He took a deep breath. *Here goes,* he thought.

'I have a problem,' he glanced up at Bertie who made no move, whatsoever. 'What I mean is, I don't know how to solve a problem.' Bertie just watched him. 'In fact, you know what? I don't even know what my problem is.'

'Now we are getting somewhere.' Bertie looked up, smiling at the young waitress as he accepted his second glass of wine before turning back to Alistair. 'What do you think your problem is?' he sipped his wine. 'Actually, don't answer that. I'm feeling rather lightheaded, no food!' he signalled to the waitress and asked for two black coffees and two packets of crisps. He turned his attention back to Alistair. 'You were saying?'

'It's Molly, I wanted to see her today and she said that she was too busy, that she would be taking Lucy out house hunting this afternoon and calls this morning...'

'And?' said Bertie waving his hands in the air. 'I don't see what is wrong with that.'

'I'm not used to being turned down,' admitted Alistair. 'Yes, alright. I admit it. I was shocked that she said "no". She's changed.' He downed his wine and looked forlorn. Bertie burst out laughing, Alistair looked at him aghast, 'What's so funny?'

'What? Is that all?' Bertie burst out laughing again. The couple at the next table turned and stared at them but Bertie just could not stop. 'I thought that it was something important,' he managed to say. 'You know life threatening or at least catastrophic. She was busy, so what? She is allowed to go out with her friends, you know. You're just upset, like a spoiled kid that she didn't come running when you called. It's about time that you learned that the world doesn't exist for your benefit.' Bertie looked triumphant as he tipped the packet of crisps into his mouth and scrunched up the bag. He sat back in his chair looking at Alistair. 'It's nice to know that you are human after all.'

'That's not all,' he pushed his glasses up onto his forehead and rubbed his eyes. 'I might as well tell you now...Molly is pregnant.' He drained his coffee and looked up at his friend.

'Bloody hell, mate. I don't know what to say. Are you pleased? No stupid question, is she pleased? Probably not, I imagine. I just don't know what to say. Talk to me, no wonder you are a mess. No, hang on a minute,' he checked his watch 'I think that we should have another coffee and get some fresh air, otherwise, I will not be in a fit state to drive back and face your mother...and in case you've forgotten, you volunteered us to do the cooking tonight.' This time, Alistair could see the funny side, and Bertie being concerned about his mother was even funnier.

'I suppose I am over reacting. It's not really my problem, is it? And we had better get something for tonight. I was a bit hasty offering to cook, wasn't I?' He stretched his back and shoulders, shaking the image of his dragon like mother from his head.

'Whoa, hang on a minute. What do you mean it's not really your problem? Of course, it is. You are going to be a father.' Bertie looked gobsmacked and shook his head at Alistair. 'Come on. Let's get out of here before I punch you on the nose.' They paid their bill and walked down to the river. 'I have done this circuit a few times. We have just about enough time to walk around the town on the old walls and back to the car park before the time runs out.' Alistair acquiesced and fell into step with Bertie all kinds of things flashing round his brain.

'So, come on Mr Worldly Wise, expert on women, what would you do?' He hunched his shoulders pushing his hands into his pockets, walking not his thing.

'Look, to begin with, you are trying to chase two women and believe me, it doesn't work. You have to make up your mind, you have to do everything you can to pursue one of them and completely forget about the other one. This is one of those situations where you cannot keep the other woman as "plan B". If you lose the one you're after, then you lose both; they do talk to each other you know...and I wouldn't mind betting that Lucy already knows about Molly being pregnant, I mean, so if you ask me, you have already lost Lucy and maybe even Molly as well.' He shrugged. Alistair grimaced, his head down. They walked in silence. Bertie checked his watch, 'Come on, we will have to take a short cut through here.' They walked down a grassy slope back onto the road and turned towards the centre of town. 'I can't help you with your decision, mate, but what I do think is that if you don't do something soon and I mean very

94

soon, you might find yourself with the decision taken away from you altogether because they just might meet someone else.'

Alistair froze, completely unnerved at the thought of losing them both; he had never considered that possibility. They made their way back towards the car park, each lost in their own thoughts. The houses were mainly red brick Victorian terraces with no gardens in front; interspersed with some older houses and one or two thatched cottages. It was a funny, quaint old town, which had once boasted its own mint. There had been a thriving port, which had made it easy for the Saxons to sail up the river and conquer the people. A Saxon sword had even been found in the river and a replica of the sword was proudly displayed on top of a pile of Purbeck stone at the entrance to Wareham. The old priory was now a fine hotel with a beautiful garden with its own river frontage. Although not strictly on the Isle of Purbeck, the people of Wareham still felt as though they belonged to Purbeck. As they walked along, Alistair noted a 'For Sale' sign outside a terraced property and thought that he might look into it, not originally the sort of place that he had been looking for but...*what's the point,* he thought, *I might just keep away from Purbeck and Trentmouth completely.*

Chapter 10

'Sorry we are late, Mrs W,' announced Bertie when they finally arrived back in Trentmouth.

'No matter dear, dinner is almost ready. It was getting late so I started without you. Are you alright, Alistair? You look rather pale.' Alistair pulled a face at his mother's fussing; he was rescued by Bertie.

'It's my fault. We stopped off in Wareham for a drink and then I dragged him off for a walk around the walls. I think that he is out of condition.' Bertie grinned at Alistair, who gave a knowing half smile in reply.

'Err, what do you mean, out of condition? I'm not a dog, you know. I'm just not used to all this walking.' They all laughed. 'I'm sorry about dinner, but please let us help now that we are back.'

They went indoors and after speaking to George. Alistair made his apologies and went to his room to change before dinner. He jumped into the shower and went over in his mind all that had happened, letting the water soothe him. It had been an eventful day, one that had bounced from elation to concern and back again. Bertie was probably right, he could not carry on like this and he hadn't been totally honest with Bertie. Yes, they are both gorgeous but he was secretly pleased to be a father even if it was a shock, he just didn't know how to handle it. He quickly dressed and went to go downstairs when he heard Bertie talking. He stopped to listen.

'Hi Molly, its Bertie.' Alistair stiffened. 'We will be in the Kings Arms tonight. Obviously, I haven't said anything to Alistair; in fact, it was his idea.' There was a pause and Alistair could hear him erring and humming. Then Bertie replied, 'Yes, I know. He's fine. We had a good day out house hunting but didn't find anything suitable; not that he could afford anyway. What about Lucy?' Another pause, 'Yep, see you later.' Alistair knocked and opened the door just as Bertie was tapping his phone against his chin. Bertie visibly jumped, startled for a minute.

'Come on, Bertie, everyone is waiting. Mother is getting anxious to serve dinner.'

'Sorry, sorry, on my way,' he spluttered.

'Who were you talking to? Your new girlfriend?' Alistair asked as they finished dinner.

'Something like that...maybe.' Bertie side stepped his question skilfully and turning to Alice, 'Mrs W...ooh,' pushing his plate back and rubbing his stomach, 'that was delicious as usual.' Alice beamed and Alistair felt piqued.

'Glad you enjoyed it. Have you any room for dessert? I have made lemon meringue pie tonight.'

'I will be putting on weight but I can't resist your cooking, just a small slice please. We had a really good day out today looking at property,' he glanced across at Alistair.

'Ah,' said George, 'I was wondering if you were going to tell us about it.' He looked at Alistair and although Alistair had intended to fill them in on the day, he hadn't found the right moment to bring the subject up. He didn't want to upset his mother. He knew she loved having him stay but the practicalities dictated that he should be buying his own place.

'In all honesty, I didn't see anything to entice me to buy but I will keep looking. I don't really know what I want if I'm honest.'

97

'Something else, you can't make your mind up about, eh?' Bertie blurted. Alistair glared at him. He knew that George had not missed it though by the quick turning of his head from one to the other.

'Do you want us to keep looking for you, Alistair?' he asked kindly.

'Thanks, Dad, but I might leave it for now.' Alistair heaved a sigh and downed his wine signalling an end to the conversation.

'No problem, Bertie. What did you think of this house business?' asked George. Bertie had just put another piece of pie into his mouth,

'Mm, well, I like Dorchester. Especially, that place where we had lunch, something with a red umbrella; I've never been house hunting before, I didn't know it could be so complicated.'

'Have you always rented?' asked George with interest.

'London is so expensive to find anything that I could afford. I would have to move well out of town and into the east end or south of the river and then it would be a very long commute, so I have just stayed put, it suits me at the moment.' He went back to his pie scooping up the last fork full; he wiped his mouth with his napkin and grinned at Alice. 'Magnificent,' he declared with satisfaction.

'Yes,' said Alistair, 'another triumph, Mother.' Alice looked pleased with herself as she began to collect the plates. Alistair pushed his chair back and headed to the snug, followed by George. They both rubbed their extended stomachs and Alistair placed a hand over his mouth in an attempt to stifle a yawn.

Alice carried a tray of dirty dishes towards the kitchen and Bertie followed with left over pie and cream.

'I really appreciate you inviting me here with Alistair,' he said to her. 'I have had a great weekend again, thank you. Can I help you wash up? Please.'

Alice chuckled, delighted and although she had considered sending him off to the snug with the others, she thought better of it.

'Thank you dear, you rinse the plates and stack them into the dishwasher while I make the coffee.' She began to busy herself arranging the coffee cups and opening a box of mint chocolates, and as casually as possible, she asked, 'Has Alistair said anything about Molly or Lucy to you?' Bertie placed the crockery into the dishwasher, carefully rinsed a large bowl and slid it on top.

'Oh, he likes both of them actually, Mrs W. I don't think he can make up his mind, who to ask out.' Alice was thrilled. She displayed the mints on one of her best chintz china plates hardly able to contain her excitement.

'They are both such lovely girls, don't you think so, Bertie?' Bertie hesitated but Alice knew that he was too late, he was well and truly ensnared in her little trap.

He clattered about in the sink for a minute, then replied, 'Actually, I agree with Alistair, it would be difficult to choose between them. In fact, we are going to the Kings Arms later and we are hoping to bump into them.'

'Bump into whom?' George had come in search of his guest and Bertie let out a sigh giving George a sheepish grin.

'Nothing dear,' Alice replied. 'I will tell you all about it later. Now, will you carry the tray for me please, dear?' She ushered George back out of the kitchen leaving Alice to give Bertie a conspiratorial glance.

'Come along, Bertie, let's all sit down and have coffee.'

Seated in the snug, brandy in hand, Alistair sat motionless gazing into the flames dancing in the grate.

'Aren't you going out this evening, Alistair?' asked George

'What? Yes, in a minute.'

'I think that I had better take you. You have had a few drinks already. I can have mine when I get back if you would like me to, of course.' George put his glass down in anticipation.

'Thanks. Actually, that's not a bad idea. We'll get a taxi back, so don't wait up for us.' Rather pleased at this suggestion, there was a time when he would have been horrified at the very thought, but he was only too aware that Bertie had had a few drinks, too. George dropped them by the entrance to the public bar. They sauntered in and Alistair quickly scanned the crowd in the Kings Arms, relieved that they had arrived first. He followed Bertie heading for the comfy couch by the inglenook fireplace with its roaring log fire.

'Come on, mate,' he said as he dropped down into the soft leather. 'You are getting very morose. If it makes you this unhappy, maybe you should forget them both,' he paused and Alistair shot him a surprised look.

'Am I that obvious?' He mumbled turning his eyes back to the fire.

'Look, I can't help you. This is one decision, you will have to make on your own, but you had better make it soon as it's eating you alive. I admit that I don't know much about women, well, probably next to nothing if I am honest, but, and I'm sure that what I am going to say next isn't going to help you that much but…'

'Hello,' said Molly. 'Mind if we join you?'

What Bertie was about to say, Alistair couldn't guess, but he jumped up to greet the two women and Bertie followed suit.

'I was hoping that you two would come in tonight. I wanted to talk to you,' he looked at Molly, 'to you both, of course.' He moved to the side and offered the spot nearest to the fire to the girls. They sat down and Bertie helped Lucy with her jacket.

'Would you both like red wine?' asked Bertie looking at the assembled gang. Lucy smiled and whispered,

'Please.'

'Not for me,' said Molly. 'I'm driving. Can you make mine a lime and soda?' Bertie nodded and he walked towards the bar giving Alistair some space.

'So, come on,' said Molly, 'you wanted to talk to us.' Molly threw Alistair a warm smile.

'Yes. But I would rather wait until Bertie comes back with the drinks. Anyway, have you both had a good day?' He sat back on the sofa turning the conversation in their direction. He looked from one to the other, his mind still in turmoil; this wanting them both was not going to work. However, much he might want it to and now that things are different...

'Yes,' said Lucy, 'we saw a few properties and I am more confused now than I was before. I loved Poundbury but it is too expensive for me and I didn't really like anything else, not enough to want to buy it. So, it's back to square one. How was your day? Did anything nice?' Her eyes transfixed him. *Bertie is right*, he thought, *those eyes could cause a meltdown*. His passion rising, he cleared his throat.

'Actually, we looked at a few properties too and that's really, what I wanted to ask you about. Ah, here's Bertie.' He leaned over to assist him and his arm brushed Lucy ever so slightly; the bolt of electricity through his veins nearly caused him to drop the glasses.

'Are you alright?' asked Bertie.

'Couldn't be better, sorry about that,' he said to Lucy.

'No problem,' Lucy smiled accepting her drink.

They settled down by the fire, talking houses, but Bertie, who had seen the exchange, realised that Alistair must have finally made his choice. He looked across at them deep in conversation. He felt a pang of regret. Lucy was gentle, vulnerable even, he wanted to take care of her but it looked as

101

though Alistair was in first making a move on her and she did not appear to mind.

'What do you think?' Molly pushed Alistair as she tucked a wisp of hair behind her ear.

'About what? Sorry, Molly, my attention slipped for a minute. I do apologise. What do I think about what?' His face flushing hot, he pulled at his collar. Molly is gorgeous, his body screamed.

'I was just saying that property is still expensive despite the downturn in the market,' allowing a mere twitch of the corners of her mouth.

'Yes, you're right. Some of the places we saw today were great, but when you looked at the asking price, you wonder if they just think of a number and double it,' he managed to say. 'Isn't that right, Lucy?'

'Yes. But…I am determined to find something of my own.' Lucy sipped her wine.

'Well, with my mum and dad here and Stella arriving tomorrow, I'm a bit busy, but I'm happy to help again on my afternoon off next week if you like?' She glanced at Alistair and back to Lucy. Alistair cut in.

'Actually, Molly, I might not bother all that upkeep. I haven't the time.'

'Why don't you let it out to holiday makers? Not long term. The holiday let market can be very lucrative. We get "grockles" all year round.' She brightened.

'Grockles,' exclaimed Bertie, 'what on earth is a "grockle"?'

'A tourist,' they all chimed.

'It's an old Dorset word,' giggled Molly. 'You're a grockle.'

'Am I? I thought that I was a visitor, you know an invited guest,' he said defensively.

102

'Too right,' defended Alistair. 'Grockles are well hmm, grockles.' They all fell about laughing.

'We have a cottage on the farm, as you know; it funds my parents' Spanish lifestyle.'

'I had forgotten that. How long are they staying?' Alistair turned his attention to Molly and began to ask her questions and Lucy quizzed Bertie.

'It must have been boring for you today...all this house hunting?'

'In a way but Alistair has been giving me a history lesson. It is a fascinating place and we had lunch in Dorchester at a place with a weird name.' Lucy nodded.

'I like Dorchester. It's an old-fashioned town and yet modern. That sounds mad, doesn't it?'

'Not really. I know exactly what you mean,' Bertie relaxed dropping his shoulders.

'It's Poundbury that does it, I think. It's most unexpected; it's new yet it looks old with such a mix of property style and shops. I think that it is like marmite, you either love it or hate it. Which do you do?' she tilted her chin and looked him straight in the eye.

'Oh, love it. Poundbury and marmite.' Bertie slid down a little on the couch. The fire crackled loudly as someone put on another log and the sparks flew into the air for a moment. Alistair was chatting amiably to Molly discussing the pros and cons of a thatch roof.

'We have a thatched roof on Honeysuckle cottage. You just have to be careful with an open fire, but we have never had any trouble. Dad replaced ours a few years ago, it costs a lot of money but then any roof would, so I don't see the difference.'

'Don't they get lots of animals or birds living in them?' asked Bertie. Everyone laughed.

'You can tell that you live in the city,' said Lucy. Bertie sat up folding his arms.

'Sorry…I don't get it, what's so funny?'

'The birds steal straw occasionally but otherwise, no residents. I'm pleased to say.' The conversation turned to more mundane topics, with Molly pounding Alistair with all sorts of leading questions, Bertie was amused.

'So, come on, what has put you into such a good mood, Alistair Warren?' Molly waited, her eyes teasing him.

'I suppose that I have had a bit of a roller coaster day actually. I set out looking for a bolt hole with enthusiasm this morning. I then became a bit despondent when I couldn't find anything that I wanted, so I made up my mind to forget it altogether. Now… talking about holiday letting, I am beginning to think that it is not a bad idea and I might give it another go. Only problem is, if I let it out, when am I going to use it? As that was the original idea,' he paused for breath and the other three all looked at him in amazement. It wasn't like Alistair to say so much and especially about his plans.

'Wow,' said Molly, 'that is a change around, especially, for you. I am wondering who this Alistair Warren is?' Bertie shot a glance at Lucy and shrugged. Lucy opened her eyes wide looking from one to the other. Alistair looked from one to the other, Bertie smirked.

'Hello,' he said, 'my name is Alistair Warren. We've never met before. Come on you lot, lighten up, I'm not usually that serious, am I? No, please don't answer that. All that I am saying is that I have been doing some soul searching recently; unusual for me, I agree but it's hard to get Trentmouth out of your blood and God knows how hard I have tried. So, I have decided to make a few changes.'

A stunned silence settled over the group. Alistair drew a deep breath, 'I am not relocating my business, so you can relax Bertie, but well, it's hard to explain really. It all started when I startled your horse, Lucy.' Molly sat bolt upright staring at him. Alistair continued, 'I was full of remorse, I am so sorry, Lucy.'

He looked at her, not knowing how she might respond but he had to get it out into the open.

'All forgiven and look my wrist is almost as good as new,' she giggled twisting and shaking her arm in the air.

'I have spent my life trying to avoid coming back to Trentmouth and that night, well, I was remembering my brother Christopher and...I suppose that I have to admit that I have blamed my parents all my life; I have never been able to forgive them for what happened. I know deep inside that it wasn't their fault; it's just one of those tragic accidents, but the problem is once you get an idea into your head, it is incredibly hard to move. I have been cold and rigid with my parents ever since. My mother has never stopped trying to comfort me but of course, I was having none of it so I came back as little as possible. What a fool I have been.' He paused. Bertie could see that it must have been very hard for Alistair to make all those admissions, he was close to hyperventilating, but Bertie knew that he couldn't help, he had to do this on his own. Thirty years is a long time to hold back and remain cold. A strange calm descended. They all looked down and fidgeted. No one knew what to say, if anything at all. Lucy reached across the table and squeezed his hand; for her, it was a natural thing to do, having trained in nursing and caring for people, but to Molly, it must have spelt disaster. She gulped but rubbed his arm in rather an awkward fashion. Bertie didn't move a muscle, he just stared at the scene in front of him in total envy; only Alistair could admit so much, lay his short comings out for the world to see in front of two gorgeous women and get away with it. They both loved him in one way or another and he felt like the outsider that he was; lucky devil.

'I had better get some drinks in. What are you going to have?' Bertie stood up pulling out his wallet.

'Can you make mine a coffee please,' said Molly.

'Not a bad idea,' echoed Lucy, 'me too.'

'Shall I make it four coffees then?' He looked at Alistair who nodded.

'…and can I have a whisky, too?' ventured Alistair.

'That's more like it,' he grinned, 'coming up.' Bertie disappeared. He ordered the coffees and carried back two tots of whisky. 'Here you are, mate?' He handed Alistair his drink. Alistair took a sip closing his eyes. In a way, they were all, four of them, lost in some sort of wilderness, not knowing which direction to take but realising their own bad choices in the past, time to just get over it and move on.

'Easier said than done,' Alistair vocalised without realising. Three heads turned in his direction, Molly had that startled look of a fawn in the forest.

'What is?'

'Oh, sorry, ignore me.' He stared into his drink as if he would find an answer there, but swirling it and looking into its depths brought nothing, no reply.

'Come on, Alistair, tell us.' Bertie took a deep draught of whisky and winced as the shock of it hit his throat.

'Well…if I may interject for a moment? For me, hearing Alistair say, what he said, made me think about my parents,' he paused and everyone sat silently, waiting. 'I guess it's much easier to blame others but trying to forgive them and yourself is "easier said than done".'

They all chorused. That broke the melancholy mood and they returned to chattering about nothing in particular.

'You're very quiet,' said Lucy, 'everything alright?'

'Yes, yes, I'm fine. What were you saying about the weather and tomorrow?' She quickly asked.

'We were wondering about going for a walk around Corfe Castle in the morning before Alistair and Bertie head back to London.'

'Oh, err, well count me out, family remember. And I have been neglecting my allotment recently. I need to do some serious digging before I go back to work on Monday.'

'Are you sure?' blurted out a puzzled Alistair, 'Just for an hour, mother is going to have another challenging feast waiting for us before we go. It will give us a chance to see you...both,' he added quickly.

'That's very kind but no, thanks. You're only going to London not another planet, and I'm sure you will be back soon as I think that you are still looking for a property to let to the grockles?' She raised her eyebrows.

'Well, yes. I suppose that's true.'

Bertie felt for his mate and was equally saddened by this turn of events, as he had grown rather accustomed to meeting up with the girls on a weekend. He looked deep into his glass trying to find one spot of whisky left that he could savour.

'Speaking of which,' said Molly getting up, 'it is going to be a sunny day tomorrow and I need an early night if I am going to get out in the garden before the slugs.'

'Ugh,' said Lucy with a giggle, 'you don't actually pick them up, do you?' Molly and Lucy discussed the merits of slug pellets but Molly was adamant that the birds come and eat the poisoned slugs, then feed them to their young chicks and before you know it, one dead slug equals a dead family of blackbirds or bluetits.

'Oh dear, I never thought of it like that; I will never buy slug pellets again,' said Lucy. Bertie had been watching Alistair's face, he had that puzzled yet defeated look about him as if he couldn't work out how he had been out manoeuvred. Alistair had always been in control and now, he had faced other people making their own decisions, what a mystifying thought that must be for him. Bertie smiled.

'What's wrong, mate?' he asked, 'we can still go to Corfe Castle; I've always wanted to climb up there.'

107

'Yes, yes,' he said half-heartedly. He turned to Lucy, 'What about you, Lucy? Do you fancy a walk out with us in the morning?' Lucy looked flustered, she quickly turned to look at Molly who just smiled.

'Well, I could do,' she said hesitantly, 'but my dad has offered to take me to see another house before he starts his shift down at Swanage railway, so I think I will pass if you don't mind.' Molly's smile broadened. Alistair brightened instantly.

'I can take you house hunting if you like, save bothering your dad. Shall I pick you up about ten?' But before she could reply, Bertie jumped in,

'Don't you mean we will pick you up? We came in my car if you remember and I'm not sure that Lucy will want the two of us tagging along with her.' He beamed in her direction and Lucy picked up his cue nicely.

'Honestly, I will be fine with my dad and anyway, I value his opinion; he was in the building trade and he will see things that I miss.'

'Okay, I give in. Just trying to be of help,' exclaimed a defeated Alistair. Molly drew herself up.

'Right, see you sometime, perhaps the next time you are down. Come on, Lucy, I'll drop you back home.' The girls left leaving the boys still pondering what had just happened to them both.

'We've been given the brush off,' exclaimed Bertie watching the girls' backs disappearing, laughing together.

'No, I'm sure that they have just made other plans for tomorrow, that's all. You'll see. But I think that we should better sort out proper plans next time or we will be totally side-lined.' Bertie nodded.

'I hope you are right, mate, because I feel like we have just been dumped!'

Chapter 11

Molly rose early the next morning, the house was still quiet. She looked over at the grandfather's clock with its brass face and gentle ticking, reminding her of the carefree days playing here at the farm with Stella when this house had belonged to their grandparents. She filled a flask, buttered some currant bread and pulled on her coat. Rex sat up in his bed ready to leap into action if he was going for a walk too.

'Come on, boy,' Molly called patting her thigh. Rex skittled across the kitchen floor, his tongue hanging out, he jumped up with pleasure. They left the kitchen and wandered down to the allotment. The air was still and her breathe created small clouds rising up to greet the dawn. She inspected the new shoots pushing their way up through the earth and tipped up the terracotta forcer to see how the rhubarb was doing. For a moment, Molly stopped and gazed at the golden light of the sun as the first rays were breaking over the hills, both hands supporting the small of her back.

'I wonder what Mum and Dad are going to tell us, eh Rex?' She looked at Rex whose ears had pricked up at the mention of his name. '...and Stella is coming too. Without the rest of the family,' she added. 'Can't be good news, can it?' Molly set about clearing weeds and the dead stalks remaining from last year, filling up the compost bin. She pruned the fruit bushes and sowed seeds in trays inside the shed. The sun was now much higher in the sky and Molly was warm and hungry. She sat down on her bench pulling out her flask and fruit bread. Rex padded over and flopped at her feet, looking up at her, hoping for some crumbs. She rubbed his ears and pulling off her gardening gloves, began her breakfast. Her phone buzzed, she picked it up from the bench and seeing Alistair's name, she hesitated for a moment before deciding to answer him. 'Hello, Alistair.'

'Molly, hi…I just thought that I would call, see if you are alright only. Last night you left in a bit of a hurry…' he paused and waited, then pushed on, 'we are okay, aren't we? I just feel that we need to talk.'

'I think you've said it all, Alistair. You are not a family man and you don't want the responsibility of a child and anyway, you have been paying a lot of attention to Lucy. That just about covers it, right?' she stopped to catch her breath.

'Not quite, I admit that it was a bit of a shock when you told me that you were pregnant, but I have had time to think about it and well, I want to be part of the child's life and…'

'Listen to yourself, "the child's life". Alistair, this is your child, not some stray dog!' she disconnected bursting into tears. Her phone buzzed again but this time, she ignored it. Rex placed his head on her lap and nuzzled her hand. Molly patted his head and ruffled his fur smiling at him. He gave a whine of satisfaction and a little 'woof'.

'Come on, boy, let's go for a walk.' She packed up her bag. Picking up her jacket, she raised her hand to shield her eyes and gazed around the allotment with satisfaction. Patting her leg, said to Rex, 'I think we will take the long way home today, boy. I need to think.' They set off towards the bottom of the field, Rex bouncing and barking with excitement. Birds were swooping up and down the hedgerows building nests, bees buzzed in and out of flowers, it felt as though the whole world had suddenly come alive. A few pink petals floated down on the breeze from the apple trees and Molly stopped to look into the stream as it bubbled along its way. She tossed in a 'pooh stick'

110

and watched it disappear before climbing over the stile and heading back up to the farm.

'There you are,' said her mother, 'we were thinking of coming to look for you. Would you like some breakfast? We have had a call from Stella and she will be here soon.' Her mother turned back to the stove without waiting for an answer, shovelling sausages and bacon onto a plate.

'No thanks, Mum, just coffee, I will make it.' Molly unpacked her bag by the sink, filled the kettle and placed it onto the Aga with a bang feeling, resentful that her mother should just walk in and take over. Rex had curled up in his basket once more and was snoring gently. A feeling of nausea came over her and she dashed out of the kitchen and upstairs heading for the bathroom.

'Are you alright?' her mother called up the stairs. Molly groaned. Sometime later, she re-joined them in the kitchen having showered and changed. Stella had arrived. They hugged each other and after a few exchanges regarding the latest updates of family life, Molly returned to the stove to make a big pot of tea. She collected mugs from the dresser and warmed some croissants. They finally all sat down to hear whatever it was that their parents had come to say.

'Well...come on, Mum, Dad, what's the big secret?' Molly and Stella looked from one to the other.

'We've put our villa up for sale and we are coming back home...' She glanced at them all. Molly and Stella sat open mouthed, each lost in their own thoughts at the implications of such an announcement.

'But you love it out there, why? Why would you suddenly want to come back here? I...we don't understand.' Stella and Molly clasped hands in mutual support.

'Yes, come on, there must be more to it than that. You wouldn't just suddenly do this and why couldn't Tony and the children come with me? You know they love to see you.' Both girls looked from one to the other.

'...and when? When were you thinking of coming back and to live where? Here?' Molly was spluttering in disbelief, this was her home now, it had been for ten years. Tom and Sandra exchanged a look and Sandra motioned for him to speak.

'I'm not sure how to tell you this but...I have cancer and I wanted to come home,' he dropped his head. For a split second, there was silence before both girls jumped up and hugged their father. They discovered that he had known for some time and had been undergoing treatment in Spain, but now they could do no more and he wanted to come back to the farm for what time he had left. Molly was distraught, partly because her father was dying but also because she had resented their return, her life was about to change, forever. Stella disappeared to call Tony and her mother put the kettle on again. Molly had so many questions. Where to start? Not daring to ask how long?

Stella went home promising to come back soon with the rest of the family and Molly, dazed with pain and anxiety, picked up her phone. She called Lucy.

'Are you busy? Can we talk?' her voice heavy and flat.

'Yes, of course, what's wrong?'

'Can I come over? Only I can't talk on the phone?' she held her breath closing her eyes to shut out the pain.

'Mum and Dad have gone shopping and won't be back till late so come on over. I'll put the kettle on.' Lucy closed her cell wondering what on earth had happened. Molly was usually the strong one. It wasn't long before Molly was sitting on her couch, tea in hand, sobbing.

'I'm so sorry, Molly. I don't know what to say,' she squeezed Molly's hand, '...if there's anything I can do, please ask, won't you? I don't suppose they have any idea how long? Sorry that was insensitive, I...I was just wondering if you had told them about the baby?' Lucy faltered, she could feel her face getting hotter and swallowed hard.

'No and no. I was going to but thought that it wasn't the right time, everyone was too upset...but from what Mum said, I don't think that my dad has long and probably won't live to see my baby.' She burst into tears again. 'I always thought that he would walk me down the aisle, you know, all the usual stuff that girls dream of, anyway, but it's not to be. Oh, I hate Alistair Warren.'

'Come on, I know you don't mean that. You will make a wonderful mum with or without him, so let's concentrate on you for now.' Molly felt better, she blew her nose loudly.

'Thanks, Lucy. You know, whatever happens, I am so happy to be pregnant and I wish Alistair was too but I can cope. It's just the shock of Mum and Dad turning up. It's the last thing that I expected. Aren't we a right pair? You back at home and now my parents have come back to me!' she let out a strangled laugh.

'Yes, well, now I have something to tell you. I have put in an offer on a house and it has been accepted.' She grinned.

'That's wonderful news, Lucy. I might be the one coming to you for a room.' She mused.

'Right, I will put the kettle on again and tell you all about it.' There was a loud knocking on the front door which startled them both. Lucy went to open it.

'Lionel...' her mouth dropped open. She stared at him, turned and looked at Molly with 'help' written in her eyes. She stammered '...you had better come in.'

113

Chapter 12

The following week, Alistair was determined not to telephone Molly. Two can play at that game, he thought but all the time, he had to admit to himself that he did miss her trips to London, it was eerily quiet. It had given him the chance to catch up with some work that he had been neglecting and although he was desperate to find out how Lucy was doing with her house hunting, he felt it best to leave her alone too. He stood staring out of the window at the traffic below and imagined himself taking her out, just the two of them, dinner, candle light, soft music...

'What are you thinking about?' came a voice from across the room. 'And don't try to deny it, I've seen that look on your face before!' Bertie was leaning back on his chair swinging a pen around and around his fingers amused at Alistair.

'Oh, just the usual,' he declared hoping to satisfy Bertie.

'I don't think so, mate. Is it Lucy or Molly this time?'

'Actually, I had been thinking of going down again this weekend, but then I thought that it might be prudent to give it a miss for a couple of weeks.' He let out a long sigh.

'Huh, right,' Bertie rubbed his forehead and sucked in a deep breath. 'You know I've been thinking...' the telephone began to ring and Alistair held up his hand to Bertie, who turned back to his computer.

'Dad, are you alright?' Alistair asked.

'No, Son. Well, yes, I'm alright. It's your mother,' George paused.

'What's happened?' he asked anxiously,

'Your mother has been taken to Dorchester hospital. I think she has had a stroke; in fact, I know she has.'

'I'm on my way.' Alistair put the phone down and turned back to Bertie.

'What's going on?' he asked.

'It's Mum.' Alistair quickly filled him in. 'I'm going down there now.'

'I'll come with you,' Bertie exclaimed jumping up.

'No, not this time, mate. Can you take care of things here and I will keep you informed.' Alistair grabbed his jacket and made for the door.

Bertie turned back to his screen and felt instantly lonely, so lonely in fact that it brought a shiver to his entire body and brain; he sat numbly staring at the screen and praying that Mrs W would be alright. The fear and panic in Alistair brought back that terrible moment when he had been told of his mother's illness. He had desperately wanted to go with Alistair, but he knew that this was one occasion when he would just be in the way. He poured himself a coffee and wandered around the office; he couldn't get any thoughts into any sense; his brain had totally clammed up. He sat down again and told himself to think, think carefully and try to get some perspective on what he had just been told. He looked at his watch. It would take Alistair about three hours to get to Trentmouth, if the traffic was fairly clear, but getting out of London at any time could be a nightmare. That meant that he should be there by five or six o'clock, he would just have to sit tight and wait. He looked at his screen and typed 'stroke' into Google. He read pages about possible side effects, causes and treatment, all this did was make him more worried, terrified, even that Mrs W might end up an invalid or worse.

'No,' he told himself, 'she will pull through this. After all, George was a doctor, he will know what to do. Why didn't he see it coming? He should have seen that she was ill.' He clicked off the awful complexities of a stroke, feeling at a loss. He could do nothing, nothing at all. He picked up the phone to order some flowers but then changed his mind, what if she doesn't make it? Flowers might be even more upsetting. He put the phone down again and paced the room. 'I wish I had someone to talk to,' he said out loud. 'Lucy,' he slapped his forehead with his palm. 'Lucy, why didn't I think of that before? She's a nurse, well, a midwife, I'm sure that's the same thing, she will know what I should do.' He grabbed his phone and then it hit him, he didn't have her number! What a bloody idiot I am! He threw his phone onto the desk, it slid across and crashed onto the floor. Now what? He thought. He picked his phone up again and remembered that he had Molly's number. Molly answered straight away and Bertie quickly filled her in on what had happened. She gave him the number for Lucy and promised to try to find out any more news and get back to him as soon as she knew anything, anything at all. Bertie felt relieved and although Molly had tried to tell him that not all strokes are major, he couldn't believe her; she was a vet and he thought that animals didn't have strokes, so she was probably just trying to stop him from worrying. He keyed the number into his phone, it rang. He waited and then it clicked onto answerphone. Oh no, where is she? He left a garbled message asking her to call him as soon as possible. All thought of work had now completely gone, he decided to pack up and go back to his flat, not that it would do much good either but he just didn't know what else to do.

George sat quietly holding his wife's hand when his mobile buzzed. He pressed the green button as he walked into the corridor away from the noise of the nurse's station.

'Dad, it's me. How is Mum?' He sounded distraught.

'It's alright, Son,' he said, 'your mother is under sedation. They have run some tests and we will know more soon.' George did his best to take the worry from his son so that he would drive carefully; he couldn't risk Alistair having an accident on top of everything else. He gave Alistair instructions of where to find them once he arrived at Dorchester and returned to sit by his wife's side. He patted her hand gently as she lay motionless.

'Alice, my darling, we can get through this.' He moved a strand of hair from her forehead and stared at her limp body, her breathing slow but methodical; he knew that she wasn't in any immediate danger but fear still held him in its grip. 'I love you so much,' he whispered, 'I'm so sorry that I took no notice when you said you were tired. Please get better, oh please get better, you are my world, my whole life. I should have told you more often that I love you and how much you mean to me. You will forgive me, won't you?' He sat quietly, just stroking her hand over and over. 'Alistair is on his way,' he said to comfort himself. He glanced at the machines steadily clicking, LED's flashing up and down, up and down. Her doctor marched into the room and took George outside and into a family room.

'Tea, George?' he asked as he motioned for him to sit down, something that George himself had done many times when he had had very ill patients to attend to, he knew the drill.

'Please,' he managed to say and sat heavily on a chair letting out a grunt of air.

'A few extra pounds round your middle there, George,' the doctor said kindly with a smile. George looked up and returned a wan smile.

'I know she's had a stroke but how bad is it?' he hardly dared to ask but he must know the answers before Alistair arrived, one of them had to be in control and he wasn't sure how his son would react; he still hadn't come to terms with the

117

loss of his brother, Christopher. George was only too aware and now his mother, poor Alistair.

'Well,' said the doctor, 'she's a strong woman, your Alice. She will need a lot of care but she will pull through this one.'

'Thank God!' said George.

'Yes, indeed, she has been doing far too much; a complete rest is called for and I mean a complete rest. This one is just a warning. We will have all the test results tomorrow and then we can formulate a programme of treatment. In the meantime, I suggest that you go home and get some rest yourself; you won't be much use to her if you are exhausted too.'

'No, I suppose not. Thank you for everything, but I will wait till my son gets here. He's on his way from London.' He glanced at his watch. 'He should be here soon.'

The doctor left George alone and he leaned back on the couch and rested his head on the wall. He felt sick and lost and alone, more than he had ever imagined. A tear squeezed out onto his cheek, he let it roll and a shudder ran through his veins. Sleep overtook him.

'Dad...Dad!' said Alistair more loudly, gently gripping his father's shoulder. Alistair had been frightened when he first glimpsed his father, he looked old. For the first time in his life, Alistair had looked closely at his father and he looked weary and frail. In fact, it occurred to him that he had never really taken much notice of his parents; they were just there and the thought had never crossed his mind that one day they might not be.

'Hmm, what? Oh, Alistair, you're here. Sit down. Have you had a coffee yet?' George sprang into action. Alistair placed a hand on his shoulder.

'Dad, it's alright. I have already seen Mum and the doctor has filled me in. We can go home for tonight and come back in the morning.'

Alistair took charge suddenly feeling the burden of being a son, realising that his father and his mother needed him. They had always done the nurturing. He expected them to always do so and suddenly, they were the ones who were vulnerable and needed him. He took his father's arm and they went to say goodnight to Alice. She was sleeping quietly but George leaned over and kissed her, telling her that he would be back early in the morning. Alistair watched this tender scene with pain and sorrow, how he envied their love for each other; he hadn't noticed before that how close they really were. The emptiness in his own life shot through him like cold steel. Molly flashed into his mind, she was carrying his child. He ached for her, his throat dry and constricted as he tried to swallow. He kissed his mother and uttered, probably, for the very first time in his life,

'Love you.' He squeezed her hand, put his arm around his father's shoulders and they quietly left the room. They said very little on the way back home. Alistair could see the toll that the strain had put onto his father and he himself could only feel a vast nothing inside, so vast that he, in that moment, felt utterly desolate. Later that evening, Alistair fell into bed very tired, his head spinning from the day's events. He remembered Bertie and his promise to keep him updated about Alice; he picked up his phone and sent him a brief text. It was very late and he thought that Bertie was probably asleep, little knowing what had been happening to him that day. He then sent a text to Molly as he guessed that she would probably already know about Alice, but he wanted to be the one who kept her informed and then he turned his attention to Lucy. He thought long and hard about what to exactly put in his text to Lucy; he couldn't sound too casual but as he was in Trentmouth anyway, he thought that this might be the ideal time to try and see her, he had some explaining to do. Texts sent, he fell asleep exhausted.

Bertie had eventually been able to speak to Lucy and asked her a thousand questions, very few of which she could answer. However, she had promised to let him know anything that she might find out about the situation with Alice assuming that he would be coming down to see her the next day. Bertie, in turn, explained that he couldn't possibly impose himself on the Warrens under the circumstances, but he would love to see her the next time he was in Trentmouth.

Bertie lay in bed turning his conversation with Lucy over and over in his mind, desperate not to read too much into it. He put his hands over his face and rubbed his eyes. *You are a wimp,* he chastised, *just tell her you like her and want to take her out.* His phone pinged and Bertie opened it to see the text message. He sat up, relieved that it was finally from Alistair confirming that Alice would recover and that he would speak to him the next day. Bertie closed his phone and got out of bed, he couldn't sleep anyway. He padded over to his laptop and brought up 'Google'; he folded his arms wondering what to look at. He browsed a few things, nothing in particular, he yawned. He typed in Trentmouth and clicked on B&B's and hotels in the area. He started to read about the history of the place, industry long gone and local events. It's funny, he mused, the number of times I have been down to Dorset and yet I have never really looked into Trentmouth itself. He settled back to read about the fishing industry, which had now dwindled to just a few crabs and lobsters; you could buy them fresh from the sea on the quayside or enjoy them at one of the excellent restaurants dotted along the quay, it read. The small port, now mainly pleasure craft, you could hire a canoe or take a water safari; that sounds good fun, he smiled. He looked at a few more sites and found himself staring at the website of a local estate agent; he typed in his details to find out what property was available in his price range including a few lettings. He noticed that there were a number of plots of land, a farm and an industrial unit.

Hmmm, that gives me an idea, he straightened and stretched as he clicked on the 'contact us' icon and ordered some details to be sent to him before finally yawning like a baby without any inhibitions and deciding to go back to bed, falling quickly to sleep, dreaming of his next step.

Chapter 13

Lucy couldn't believe that Lionel was here on her doorstep and stared at him in disbelief; her mind racing, she held the door open. Lionel stood looking at her, his face wreathed in smiles, he followed Lucy inside. He thrust a large bunch of flowers in her direction and Lucy took them as he walked past her into Honeysuckle Cottage.

'Aren't you going to say "hello"?' he asked, '"nice to see you, I've missed you" or something?' Lucy felt as if she had been struck dumb, all she could think about was their last conversation which had seemed so final.

'Hello,' she managed, 'I'm just so surprised to see you and especially here.'

'Tut, tut,' he exclaimed, 'now come on, Lucy, let's not rake over old ground. I'm here now and you didn't tell me that you had had an accident. I'll have a coffee if you are putting the kettle on.' He followed her into the kitchen and she watched as he scanned the room before he walked over to the mantel picking up some old curled up photographs of Lucy, half stuffed behind the clock; she grimaced as he smiled at her pictures. Lucy filled a vase with water for the flowers and switching the kettle on, she lifted two mugs down from the shelf and picked up the jar of coffee. Coffee! Poor Molly was in the sitting room.

'Excuse me a minute, Molly is in the other room. I'll be back in a tic.' Lionel pushed the photographs back and followed. 'I…I'm sorry, Molly, but Lionel has turned up and…'

'Please introduce me, Lucy,' he exclaimed marching across to Molly, hand outstretched. 'Hello, Molly, Lionel,' he said not waiting for an introduction. Molly politely shook hands and rolled her eyes at Lucy, excused herself and headed out of the door.

'Call me and if I don't hear from you in half an hour, I'll come back. Okay?'' She mouthed. Lucy nodded as Molly disappeared. Lucy went back to making the coffee, her hands shaking, her mind in turmoil. She held out a mug and Lionel took it letting his hand caress hers. Lucy quickly pulled away, she wasn't falling for that old trick again.

'No biscuit?' Lionel said raising his eyebrows.

'Look, what do you want? I haven't heard from you for weeks and then you turn up here out of the blue and...'

'I would have thought it was obvious,' he looked her straight in the eyes turning the charm up to full volume. 'I've missed you and I didn't think I would but well, I have, so here I am.' Lucy could feel herself tingle, this was the old Lionel the one she had first fallen in love with. *Be strong*, she told herself, *you are not falling for that again*. She pulled herself up to her full 5 feet 3 inches and demanded.

'Just like that, you think that you can walk in here, all would be forgiven and we would drive off into the sunset,' she marvelled in disbelief.

'Oh, drive off into the sunset, now that does sound nice. Yes, if you like, we can do that,' he drawled.

'Don't make fun of me,' Lucy felt exasperated. 'You know what I mean,' she began to feel rather annoyed, he was toying with her, 'you said that you never wanted to get married or have children. What did you expect me to do? Just roll over and accept that as my life? I want more from life than a career and living with you. I want marriage, a husband, children, is that too much to ask?'

Lionel visibly winced at the word 'husband' and shuddered.

123

'I hadn't quite thought that far. Come on, Lucy, you know my feelings. One thing at a time, eh. Come home with me and I'm sure that we can work out everything else; we can discuss it again in the future.'

He walked towards her with his arms outstretched. Lucy felt her knees start to buckle. She had loved Lionel with all her heart once and it would be so easy to fall straight back into his arms and life. He had missed her, he wanted her back and he had driven down to Dorset just to find her. That must mean something.

'I, I don't know,' she looked at him and pushed her long hair behind her ear. Lionel smiled.

'You know you want to and I know you love me, Lucy, you always have. We can leave today, everything is as you left it...our home,' he paused. It was a large house on the outskirts of Harrogate, Georgian with many of its original features intact. Lucy loved that house, she had had such dreams and hopes, plans for the future, fantasised about being Mrs Lionel Maddox. He touched her arm, kissed her wrist ever so gently. 'Is it better now?' he asked staring up at her with his dark green eyes that always captivated anyone who looked into them, pulling you in, mesmerised like some innocent prey caught in the headlights.

'Yes, it's fine now,' she hesitated feeling the warmth of his lips on her wrist; the goose bumps slowly climbing up her arm, steadily making their way into her blood stirring up forgotten memories. 'Mm,' she uttered quietly. 'How did you know about my accident?' she asked waking up again, 'I didn't tell you.' Lionel let go of her arm and walked around the room. The spell momentarily broke.

'Oh, I heard from someone or other, I can't remember but that doesn't matter. I'm here now and ready to take care of you.' He turned and looked at her, tilting his head to one side and held out his arms once more. Lucy wavered but something deep inside still held her back. 'You know how special we are together,' Lionel crooned. 'We could get engaged,' he beamed, his final concession.

'Are you proposing to me?' she asked in excitement stepping towards him full of hope, teetering, her heart lay bare.

'No, just engaged so that you can show a ring off and feel more secure.' Her face dropped together with her hopes and dreams crashing to the floor, shattered for good.

'Is that all I mean to you?' she asked quietly. 'Someone to show off on your arm and have sex with?' Lionel dropped his arms and marched purposefully across the room to her grasping both wrists. Lucy flinched and half fell backwards but Lionel was holding on tight; he slid one arm around her waist and pulled her to him. He pressed his lips to hers but Lucy struggled and pulled away.

'No. Stop it,' she gasped. 'I'm sorry, Lionel. There was a time, I would have done anything for you but...'

'But what? You know you still love me. I can see it in your eyes. You want to come back to me, don't you? I know you do. So, come on, we can make love all night just how you like it and go shopping tomorrow for that ring.' He was pleading and Lucy stood rigid, her eyes filling up with tears. Why was he saying this now? Why couldn't he have said it before? why, why, why? The questions were endless and she knew in that moment, she had one chance to go back to Lionel or say goodbye forever. They stared at each other, both knowing that time was almost up. The next word, whoever it came from, was it, final. There was a loud knock on the door which startled them both, the door opened and Molly marched in.

'Molly,' Lucy exclaimed, she had forgotten Molly's promise to come back and was here to rescue her. 'Thank goodness,' she breathed a sigh of relief.

'Are you alright, Lucy?' asked Molly as she quickly surveyed Lionel. *He looks like an aging Tom Cruise*, she smirked to herself. Lionel eyed Molly up and down, stroking his chin. Lucy knew the signs.

'You bastard! How dare you? Get out, get out. I never want to see you again,' her nostrils flaring, she paused for breath.

'Come, come now, Lucy. Don't be such a banshee. I am merely being friendly to Molly.'

'It's alright, Lucy. I'm not about to fall for that old trick,' said Molly.

'How about we all calm down. I'm sure that we can then sort this out. No one is in any danger, are they?' Lionel looked from one to the other, outnumbered, throwing Lucy a sharp look. 'Why don't you put the kettle on?' he said, 'There's a good girl. We can sit down and have a civilised conversation.' Lucy, on autopilot, walked into the kitchen obediently putting the kettle on, feeling sick to her stomach; she just wanted him gone out of her life, forever. She could hear low conversation going on in the sitting room, but she just couldn't be bothered to go and listen. She threw her head back and puffed out her cheeks as she let the pent-up air out of her lungs. 'To think that I once loved that man,' she muttered to herself, 'I am such an idiot but not anymore.' Tea made, she carried the tray into the sitting room to find Lionel and Molly deep in conversation on the couch.

'That's better,' said Lionel looking up at Lucy. 'Come and sit down. I was just explaining to Molly that I had come to see you as soon as I heard about your awful accident; you poor thing, handling it all on your own.'

'I'm not that incapable.' She glared at him, appalled at his patronising attitude.

'Well, now I'm here for you. You can pack your things and come back with me.' He smiled warmly as if the previous exchange had never happened and as if he was the kindest, most caring man in the world who loved her very much. She thrust a cup of tea in his direction and snapped.

'I don't think so, not this time and you never finished telling me how you found out about my accident, did you?' determined not to let it drop. Lionel sighed heavily, glancing at Molly and turned to Lucy.

'Your very good friend, Molly here, told me,' he paused.

Molly looked horrified but it was Lucy who said, 'What? I don't believe you. Why would Molly tell you about my accident?' Lionel opened his mouth to reply but then closing it again, turned to look at Molly instead. Molly grimaced.

'The truth is...the truth is that when you first had your accident, you were crying all the time, telling me how much you loved Lionel, how much you missed him and that you couldn't live without him. You sounded desperately upset that he hadn't been to see you. You were distraught, you know that and well, I suppose I thought that I was helping you. I honestly thought that is what you wanted. I'm sorry if I got it wrong.'

Lucy knew that this was all true and that Molly was only trying to help; she wasn't to know how things would turn out.

'No, I'm the one who is sorry, if you had come to see me straight away,' said Lucy turning to Lionel. 'Things might have been different. I probably would have come back with you but now I'm not so sure.' Lionel jumped in with,

'So, you're not certain then. Well, let me help you, you come back with me now and if it doesn't work this time, then...', he shrugged his shoulders, '...it's up to you.'

Lucy held her head, dragging her fingers through her long hair.

'It suits you like that,' said Lionel changing the subject, 'you should keep it long.' She dropped her hands torn by indecision. Molly got up from the couch and sat by her friend, she put her arm around her shoulders.

'Isn't this what you have always wanted?' she asked.

'Not like this,' Lucy choked back tears. 'Once, I would have run to him. Well, I did, but now, it's not what I want anymore. He is not what I want anymore.' Lionel stood up.

'You've had your chance, Lucy, and I have to get back. I really thought that you loved me and wanted me but clearly you don't. Perhaps, you never loved me, I have been fooling myself all along.'

'Fine,' said Lucy pausing, '…think what you like but I don't want that life or you anymore, it's too late.' Lionel picked up his jacket turning to Molly.

'Nice to have met you Molly. May I take you to lunch by way of a thank you?' he smiled.

'Err,' Molly looked unsure about this and glanced at her watch. 'No. Sorry, thanks anyway.' There was a loud banging on the front door, matching the thumping in Lucy's head. She opened the door to see Alistair standing there and without hesitation, she threw her arms around him.

'Alistair, thank goodness, it's you.' Alistair's mouth dropped open, he looked startled and shot a look around the room at the assembled group. He placed his arms instinctively around her and hugged her to him.

'What on earth is the matter, darling?' he said.

'So, that's it, Lucy, you've found someone else. Nice of you to tell me. No wonder you were reluctant to come back with me.' Lionel acted the hurt, abandoned male but Lucy didn't care. Turning to Alistair, he offered a parting comment, 'Good luck, you'll need it.' He put his jacket on and turned to Molly, who had been staring at Alistair as he had his arms firmly around Lucy. 'Molly, my dear, I think that we were heading out to lunch.' He proffered his arm to Molly. She glanced at Alistair and Lucy held on tight, she grabbed her bag and left trailing after Lionel.

Chapter 14

Lucy dropped her arms letting go of Alistair.

'I'm sorry about that.'

'No, don't be, I'm always happy to help. I'm just glad that I turned up when I did. What has been going on?'

'Oh, it's a long story but the main thing is that Lionel has gone.'

'So, that was Lionel, eh?' Lucy shot him a look.

'Sorry, I didn't mean it to sound sarcastic.'

'Oh, that's alright. I'm just a bit fragile, I suppose. I'm glad he's gone…' she paused. 'Let's have a drink. It's not too early for a glass of red wine, is it?' She moved over to the sideboard, where her mother kept a secret supply, opening the door, she rummaged for a red.

'Never,' said Alistair. Lucy handed the wine to Alistair for him to open and placed two glasses on to the table. They chatted, relaxed and comfortable like an old pair of slippers that you can't quite bring yourself to throw out.

'I'm worried about Molly. Lionel did rather drag her off.'

'Don't worry about, Molly,' said Alistair, 'she can take care of herself. She won't fall for any of his tricks, not our Molly, you'll see.' She smiled in reply sipping her wine, letting the alcohol do its job, her eyes gently closing. 'That better…?' asked Alistair staring at her. Lucy suddenly opened her eyes remembering that Alistair had come knocking on her door.

'I'm so sorry, Alistair. You came to see me and I acted in such an appalling manner, grabbing you like that without any warning. Is there anything I can do for you?' She looked him in the eye, picked up the bottle of wine and topped his glass up. She saw Alistair swallow hard and realised that her phrasing could have been better.

'Oh, well, I was just coming to give you an update on mother.'

'Oh, Alistair, I'm so sorry. I forgot about Alice, please forgive me. How is she today?' She leant forward looking attentive. Alistair coughed smothering a grin.

'That's okay, you were rather busy caught up in a bit of a drama yourself when I arrived.' Alistair visibly relaxed and he brought Lucy up to date adding, 'I'm sure that you know more about these things than I do.'

'That's funny,' she said, 'that's exactly what Bertie said last night. He was very worried but I explained to him too that being a midwife doesn't qualify me to know all about someone who has had a stroke,' she began to feel a bit woozy and sleepy.

'Bertie...?' He sounded surprised raising his eyebrows, he pushed his glasses up on top of his head rubbing his forehead.

'Yes,' said Lucy with a smile, 'you remember, tall, lanky guy, works with you.'

'Yes, sorry. It's just that I forgot to call him, I'll catch up with him later.'

There was a beep and Lucy looked at her phone; it was a text from Molly, there was one word, 'HELP'. She stared at it for a moment and then snapped it shut.

'So,' they both said together. Alistair looked rather awkward, uttered a strangled laugh.

'Please, you go first.'

'No, no. I was only going to ask if you wanted more wine,' she lied.

'Better not. I do have to drive over to the hospital to see Mum and pick up Dad.'

'Of course,' she topped up her own glass and sat back to listen to him.

'I was only going to ask about your house hunting last week with your father.'

'Gosh, yes, I had forgotten all about that. It is great, needs some work of course, but I really like it. I am going for a second look next week.'

'Great,' Alistair shuffled and sat back his shoulders dropped. 'Where is it? Dorchester, I presume?'

'Actually, no. It's in Wareham and not what. I had originally planned to buy at all. It is Victorian, quite large, with a long garden and it has a parking space at the back. I thought that I would be better off with a more central location.'

'That's true and there is a direct link into London too.' Getting up he continued, 'I hope it works out but right now, I had better go. I promised dad that I would not be late.'

There was another beep on Lucy's phone. She looked at it and this time Molly had written, 'URGENT, PLEASE HELP', she looked at Alistair.

'It's from Molly,' eyes open wide. 'She's asking for help.'

'Molly! Where is she?'

'I don't know,' said Lucy. 'But what can we do?'

'Let me think. I know, send her a text saying "Emergency at the surgery, come at once".' Lucy texted as quickly as she could. A moment later, one came back, 'Will do, see you there.'

Lucy sighed with relief.

'That seems to have done the trick. I'll take a walk over there and make sure she's alright.'

'Do you want a lift? I'm going that way,' asked Alistair.

'No, you go and see Alice and don't forget to speak to Bertie.' She pushed herself up on to her toes and kissed him lightly on the cheek. Two red spots flashed onto his cheeks making Lucy smirk.

'Right, I'll give you a call.'

131

'Okay,' said Lucy picking up her jacket and handbag.

'Oh,' said Alistair opening the window of his car, 'let me know what happens when you view that house next week.'

She waved goodbye and wandered down the lane to Molly's surgery to wait for her. She didn't have to wait long. Molly came tearing up the road, screeching to a halt, she jumped out and ran into the surgery. She gently closed the door, leaned back, closed her eyes and took a deep breath.

'That better?' said Lucy. Molly opened her eyes again.

'Lucy, come into my office,' it sounded like an order but Lucy obeyed anyway. 'Put the kettle on, will you? And make us a coffee.' Molly threw her bag down and began marching up and down, dragging her fingers through her hair.

'Hey,' Lucy came back with two mugs of strong coffee and handed one to Molly. 'Are you alright?' Molly slowed and sat on a stool.

'That man,' she said, 'that man,'

'Go on, obnoxious, arrogant and a chauvinist, I won't be offended!'

'…that man thinks that every woman will just fall at his feet.'

'They usually do,' said Lucy.

'But you have the advantage of knowing a lot more about him than most.'

'I suppose you are right. I was beginning to think that I would never escape.' She opened a drawer and took out a packet of biscuits offering them to Lucy and taking a couple for herself.

'I've been thinking,' said Lucy settling into a chair opposite her friend,

'Why did you really tell Lionel about my accident giving him the impression that I couldn't live without him?'

There was a long pause. Molly realised that it was no use telling her friend anything but the truth, sometimes, no matter how painful or what the consequences might be, you had no choice. She regarded her for a moment and after taking another gulp of her coffee, began her story. Molly told how she had seen Alistair look at Lucy after the accident and all she could see was that he appeared to be falling for her. Molly looked at Lucy waiting for a reaction but none was forthcoming, so she ploughed on.

'So, a case of plain old jealousy and well, you know the rest.' Molly sat munching a chocolate digestive and shrugged her shoulders. Lucy let out a belly laugh that she couldn't control; she hugged her stomach and rocked in her chair. Molly was stunned.

'God,' she said, 'what a mess, Alistair! I think he is a really nice guy but that's it.' Tears were now rolling down her cheeks. 'Boy, I feel better for that. Anyway, truth is you did me the biggest favour ever, finally, ridding me of Lionel and quite spectacularly.' She grinned and Molly seeing her face smiled too.

'Forgiven?' she asked. Lucy nodded.

'Forgiven,' they hugged each other and Molly vowed never to interfere with anyone's love life again. She felt empty, bereft.

'It's over now, anyway.' she said at last.

'Really...why?' asked a puzzled Lucy.

'He called you "darling", I thought that you two were an item now?' Molly gave her a sideways glance.

'No...' half laughing, 'no never, you do jump to conclusions.'

'But he came to see you.'

'Yes, but only to tell me about Alice. He was so surprised when I opened the door and grabbed him, he just acted on instinct. He was mystified as to what was going on and then you left with Lionel and he play acted as I had whispered to him to

133

go along with me.' Molly burst out laughing now too '…and I want to know everything about you and Alistair,' said Lucy getting caught up in the moment.

'Alright, I owe you that much. How about tonight? You could come over to my place, watch a DVD and I will fill you in on all the "gory" details.'

'Great and then, I can tell you all about Bertie.'

'Bertie?' quizzed a surprised Molly.

'Yes, Bertie. Later, we need some serious girl talk.'

Bertie had not been able to work properly; his head going round and round with thoughts of Mrs W, Lucy and Molly, even Alistair. They all crowded his head vying for position. His phone buzzed and Bertie grabbed it.

'Alistair, thank God. How's Alice? When I didn't hear from you, I was beginning to think the worst.'

'Mum is going to be alright. I'm just on the way to the hospital now to pick up Dad. I'll be back tomorrow. And I have something to tell you. I will fill you in with all the details on Monday but it's Lucy, she and I, well, what I mean is, I think that we…look, I can't talk now. I must go.'

'Hang on a minute, what do you mean? You and Lucy what?' he asked urgently.

'What? This line is bad. All I can say is that what you said and seeing mum and dad at the hospital finally made me realise that I have to take action. It's a long story. I haven't time to tell you now. I just wanted to let you know about mum. See you Monday, okay?'

'Hang on, have you told Molly?'

'Molly! No. I'll call her later. Bye.'

Bertie flipped his cell shut and collapsed onto the couch. He sat turning his cell over and over. He flipped it open and closed it again. He pulled himself up and took a beer from the fridge.

'It's too late, you idiot. You should have made your move when you had the chance,' he chastised himself loudly. He turned over the options in his mind that he could carry on and pretend that he was pleased for them both. He could immigrate to Australia or…he grabbed his phone. 'Or you could just get over yourself,' he muttered.

'Hi, Molly, it's me.'

Chapter 15

George crept quietly into the private room watching Alice gently sleeping. He sat down by her bed and picked up her hand. He stroked her fingers and touched her wedding ring, it was wearing thin but still sparkled. He thought of all the love that she bestowed with her hands; she cared for him in ways that he hadn't really noticed before. Despite the fact that he had retired and spent most of his time fiddling in the shed or tinkering with an old radio, it dawned on him for the first time that Alice had not retired, could never retire. It was her life's work to cook and clean and do the garden. He lowered his head in shame, Alice never complained. He sat tracing the lines on the back of her hand resolving to do more, take his beloved shopping and any other little jobs that he could do to make her life easier and to ensure, albeit for a selfish reason, that they would spend many, many more years together. He couldn't bear the thought that she might be taken from him and that he would be left alone. Alice stirred.

'Are you alright, my darling?' he whispered. Alice made no reply. He sat down again and began to talk to her, telling her that Alistair had been to see her and that he would be back again very soon. He talked and talked about old times, holidays, silly things that had happened in the past and more importantly what they were going to be doing when she was well enough.

'We can book that holiday you've always wanted,' he said. 'I'll look into it tomorrow. Switzerland I think is where you wanted to go and Austria, we will do it as soon as possible, you'll see,' he said with enthusiasm. He fell quiet for a moment and then as if it had been a burden to him, he said, 'I'm sorry, my darling. I have neglected you. You mean the world to me, you know that, don't you?' Alice stirred again but her eyes remained closed. He patted her hand once more. 'I'll even go on a cruise.' He had always resisted going on a cruise, felt that it would be full of old people or worse rowdy young ones and then you are trapped, can't get off the wretched thing to escape. He let out a sigh of resignation. He leaned back in his chair and watched her, she is still beautiful, he smiled, it's nearly 40 years since our wedding day and she is just as wonderful. He pictured the day in his mind, how utterly happy they were, they didn't have a lot of money and had to forgo a honeymoon always promising themselves that they would 'do it later'. Med school had taken all the money that George could get together. His parents had not been able to support him, but it was what he had always wanted and he and Alice had agreed that it was worth the sacrifice. In that moment, George made a decision: We will have our honeymoon, he thought, straight after a celebration for our Ruby Wedding Anniversary and we will take a world cruise. He jumped up clapping his hands with satisfaction, making Alice stir once more; she let out a low moan and George leapt to her side.

'Alice, Alice,' he whispered. Alice turned her head.

'Hmmm,' she moaned. George grinned, she was going to be just fine. He pressed the buzzer to call for the nurse and sat down once more.

'I'm here,' he said, 'I will always be here.'

The nurse came in.

'Could you wait outside please, Dr Warren. We have a few checks to make and then you can come back in to see your wife.' George obediently left the room and wandered along the corridor to find a coffee machine. He walked around the corner feeling elated. He heard someone calling his name and

137

recognising the voice, he turned to see Molly with a bunch of flowers.

'How is Alice?' she asked. 'But by the look on your face, I would say that she is alright.' George kissed her lightly on the cheek.

'Yes, I am pleased to say that she has just woken up and I'm waiting for the doctor to give me his report but the signs are good…very good.'

'That's wonderful news. We have all been so worried. I wasn't sure if I would be allowed to visit so I just took a chance and here I am.'

'It's very nice to see you, my dear. Of course, you can visit. Alice will be delighted to see you but I think that it may have to be another day.' He fell into his old habit of patting people on the hand; it wouldn't be allowed these days but when he was practising, he found that patients took comfort from a doctor patting their hand.

Molly held out the flowers.

'I won't stay but could you give these to Alice for me and give her my love, please.'

George took the flowers saying 'Of course, my dear. I will give you a call tonight.' Molly rose to her feet, they kissed once more and Molly squeezed his hand. She left George making his coffee as he waited for the medical team to finish and allow him to return to Alice.

***

Alistair was busy in London trying to reschedule his diary; he wanted to get back to Dorset and see his mother as soon as possible and he couldn't deny it but Lucy, too. Since he had arrived at Honeysuckle Cottage that day and Lucy had grabbed him, it was all he could think about. He desperately wanted to take her out, to talk to her; he just couldn't wait to tell her how he felt but all that was going to have to wait. His father needed him and his mother too. For the very first time, he wished that he lived nearer but then perhaps, that wouldn't be such a good idea either, he laughed to himself.

'Bertie, I think that I have sorted everything for the next couple of weeks; you can manage here on your own, can't you? I'll take my laptop and if there is anything urgent, I can deal with it in Dorset.'

'Sure, no problem,' he replied chewing the end of his pen.

'You alright?' asked Alistair, 'You have been very quiet since I got back. Nothing you want to tell me, is there?'

'No, no, I'm fine. You worry about yourself and Alice. I can hold the fort.' He twiddled with his pen turning it over and over. Alistair poured out two coffees and sat down next to Bertie pushing one of them in his direction.

'Come on, I know you better than that. Fess up, what is bothering you?' Alistair waited. 'At the beginning.'

'What? Nothing. I'm fine,' he quipped.

'I know there's something wrong so you might as well tell me now and then we can get on with some work before I go home.'

'There's nothing, really. Just a bit confused, that's all.'

'Good, now we are getting somewhere. I suggest that you tell me your worst fear first. You know what they say about swallowing the biggest frog,' he exclaimed with a grin.

'You always say that. Is it some sort of West Country thing?' he mused. 'But alright, you win, this is getting to be a habit,' he half grinned. 'Well, if you must know, Lucy, Mrs W and my job, what order would you like them in?' Bertie threw his pen onto the desk and it skittled onto the floor. He folded his arms in resignation and looked Alistair in the eye. Alistair jumped up.

'If it's that bad, I had better get the packet of chocolate hobnobs. Hold on a minute.' He collected the biscuits and returned taking a couple from the packet and pushing the rest towards Bertie. 'Right, come on then.' Alistair began to munch on his first biscuit. It's not that he didn't take Bertie seriously but he knew from over the years that Bertie usually turned a small episode into a gigantic saga.

'I like Lucy,' he began and then stopped.

'Yes, so do I, carry on.'

Alistair glossed over his first statement trying to get all his thoughts from him so that he could straighten Bertie out.

'What I mean is…it's just that, well…have you told Molly yet?' He looked defiantly at Alistair.

'Look, what happened between me and Molly is none of your bloody business. However, I can see why you would be concerned about Lucy. I like Lucy, I like her a lot and I have learnt my lesson and I do need to try and make amends, you see that, don't you?'

'Right, sorry, I should have kept my big mouth shut. I am such a bloody fool,' Bertie rubbed the back of his neck with the palm of his hand. Alistair let him squirm. Bertie was trying to look up at him, it was obvious that he had more to say and was struggling. 'Sorry,' he muttered. 'It's just that I thought that you had already taken her out,' he paused pulling a biscuit from the packet scattering crumbs everywhere. 'I'm digging the hole deeper, aren't I?'

'Pass me the biscuits, you idiot. I can see that this is going to take longer than I thought.' Alistair reached out and took the packet.

'You don't owe me any explanation,' Bertie looked at him apologetically, 'you're right. It is none of my business.'

'No, I don't but in the interests of a happy working relationship, I prefer to discuss it but then that's it, alright?' Bertie nodded. 'And after that, can we get back to work?' Bertie put his pen down and grabbed the last two biscuits. Alistair explained what had happened at the cottage when he had turned up unexpectedly, only to find Lionel there. Things began to make sense, Bertie grinned.

'I've done it again, haven't I…? Got it all wrong as usual?'

'Too right. You have. I'm not even going to say anything to Lucy at all for the moment. I have mum to worry about and I don't want to complicate things. Keep it to yourself too, I will speak to Molly.'

'Fine by me,' Bertie drained his coffee.

'Actually, I have a confession, too,' Alistair changed his tone to one of almost sadness.

'Oh, what's that then? You have me really worried now.'

Alistair opened another packet of biscuits fiddling with the seal, trying to put the words in the right order before he spoke.

'The thing is, when Mum was desperately ill, I saw a side to Mum and Dad that I have never seen before. Dad was so loving and caring, he was lost without mum; it had never occurred to me before how much they love each other and what they share in their lives together. To be honest, that is the sort of relationship I want. I never did before, in fact, I didn't really know that it existed. It was all about sex, not two people who love each other, who want to be together. I thought that it was just some female ploy to get their hooks into you; I never appreciated the other side to a relationship.' He stopped and looked intently at Bertie. 'Do you know what I'm talking about Bertie?'

'I think so, I mean I have always wanted that special together relationship. I have wanted marriage, you know the big white wedding and all that and children even, but lots of women these days just say "don't read too much into it, we're just having fun". They think that we, men, only want sex anyway. I suppose we do half the time but I have always been looking for a Miss Right, it's not one sided like they think it is.'

'Well, you know that I have always subscribed to the sex only camp, no commitment, just have a good time and move on, but it does get wearing. I envy my mum and dad and what they have together and I want some of it for myself. I'm not saying that I want to get married at the moment, but I am not saying "no" either.' Bertie just nodded. This Alistair was new and scary. They both fell silent for a moment. 'Right, that's Lucy off your list, what next?' Alistair swung round on his chair and picked up the mugs waving them at Bertie. 'Another before we get to problem number three?'

'I thought that you had forgotten.'

'No chance. C'mon.'

'Well, I have been very worried about your mum, obviously, and I suppose it has a knock-on effect with here and everything…' Alistair stopped and watched him for a moment looking for a further reaction, nothing, Bertie heaved his shoulders and glanced out of the window as he heard the siren of a police car as it flew screeching past.

'I admit,' said Alistair, 'there will have to be changes. I haven't had the full picture yet from Dad, and I feel that it is more important than ever to get my own place as I can't expect mum to run around after me anymore or dad for that matter but I don't see any other changes. Do you?'

'Nicely thrown,' Bertie muttered. 'I was rather hoping you would catch that curved ball.' He sat swinging on his chair for a moment, huffing and puffing.

'Well?' prompted Alistair reaching for another biscuit.

'I can see your position for needing a house; that makes sense and I suppose at the moment, there is no need to change anything else but thanks for putting me in the picture anyway.' Bertie swizzled his chair as if to put an end to the conversation, but Alistair knew that there was more to it than that.

'Come on, Bertie,' he pushed. 'You're just miffed as you think that this is the end of your trips to Dorset because of mum, aren't you?' Flabbergasted, Bertie's mouth dropped open. Alistair coughed as a crumb caught in his throat. 'You can't

142

bluff your way out of this one mate confess all deny, everything or what?'

'You're right and you're wrong,' he announced, 'but before we go any further, I need another coffee and you've eaten all the biscuits,' he grinned. The tension evaporated, Bertie looked visibly relieved. He made yet more coffee, found that the biscuit bin was empty. He headed to his desk opening the drawer and waved a bottle of whisky in front of Alistair.

'It's for when I work late', he grinned, 'or, in this case, an emergency.'

'That's more like it but you had better make it a small one,' he smirked whilst holding up his fingers, indicating a measure more the size of a double. The original questioning appeared to be forgotten and Bertie dropped down onto his chair. They chinked glasses and talked instead about the next F1 due the following weekend.

Later that evening, Bertie collapsed into the depths of despair; well, that's what it felt like, he convinced himself. He opened his laptop and brought up the analysis page he had been working on; he scanned over it and sat staring at it as if the answer to his dilemma was going to jump off the screen. He had decided to put down his current situation, all his options and possible outcomes, none of which he was happy with. He tried to be rational and keep his outcomes positive, but it seemed that all roads led into the same cul-de-sac. One thing he did know and that was he couldn't carry on as he was. The thought of never being able to go to Trentmouth again just did not seem an option that he was prepared to accept, but how was he going to bring about his greatest desire?

'What is my greatest desire?' he asked the screen. He paced up and down his apartment. He wandered over to his gym equipment and began rowing faster and faster his mind completely elsewhere. 'What is my greatest desire?' he asked himself again and the more he asked, the more the same answer came back, 'I don't know'. He stopped rowing, sweat was pouring down his face; he shook his tortured head. Bertie stood in the shower, letting the water run over him, his eyes closed to try to shut out the gnawing question about his future. Suddenly, his eyes popped open, he slapped his forehead. 'Eureka!' he shouted punching the air. He scrambled out of the shower, dressed and returned to his laptop and self-analysis chart. He typed, furiously feeling much better. He sat back exhausted and allowed himself a smile which broadened into a grin.

'Right, that's it, I have a plan and this time, I am not going to let Alistair Warren put me off.'

Alistair had had rather a different evening. He talked to his father to get the latest update on his mother and arranged to go the following weekend. 'Bring Bertie,' his father had said but Alistair had declined saying that he preferred to come on his own, so that he could see his mother without wondering what to do about his guest and anyway, it wasn't fair on his father with mum being in hospital.

'Okay, Son, as you wish,' he had replied.

Alistair had gone to bed feeling guilty. He was more than a little interested in Lucy despite his protestations to the contrary, but he now knew what he wanted to do. He pondered his two unanswered questions from earlier that day. He had been indignant at Bertie's assumption that he was just playing with Lucy, also knowing that Bertie would stand back and not interfere. He turned over and looked at the clock. Two o'clock and he was no nearer sleep. Bertie's other two questions were easy: his mother would recover although it may take time and his job? Alistair had considered moving his whole business to Dorset and he still might do this, times had been difficult recently but not so much that he needed to let Bertie go and anyway, feeling selfish. He needed Bertie to run things in London. If he did relocate, he would still need someone and who better than Bertie? As his eyes finally began to crash down from exhaustion, his phone made a ping to let him know that he had a text, but Alistair decided to leave it till tomorrow, whoever it was, they could wait.

Chapter 16

George woke early the next morning, as he had every day since his wife had been admitted to hospital, to the still quietness of their large home. He stretched out his arm to touch her knowing that she was not there but instead in some noisy ward surrounded by rushing, busy people. Hardly the environment for rest, he mused. He wanted her home where he could take care of her, himself, where he could give her the peace and quiet needed for full recovery. He touched her nightdress still folded where she had left it and for the millionth time, whispered, 'I love you, please come home soon.'

His day was perfunctory, just wasting time till he could go to the hospital and see her, be with her for a few precious hours. His telephone rang and he dashed towards it thinking the worst from the hospital. Grabbing it breathlessly, he simply said,

'Hello.'

'Hello, George, its Molly.'

'Hello, my dear, what can I do for you?' Old habits die hard, he thought. 'I'm sorry, my dear, how are you? No, let me try again. Hello, Molly,' they both laughed.

'I was ringing for two reasons: first, I obviously want to know how Alice is and second, I wondered what you were doing for lunch today?' she asked.

'Alice is coming along nicely, thank you. The speech therapist is visiting today and she is very pleased with Alice's progress. She will soon be home, I'm sure and as to your second

146

question, I will probably have a sandwich before going to the hospital. Why do you ask, my dear?'

'Great news about Alice. I was wondering if I could go to the hospital this afternoon to see her...' Molly paused, giving George his opening.

'Alice would be pleased to see you. It can get very boring in there and with just me as a visitor, too. I'm sure that she would enjoy some "girl talk" as you call it,' he gave a chuckle. He found himself looking forward to listening to this conversation that he was not normally privy to.

'Good,' exclaimed Molly, 'because I have made a casserole. I could bring it over and we can have lunch together before going to the hospital as I have nothing scheduled for this afternoon.'

'That would be wonderful,' declared George. He hadn't had a proper meal since Alice went into hospital; not that he couldn't rustle something up himself but he just hadn't felt hungry and the sound of a casserole from Molly made his mouth water.

'Right, I will be with you about one, is that alright?' She asked.

'Fine, I will look forward to it.' George put the phone down and smiled to himself. Alice was improving and he had a lunch date with a stunning young woman. 'Ah,' he said and disappeared into the kitchen to collect the cutlery and plates to set the table in the dining room, do things properly. George looked at his watch and realised that he had just enough time to make a coffee and sit in his study to do the crossword. It was the first time in the last week that he had the inclination to tackle it, Alice and he usually did it together. The warmer weather meant that he had not been lighting the wood burner but he had cut the lawns, although he was at a loss as to how to tackle the roses and flower borders. It had always been Alice's favourite pastime; it crossed his mind that he would have to find

147

a gardener. *I will ask Molly if she knows anyone who would like a little job, not so little in reality.* He got up and wandered over to the window to survey their large garden, *we will have to look at other changes too, maybe even get a cleaner, although Alice won't like it.* He shook his head, brought out of his reverie by the clock chiming and Molly coming up the drive, he dashed out to meet her. They soon settled down to lunch and George couldn't help but savour the moment.

'You are a very good cook, my dear. You grew the vegetables yourself, I presume.'

'Mostly. It's a bit early in the season for some things but I like to try to be self-sufficient and I am experimenting with one or two new veggies this year.' They chatted about the weather and soil types, Molly's successes and failures on the allotment and George confided his concerns about his garden and needing a handyman. 'I'll put a few feelers out,' she replied. 'I'm sure that someone in the village would be grateful for a few hours' work each week.'

'Are you alright, my dear? You're looking a bit peaky, if you don't mind me saying so?'

'Can't stop being a Doctor, eh, George. I'm fine, thank you, just a little tired, nothing to worry about.' Molly looked askance at George, he held his fork aloft for a moment but thought better of it merely tucking into his casserole.

'I've been meaning to ask you how you are coping with your parents back. How's your father by the way?' he asked as they cleared up the lunch table.

'Well, not good at times. I'm afraid. It feels very strange having them back. They can do nothing else for Dad and Mum keeps crying all the time. Dad seems resigned to the situation.'

'It must be difficult for you all, especially for you having them turn up as they did.'

'Yes, it is, and I don't know if they have made any plans or what they want to do. I can't seem to find the right time to ask. We had better hurry up, Alice will wonder where we are.'

They set off to the hospital with George relaxing beside her, his head rolling about as he began to doze a little in the Land Rover which brought an instant smile to Molly. How alike are Alistair and his father, she thought, especially when they are asleep. She resisted the temptation to brush his hair back from his face, it flopped forward just as it did with Alistair, inside, she ached to be back in his arms. Nearing the hospital, Molly gently woke him up; George was full of apologies for having fallen asleep in company and sought assurances that Molly would not tell Alice. They walked up to the ward and George went in first, he emerged a few moments later beaming.

'Please go in, my dear. Alice is delighted that you have come to see her, but be warned, she tires easily and her speech isn't back to normal yet; I will go and chat to her doctor for a moment or two.' George disappeared and Molly went to find Alice.

'Molly,' she beamed and held out her arms. Although shocked at how much weight she had lost, she gave her a gentle hug.

'How are you feeling?' she asked, 'And please, nod and shake your head if that is easier.' Tears welled up in Alice's eyes as she squeezed Molly's hand.

'I'm alright, my dear,' she said slowly and carefully. 'You talk to me and tell me everything that has been going on.' Molly realised how desperate she was for news and began to tell her all the gossip from the village, filling her in on the forthcoming events at the village fete, her allotment and finally she mentioned Alistair. 'Go on,' Alice managed to say.

'Well, to tell the truth, I haven't heard from Alistair only to tell me about you, of course. I sent him a text last night but I haven't heard from him.' Molly looked briefly down at her hands and then brightening, she continued, 'I have spoken to Bertie and he sends his love and Lucy, of course.' She went on to tell her about the lunch that she had made for George and herself, promising to come and help Alice with the cooking when she returned home.

'Thank you, Molly. That would be lovely.' Alice laid her head back on the pillow and Molly could see that she was tired and she sat quietly looking at how this stroke had aged her so quickly. George appeared with a smile on his face.

'My dear,' he said patting her hand, 'you can come home on Friday, isn't that wonderful news?' George was clearly relieved and more than happy to be taking his darling wife home. Alice's face dropped but she managed a smile for George.

'Yes,' she said simply.

Molly stood up to leave giving them some privacy.

'I will go and get a coffee and see you later, George. I will wait in the entrance and don't hurry, I have all afternoon. Bye,' she said to Alice kissing her on the cheek. Alice took her hand and gave a little squeeze.

Molly bought a coffee and a cake from the little café and sat outside on the terrace. She took out her mobile and checked for messages, nothing from Alistair. She flipped it shut and began to consider her future now that it was clearly not with Alistair. Her phone beeped, Bertie, she opened it, pleased to talk to someone, however, tenuously linked to Alistair.

'Good day, mate. How are you?' she tried in her best Aussie accent.

'Hi, Molly, sorry. "Good day, mate," great and I guess you are too from your tone.'

They talked about Alice and Bertie said that he would like to visit her but Alistair had, quite rightly, made it clear that it would not be appropriate for him to stay at the Warrens' and did she know of a good B&B?

'Tell you what? The cottage at the farm is empty till next week. Why don't you come and stay there and you can help me with the allotment as payment.'

'Brilliant. Nothing would give me greater pleasure.'

'Hey, don't be too sure. It's hard work digging an allotment, you know.' Arrangements were made for the following Friday, the day that Alice should be home and Molly would speak to George to see if they could call on her on the Saturday morning. Molly relaxed, at least she would see Bertie. His childlike enthusiasm for the allotment made her smile. She would get him to do the heavy part for her so that she could do some pricking out and pruning, there was lots to do as the nettles and dandelions grew just as well as her crops. The rest of the week passed quickly. Molly visited Alice again, who was now making good progress, promising to call in on her as much as possible. Friday arrived and Molly sat at the kitchen table rubbing Rex around the ears, it occurred to her that Lucy was probably going to have dinner with Alistair. Bertie was due early evening and Molly had suggested the Kings Arms for dinner as she had heard nothing from Alistair despite the message she had left him and Lucy was busy too. She sniffed back a few tears, shaking herself out of it, telling an attentive Rex,

'I have more important things to worry about, don't I, boy?'

Bertie arrived and Molly took him over to the cottage so that he could dump his stuff before going off to the pub.

'What can I get you to drink, Molly?' he asked as he had pulled out her chair for her to sit down.

'Quite the gentleman,' she quipped feeling that someone cared for a change. 'Can I just have an orange juice, please? I have an early start tomorrow, actually, so do you,' she grinned.

'You're probably right, I will have the same as I must make sure that I dig the allotment properly, then maybe I will be invited to come again?' It was a thinly disguised question as he looked up at Molly with his best pleading face.

'No promises. Let's see how you get on tomorrow first.'

'That's good enough for me,' Bertie grinned and he disappeared to order orange juice for two.

'So, come on then. What exactly do you want me to do tomorrow?' asked Bertie sometime later as they perused the dessert menu.

'Well, there is quite a large area that needs double digging and if you have any energy left, we can put up the canes ready for the runner beans. That should do it for one day.'

'Great,' smiled Bertie. 'I think I will have the Dorset Apple cake, what do you think Molly?' He glanced up at Molly, she shook her head.

'You won't be so pleased tomorrow,' she grinned. 'And I have to make a cake, first thing in the morning for Alice, remember; I'm going to give dessert a miss, maybe just a coffee.'

'Okay, I forgot. Coffee it is.'

Molly caught sight of Alistair entering the pub with Lucy; she grabbed Bertie by the arm,

'Look, who just walked in.' Bertie turned and Molly saw Bertie's face tighten as he clenched his jaw, but he raised one hand beckoning them over.

'Hi, come over here and join us,' his voice was friendly but shaking.

Lucy waved and headed straight over to their table, Alistair followed a lukewarm smile fixed onto his face.

'We don't want to disturb, you guys, in the middle of your meal,' he said gallantly.

'Nonsense, we were just about to order coffee, come on, sit down.' Bertie got up and held the chair for Lucy and she smiled up at him. 'What would you like to drink?' he asked them both.

'No, I'll get these,' said Alistair. 'What would you all like?'

'Make mine a latte,' said Molly.

'And me too,' agreed Bertie.

'You are joking!' laughed Alistair. Molly glanced at Bertie.

'Early start, I have an allotment to dig.'

'I'll have a brandy coffee, please,' said Lucy.

'That's more like it, coming up.'

Alistair disappeared to the bar leaving Bertie with the two girls. The girls began to chatter and Molly, although desperate to ask about Lucy's night out with Alistair, was determined to keep off that particular subject. To her surprise, it was Bertie who asked the question.

'Had a good evening, Lucy? Sorry, maybe I shouldn't ask,' he looked sheepish and fiddled with his napkin before tossing it onto the table, Molly wanted to hug him.

'Very nice, thank you. We had dinner in Wareham by the river; they have an excellent veggie menu, too, for you, Molly. Perhaps, we could all go one evening?' They were becoming more than friends all of a sudden, pairing off and Molly for one was not very happy with the situation but what could she do? Bertie had that something else that was hard to define, but he wasn't Alistair and it was clear to her that he had Lucy on his mind.

'Great idea,' said Molly, 'but not this weekend. Bertie and I have a full day tomorrow already.'

'That's right, but another weekend if I can find somewhere to stay.' Bertie looked from one to the other.

'You're fishing again, Bertie, behave. I'm sure that we can find you a bed somewhere,' said Molly. Alistair returned with a tray of drinks.

'What are you all laughing about? Have I missed something?' They all tried to speak at once enjoying the moment.

That evening, Molly lay in bed unable to sleep, going over and over the events of the day. Was it her imagination or did she sense that Bertie had more than a passing interest in Lucy, she couldn't be sure. He had looked at her in such a way that she was sure that he was trying to say something with his eyes but hadn't quite got the message through. Thoughts chased each other around in her head vying for supremacy; she tossed and turned getting nowhere. Finally, she got out of bed. It was pointless to lie in bed wide awake, she padded downstairs and made a cup of tea. She sat by the Aga in her cosy rocking chair curling her feet up and pulling her dressing gown tightly around her. Warming her hands on the mug, she sipped her tea and began again, trying to sift fact from fiction, feelings from fears. *It's no good*, she thought, *I will have to try and see Lucy somehow tomorrow*. This decision did not help her sleep but at least she managed a few hours of rest. The next morning, Lucy sent a text to Molly, 'coffee?'. It was short and to the point but Molly only sent back, 'tomorrow'. As much as she wanted to see Lucy, the allotment was more important, for now.

Molly and Bertie walked companionably across the farm yard, their breath creating clouds of vapour in the fresh but nippy air as the sun was still weak and low in the sky. Bertie was grateful for his fleece, which he had pushed into his bag at the last minute, as he pulled up the zip. They collected the tools from the shed and sat on the bench which Molly had placed by her garden in order to survey the task ahead. It was sheltered by the old, dry stone wall and Molly took out the flask of coffee and poured out two mugs.

'So, come on then, what on earth are we doing out here at this unearthly hour, Molly?'

'It's the best time of day: dawn breaking, the birds collecting twigs and moss to build their nests. I just love it and I thought that you might, too.'

Bertie looked around, it was indeed a beautiful time of day, quiet and peaceful; he couldn't hear a thing other than the birds singing, of course. He looked across the allotment, it was not a small scrap of dirt as he had envisaged; to him, it looked more like a field. He shook his head and turned to Molly.

'There is no way I can dig all this today, it will take weeks.' Molly burst out laughing.

'Hey, I didn't think that it was that funny, I mean it. I sit in an office all day, I'm not used to proper work.'

'You are funny, Bertie,' she said stroking his arm. Bertie experienced a shock of electricity through his veins; this is getting to be a habit but he didn't mind one bit.

'So, do tell me what is so funny?' he smiled warmly at her feeling very comfortable.

'It's not that bad if we can dig this area here today,' she said pointing to an overgrown patch of weeds and nettles. 'I will be very pleased.'

'You and me both. If I survive this trauma, will you let me cook for you tonight in the cottage?'

'That would be very nice,' exclaimed Molly.

'Yes, and don't sound so surprised,' he teased.

'Alright, you're on,' she beamed. 'Come on, lazy bones, we have work to do.'

An hour or so later, Molly indicated that they should go back up to the farmhouse where she set about making sausages, eggs, mushrooms and tomatoes. Bertie was despatched to shower and come back ready to eat breakfast before they went to visit Alice. He tucked into the best breakfast that he had ever had, apart from Mrs W, he licked his lips and downed his tea.

'Molly, this is fantastic, I love these sausages.'

'You've earned it. That digging would have taken me all day,' she picked up her mug. 'I'll take my tea upstairs and get ready while you finish and no feeding the dog.'

Bertie ruffled Rex's ears, who had taken up position under the table as soon as Bertie sat down.

'Sorry, mate, the boss's orders,' he said to Rex, 'but I won't tell if you don't,' as he slipped a bit of sausage under the table for Rex.

Once ready, they set off for the Warrens'. Molly had carefully placed a coffee and walnut cake into a tin to take to Alice.

'I don't know how you do it, Molly. Baked a cake and digging the allotment, all before most people get up in the morning.'

'Well, I'm just used to it, I suppose,' she said. 'I've never really thought about it before.'

Alice was absolutely thrilled to see them both and George disappeared to make coffee so that they could sit and chat in the snug. George, the happiest man in the world today, had his wife home safe and sound; his son was staying for the weekend and now Molly and Bertie had arrived. Life doesn't get much better than this, he thought, except it would be nice to see Lucy, too. He wondered if Molly and Bertie were now an 'item' to use his son's expression but he was not about to ask. Alistair joined him in the kitchen in order to help.

'You join the others, Dad. I will carry the tray.'

George was pleased to see this change in his son. He wasn't sure exactly what had brought it about but happy, nonetheless, and hoped it would stay that way. Bertie sat staring out of the window at the bedraggled plants, dead leaves filled the borders and daffodils were bent from the wind looking forlorn. He chastised himself forgetting to bring flowers, shaking his head, and even though Molly had baked a cake, that didn't excuse

156

him. Next time, he mused, that sounds good; he was really enjoying being part of the way of life down in Dorset. Alistair came in with the coffee closely followed by George with Molly's cake proudly displayed on a 'chintz' plate. How quaint these people are, he smiled, what a life. He felt envious and couldn't help comparing his parents to these good people, he suddenly longed to see his sister.

'Bertie...Bertie, come back, mate, where were you?' Alistair was holding out a cup of coffee wielding a cake knife in the other hand.

'Oh sorry, nothing. Thanks for the coffee and only a small slice of cake, please'

'What, you alright? This is Molly's cake. Remember, you won't taste better,' he grinned, 'except Mother's, of course.'

'It's not that I don't want it but you should have seen the size of the breakfast that Molly made me this morning.' Alistair froze, this information was doing cartwheels in his head, not to mention the somersaults in his stomach. George watched his son, he knew that look; he quickly glanced at Alice and then Molly and saw a little smile dancing on her lips.

'I'll have that slice please, dear,' said Alice to Alistair. She gave a shudder, 'Has it gone cold in here?'

'I never say "no" to cake,' chipped in George. Alistair moved in slow motion cutting the cake and serving everyone. He stared at Molly, who was quite flushed in the face for some reason. Had they, did they? Alistair was tormented but his mouth felt that it had been glued shut. Finally, it was Alice who broke the spell.

'Where is Lucy this morning?' she said to the air in the room, '...anyone know?'

'Lucy,' exclaimed Alistair. 'Oh, I am taking her out to lunch actually and I was thinking of bringing her to see you later if you're up to it, of course, Mum.'

'That would be wonderful, my dear. Of course, I am up to it.'

'Now, now dear, you mustn't overdo it,' he saw the look of disappointment on her face and changed his mind. 'What I mean is, after you have had a nap.'

'That's fine, Dad. Lucy has been asking about mum, she would really like to see you both.' Everyone settled back into general conversation but not without an awful, lot of unasked and unanswered questions by all in the room, each one with a different agenda. Alistair felt his cell vibrate in his pocket, he quickly looked at it. There was a text from Molly.

'Call me,' it said.

Chapter 17

Bertie busied himself in the kitchen, the events of the day going round and round in his head. He was trying to find a better time in his life but decided there wasn't one. He could not remove the grin from his face, it felt permanently attached. His body ached from all the digging he had done, he stretched up touching the beams to ease his back and catching sight of a spider as it scuttled back into its corner. He checked the recipe book, making veggie food is quite fiddly but he wanted to make an impression on Molly to thank her. He opened a bottle of Australian red wine from the Barossa Valley, one of his favourites and one that he knew Molly loved too, to let it breathe. Next, he put candles on the table and hedgerow flowers in a small vase; he stood back admiring his efforts. He wasn't into desserts very much, unless someone else was making them, so he had settled for a simple fruit salad and plain yoghurt.

'Just enough time to have a shower and I'm ready for my guest,' he smiled triumphantly to himself. Bertie leapt up the stairs two at a time with renewed energy; he felt his phone vibrate and flipped it open, Alistair.

'Hey, mate, everything alright?'

'Yes, fine, just wondering what you were up to tonight, see if you fancied going to the pub or something.' Alistair sounded strained, his voice had an edge that Bertie couldn't quite make out.

'Sorry, mate. I am cooking dinner for Molly, she will be here in a minute.' There was silence at the other end of the phone.

'Alistair, are you still there?'

'Oh, I see,' he said. 'That didn't take you long to get in there, did it?'

Bertie gasped at the vehemence in his voice saying,

'Come on, mate, that's not fair. You have made it quite clear that you and Molly are over and well, now that you are seeing Lucy, I thought...'

He was cut short by an angry Alistair.

'You thought that you would take advantage, is that it?' Bertie, shocked, took a moment knowing that Alistair was being unreasonable, sometimes his mouth took over before his head is in gear. Bertie took a deep breath trying to remember that Alistair was also his boss.

'Look, she asked me to help her with the allotment in exchange for a couple of night's free accommodation in her parents' cottage. I am saying thank you by making dinner and that's it. There is nothing going on, although I don't know why I am bothering to explain myself to you.'

Alistair immediately calmed down, his anger fading.

'I'm sorry. I don't know what got into me. I had no right. You can do what you want. I'm staying on for a few more days, you can take care of the office, can't you? I'll ring you next week.' Bertie snapped his phone shut.

'What if I do make a go of "getting in there",' he said out loud staring up at the ceiling, 'it's my bloody life.'

He was fuming, not the mood he wanted Molly to see when she arrived. Molly, she will be here any second, he dashed into the bathroom, cleaned his teeth again and splashing cold water on his face, he looked in the mirror. That's better, he mused. Straightening up, he calmly walked back downstairs. As he passed by his bedroom, he caught sight of the unmade bed; he quickly pulled the covers back and patted the pillows. He grinned to himself, well you never know. There was a knock on the front door. Bertie leapt into action, put on his best face, ran down the stairs and calmly opened the door.

'Molly, perfect timing. Come in, dinner is almost ready.' He kissed her lightly on the cheek and took her jacket. Molly scanned the room, letting her eyes rest on the table with its candles and the lovely flowers.

'Bertie, you shouldn't have gone to all this trouble but I do like the flowers,' she beamed, tracing a finger along the edge of the table. 'Can I help you in the kitchen?' she asked as she followed him.

'No, definitely not. If I make a mess of it, I want it to be all my mess, if you see what I mean.'

Molly wandered around the room. A room she had been in thousands of times but, somehow, today it seemed different. She looked out of the window and could see her allotment and the evidence of all the hard work that Bertie had put in. She could hear the clatter of pots and pans being stacked up in the sink, the tap turned on, the sound was very comforting somehow. She sat on the couch looking again at the flowers that Bertie had managed to find along the lanes nearby and spotted the red wine.

'Dinner's ready, Madam,' announced Bertie with a flourish placing a tea towel over his arm and bowing ever so slightly. She got up from the couch.

'Why thank you, kind, Sir,' they both burst out laughing. He pulled out her chair for her and draped the napkin across her lap.

'Would Madam care for a glass of wine?' he said as he picked up the bottle.

'Err, yes please, just a small one and could I have a glass of cold water?' Molly turned her pleading eyes towards him.

161

'Coming up,' he dashed into the kitchen and returned with a tall glass of water. 'No ice, I'm afraid,' he said as he placed the glass onto the table.

'That's alright. I'm just thirsty, that's all.' Bertie relaxed and disappeared in order to serve his main course. He placed a number of dishes onto the table, a Mediterranean pasta dish, fresh bread and a salad.

'I haven't made a starter, I hope you don't mind but I do have a dessert.'

'It smells wonderful, Bertie. I probably couldn't manage a starter as well as a dessert anyway, and I didn't know that you were such a good cook. Sorry, I didn't mean it how it sounded.' She flushed with embarrassment.

'Now whose digging?' he grinned.

'You're right, let's just eat, shall we?' They chatted about gardens, food and vegetables in season. Bertie sat riveted, listening to her as if he was really interested, Molly mused. He put his fork down to take a sip of wine, picked up the bottle and began to pour it into her glass. 'Oh, just a small one please, Bertie, long day tomorrow and I will have another glass of water if you don't mind.' Bertie jumped up to refill her glass.

'Sure. You alright? You never usually turn down the best red wine that the Barossa Valley has to offer, it's one of your favourites if I remember correctly.' He gave her a lop-sided grin.

'I know but not too much tonight,' she leaned across and rubbed the back of his hand; She pondered if she should say more but thought better of it. Bertie lingered for a moment before jumping up to collect the plates.

'Time for dessert, I think.' Molly felt a pang of guilt, Bertie was a really good guy, not many of those about but... Bertie came back bearing a large bowl of strawberries, raspberries and blueberries and a pot of yoghurt.

'Perfect,' said Molly as she gave him a little smile, 'and yoghurt rather than cream, how did you know?'

'I just guessed and anyway, I'm not a fan of cream myself. I like to keep fit,' he said as he patted his six pack and grinned.

'I had noticed,' smiled Molly, 'and all that digging helped today, are you up for it again tomorrow?' Bertie leaned back in his chair, hands behind his head, stretching from side to side.

'You bet I never knew that gardening could be so much fun. What have you got in mind for me tomorrow? Not forgetting that I do have to drive back to London later?' He took a sip of wine. 'Alistair rang earlier. He's planning to stay on for an extra few days with Alice just coming home and all that.'

'Oh, is he? I didn't know that. I wonder if he is planning to see Lucy…' She cast her eyes down and then looking at Bertie. 'Sorry, I shouldn't have said that. He can do what he likes, it's nothing to do with me, is it?' Bertie fell silent, his eyes cast down.

'I wish I hadn't mentioned it. I don't want to spoil your evening.' Molly squeezed his arm, Bertie squared himself up. 'Well, come on then, you haven't told me yet what you want me to do on that allotment of yours.'

'Tell you what,' Molly announced. 'Let's do the washing up, I'll make coffee and we can plan our day. Let's not worry about Alistair and Lucy, eh?'

'That's more like it,' he enthused. 'Great, but you are my guest, please relax on the sofa and I'll clear up and make the coffee.'

'Bertie, we're mates, friends having dinner together, I insist on helping to say thank you for that superb meal and I want to know how you made it.'

Bertie gave in and they were soon relaxing again over coffee. Molly picked up a CD and read, 'Lounge Jazz, interesting…you have some good stuff here,' she said. 'Can you put this on? I don't think I know it.' Bertie did as he was bidden

163

and Molly sat down on the couch, opened her bag and produced a bar of organic dark chocolate. She waved it at him. 'To go with the coffee,' she said as she broke it into pieces and placed it onto the coffee table.

'I don't eat much chocolate but I do like dark chocolate, now it's my turn to say, "how did you know?",'

'Secret,' she said with her mouth full of chocolate.

On the table was a piece of driftwood and a few shells that Bertie had picked up on the beach. He had cleaned them and stuck them together into a collage of sorts that he rather liked. Molly picked it up and carefully inspected it saying,

'I've never noticed this before. I wonder where mum got it,' turning it over, looking for a maker's mark.

'I made it,' he grinned. 'It's for you if you like.'

'You made it!' She exclaimed. 'But when and where did you find the wood? It's very good. I didn't know that you had such talent.' Molly looked at it turning it around and placing it back onto the table.

'There's a lot you don't know about me,' he raised his eyes to look into hers.

'I'm beginning to see that, tell me more.'

Bertie sat beside her on the couch and stroked her cheek lightly.

'I'd rather talk about you,' he said. He felt her stiffen at his touch and dropped his hand.

'My mistake,' he muttered. 'Sorry,' dropping his eyes and staring at his hands.

'Bertie,' she said softly. 'Please, Bertie, look at me.' Reluctantly, he lifted his eyes. 'I've something to tell you. I wasn't going to tell you but I think that I owe you an explanation.'

'You don't owe me anything. You don't fancy me, I can see that and you are still in love with Alistair, aren't you?' trying to make it sound casual without bitterness, but he knew that he was failing miserably.

'It's not that. In fact, I do like you, I like you a lot actually. Another time, another place maybe but there's no easy way to say this so here goes: I'm pregnant.' For a moment, an icy shiver ran around his body and Bertie shuddered. He opened his mouth to speak but nothing, nothing came out. He picked up her hands gently stroking them before lifting his eyes to hers once more.

'I...I know. But what I don't understand, you and Alistair? I mean, I presume it is Alistair's, why?'

'You know? But how? Who told you? Alistair, I presume.' He poured himself a glass of wine and stared at her, his mind in complete overdrive wondering how much to say. He held the glass of wine tightly and tried to make some sense of everything. Molly was clearly annoyed but sensing that she had more to tell, he remained quiet. 'Let me start at the beginning, then you might understand better.'

'If you don't mind, because I am feeling like the biggest idiot on the planet at the moment.' Molly smiled at him, taking his hand and squeezing it. She took a deep breath, opened up to him, relieved to finally tell someone, including that awful day when Alistair had said that they should cool it for a while. She explained about the allotment and apologised for using him to do the digging because she couldn't do it not now that she was going to have a baby...

'A baby,' said Bertie as if he had just realised that being pregnant meant that you were going to have a baby. 'A baby, I could thump Alistair, thump him all the way to the moon and back,' he punched his right fist into his left palm.

'No...no,' she laughed picturing Alistair being bounced around the universe. 'I have left him a message and sent a text to call me but he's ignoring me.'

'Bloody fool, I know his head is in a mess but to abandon you is…is unforgivable!' he fumed.

'I don't know. I really don't know but I have decided that for now, I am keeping it to myself. With Mum and Dad back, I don't want to give them anymore grief and I think that he thinks it's some sort of stunt or another to get him back and I don't want him on those terms. He's always wanted our relationship kept secret, I have often wondered why myself. All I can think is that for some reason, he prefers to keep his private life private, even from his parents.'

'Does anyone else know? About the baby, I mean.'

'No, only Lucy, but I'm glad that I've told you. I couldn't keep it to myself much longer. Actually, I'm pretty tired. Do you mind if I go home, Bertie? We have an early start again in the morning, that's if you are still willing to do all that digging for me?'

'Of course, I am. No problem, if you're willing to cook me a big breakfast again?'

They hugged each other and Bertie caressed her hair not letting her go. She lifted her face up to him and they kissed tenderly and deeply. Molly pulled away and disappeared across the farm yard back to the house, he watched her go, head down. Bertie closed the door with his head spinning; he opened his laptop and brought up a spread sheet and stared at the page trying to come up with all the options he could think of as he finished the bottle of wine. It's not my problem, he told himself, I should just walk away, go back to London, keep my head down and pretend none of this has happened, but he also knew that it was not going to happen. He finally went to bed, he had a garden to dig tomorrow.

The next morning, Bertie worked with gusto as he tried and failed to come up with a solution to Molly's problem, which he felt now to be his own. He could help her with the allotment— that was easy—but what about everything else, he longed to discuss it with someone but when he turned over his options, he realised that there was absolutely no one he could turn to, so he would have to make up his own mind and take it from there.

'What a frightening thought,' he said out loud.

'Hmm, what's that Bertie? I didn't quite catch what you said.' Standing by the door of the shed, Molly was pricking out seedlings, looking gorgeous in her dungarees and wellie boots. Bertie couldn't help himself smiling at her.

'I said I thought that it might be time for coffee and a biscuit maybe,' he leaned on the spade trying to put on his best pleading look. Molly turned to look at him.

'Alright, give me a minute. I've nearly finished, then we can have a sit down.' Bertie went back to his digging. *I wish that baby was mine,* he thought. A robin landed close to his boots and they eyed each other before the robin made a grab for a bug of some sort and flew off. He returned to his digging as he saw Molly coming back with a tray deciding to say nothing for now.

'Come on,' she called, 'let's sit down for five minutes.' Bertie left his spade and walked across to the seat where he flopped down in mock exhaustion. On the tray, Molly had brought scones that were still warm and slices of lemon drizzle cake.

'When did you make those?' He looked up in awe. 'You're a domestic goddess if you don't mind me saying.' Molly laughed.

'Oh, easy. I was making breakfast for you so I put them into the oven at the same time,' sounding quite matter-of-fact as if she did it every day.

'This is delicious, I will be getting fat. Oh, sorry, Molly. I didn't mean anything by that, about you, I mean.'

'Forget it, Bertie. I already have.' They finished all the cake and scones with their coffee and Bertie asked about the allotment and the trees that were now in full blossom.

'We have apple, eating and baking, plums, cherries even a fig tree and then over in the cage, I have raspberries, blueberries, strawberries and gooseberries.'

'What do you mean by that?' he asked quizzically.

'By what exactly?' she asked giving him a sideways glance.

'Well you said "we" have apple trees and so on and then "I" have raspberries and blueberries. I just wondered why it was "we" and then "I".'

'Oh, I see. Strictly speaking, the orchard belongs to Dad. Although he lets me sell the fruit through the farmer's market, what I can't use that is but I planted the fruit cage for myself.'

'Ah, I see.' He fell silent before asking, 'Are you planning to take over the farm one day?'

'Don't know. I never wanted to, Dad was into cattle and sheep, I would rather have a few chickens and ducks, maybe a goat but that's all...and of course, now that they are back, I don't know what will happen...then there's Stella, of course.'

'Stella! Who's Stella?'

'My sister, she lives over in Beaminster with her husband and three children. She's not interested in farming, she's too busy running her cake decorating company and she's had a couple of novels published, too,' Molly looked at Bertie who was staring at her dumbfounded. He let out a low whistle.

'I don't know how you do it, both of you. I feel lazy by comparison. I don't mean to sound patronising but all this...' he waved his arm in the direction of the allotment, 'and your business and now a baby...' Bertie gazed at her.

'Things are going to have to change soon. I don't know what I am going to do to tell you the truth.' They both fell silent with their own thoughts. 'Come on, back to work and no arguing, you are staying to dinner with me before you go back to London, okay?' She turned to collect the dishes then said, 'Bertie...sorry about last night.'

Bertie quickly grabbed her hand, he stood up pulling her to him.

'I'm not Molly, not at all.'

He leant in and they kissed again. Feeling happy, very happy, he worked hard for the rest of the morning; he noticed the robin return hopping about, following him around the allotment, pinching worms when he thought that Bertie wasn't looking; it made him smile with contentment. He was determined that he would not let Molly out of his life, even if it pained him to see Alistair with Lucy.

Chapter 18

Alistair picked Lucy up at Honeysuckle Cottage to take her to lunch; he stared at the once despised thatch with its wisteria entwined around the porch.

'Who would have thought of it,' he shook his head in disbelief. He felt contented that his mother, now feeling much better, was home again and here he was about to take Lucy out to lunch, just as friends but still...perhaps, now was the time to move things along with Molly? He opened his phone and pressed the button. Lucy came out of the cottage looking radiant. He closed his phone, he would call her later.

He kissed her on the cheek and opened the car door. Lucy chatted endlessly about the house that she had found, her offer had been accepted and she was now waiting for the solicitors to sort it all out. She had been lucky that property here had been within her budget so the money she had received from Lionel meant that she could make a cash purchase.

'What about Lionel?' asked Alistair. He was still rather cautious with regard to that debacle.

'He is being very co-operative, he knows that it is all over and he wants everything finalised as quickly as I do. I have moved on.'

'And have you?' asked Alistair.

'Definitely, I shall be glad when I sign the final paperwork. Lionel is even sending the remainder of my things by courier so I won't even have to see him.'

'So, what happens next?' he enquired.

'Well, I will be staying with Mum and Dad until I have upgraded the house; I have a lot of plans and it will probably take a month or two but that doesn't matter. I am not in a hurry. I would love to get back into midwifery but for now, my two part-time jobs will have to do, at least they give me time to work on my new house.'

'You've got it all worked out, anything I can do to help?' He asked.

'Probably, thank you. I'll let you know.' Lucy looked out of the window, her attention caught by dozens of gulls circling behind a tractor, screeching incessantly. She watched them for a moment and turning back to Alistair asked, 'Have you heard from Molly or Bertie this morning?'

'No, not since last night, have you?'

'No. I sent a text yesterday asking Molly to coffee, but she must have been busy as she suggested another time. I was wondering what they were up to, any idea?'

'Sorry, can't help. I spoke to Bertie last night and he was preparing dinner for him and Molly.'

Lucy let out a faint, 'ooh' as she slumped, head down twiddling with her bracelets.

'You're quiet,' said Alistair, 'everything alright?'

'I'm sorry, I was just thinking that after lunch, perhaps we could swing by Molly's place and see them. I expect Bertie will be off back to London today.'

'Of course, we can. I need to speak to Bertie and Molly actually,' Alistair indicated and turned up a long gravel drive with lime trees on either side just bursting into leaf with carpets of bluebells adorning the verge. 'Here we are, I thought that you might like this place. I've heard that it is very good.' Alistair pulled up outside a large Victorian building that had once been a school but was now a popular wedding venue with extensive gardens.

'You didn't have to do this, Alistair. I have forgiven you. You must let me pay my half.'

'Sorry, no, can do, my treat.'

'Okay, but then really I insist you have paid your debts,' Lucy gave in.

Alistair talked about his business, his life in London and his parents; Lucy quizzed him about how he knew Molly? Why he had left Trentmouth? And why did he really want to buy a place back here again? They polished off a bottle of red and relaxed feeling soporific.

'Let's move to the lounge, there is a lovely log fire in there and we can have coffee,' Alistair suggested.

'Great. What a lovely idea. Will you excuse me for a minute?' Alistair nodded, ordered coffee and wandered out into the lounge. It was a sumptuous room, with rich tapestry chairs arranged intimately. The fire crackled and popped reminding him of his parents' wood burner. He sat down and thought of Molly, he was going to ask her to marry him.

Molly's phone buzzed, she pulled it out of her back pocket, it was Lucy.

'Hi, Molly, how are you?'

'Great, aren't you supposed to be having lunch with Alistair today?'

'Yes, we are just about to have coffee. I was wondering has Bertie already left for London?'

'No, we're just washing up. I made lunch for us, he has worked very hard digging the allotment for me this weekend. Do you want to speak to him?'

'No, no. It's just that we, I mean Alistair and I, were wondering if we could come over and see you both, if you're not too busy that is.' Lucy stumbled over her words and Molly gulped as her throat tightened, dreading the thought that they might be coming over to make an announcement. She froze, a

172

knot tightening itself in her stomach. Her head ached as a feeling of nausea swept over her.

'See you in a bit, I'll put the kettle on,' she managed to say before turning to Bertie, she clutched her stomach and bent over double. Bertie was there like a shot, he put his arms around her.

'Are you alright? Sit down, should I get a doctor?'

'Just a glass of water, that's all.' Bertie dashed to get the water; he came back as quickly as possible and pulled up a chair next to her. She squeezed his hand, 'Thank you, Bertie. I'm so glad that I confided in you, you're a good friend.' Bertie had no experience of such matters and was at a loss as to what to do.

'Are you sure you're alright? Should you lie down or something?' Molly managed a grin.

'You're amazing,' she said at last allowing him to hug her.

'I've never been called that before. What's the problem anyway, is something wrong with Lucy?'

'No, they are coming over to see us before you go.' Molly tried to talk nonchalantly to disguise her fear, 'That's not a problem, is it?'

'No, but I'll have to go soon. I'll finish clearing up and you will sit down there and not move.' Molly smiled. Bertie picked up the tea towel and began to wipe the dishes.

'Actually,' he said turning to face Molly, 'I was wondering if you would like some more help again next weekend? I could go bowling with a few mates but if you need me, I'm here.'

'Bertie, that would be great. The cottage is occupied I'm afraid, but if you want to, you can stay here at the farm with me. I'm sure Mum and Dad won't mind. It's the least I can do in exchange for all your hard work.' Bertie grinned.

'Great, I'll call you in the week to see how you are and sort out the weekend. I have a few things to sort out regarding my future this week but it can wait.'

'You didn't tell me about this,' said Molly, 'Keeping secrets?'

'No secrets,' he grinned, 'but I will fill you in next week. There's nothing very much to tell, to be honest, but I've been working on one or two ideas, nothing definite...I promise to tell you all about it soon.'

They turned hearing a car pull up outside and Molly got up to open the door. Lucy went to kiss Molly on the cheek, the two girls hugged each other. Lucy then stepped up to kiss Bertie and he bent forward so that she could reach him, her lips brushed his cheek. 'Hi,' he crooned. Bertie shook hands with Alistair and they all sat around the range cooker in the kitchen.

'Nice lunch?' Molly managed to say carefully side stepping any closeness with Alistair, opting instead for the merest peck on the cheek. Rex was delighted to have so many people to make a fuss of him, so many new smells, he wagged his tail furiously.

'Would you like me to take Rex for a walk before I go?' Bertie looked at Molly. 'Then you two girls can have a private chat.'

'Thanks, that's a great idea. I'll have tea ready for you when you get back. I'm sure that I can find a few crumbs.'

'Great, come on, Alistair, let's go.' He picked up Rex's lead and Rex was out of the door and down the lane before Bertie could pull on his sweatshirt.

'What! Me too?' said Alistair feigning surprise. 'I haven't got the right shoes on.'

'They'll do,' said Bertie looking at his shiny loafers, 'we're not going far.'

The men set off amiably following Rex down the lane and as soon as the door closed, Lucy began to fill Molly in on their lunch; all was fine till Lucy had returned from the ladies. Alistair had ordered coffee and a brandy which Lucy enjoyed so she didn't mind that at all but...

'I thought he was going to ask me out again,' she confided.

'I thought that is what you wanted,' Molly uttered softly.

'No! I told him that it was too soon after Lionel, I need breathing space. I don't want another relationship just yet. I am trying to sort my life out and I really don't want it complicated. I am looking forward to doing my own thing, you know? I just want to be friends.'

'I can understand that,' said Molly feeling less stressed as her headache eased.

'What about you and Bertie?' asked Lucy as she helped put plates and mugs onto the table.

'Not jealous, are you?' smiled Molly.

'…course not. I just wanted to know how things were between you, that's all.'

'Well, before anyone else tells you, Bertie is coming again next weekend to help me with the allotment and he will be staying in the farmhouse…in the guest room.' She paused for breath, Lucy smiled leaning back in her chair, nibbling some cake.

'That's good. I mean that's good that he wants to work on the allotment, but I didn't think that it was his kind of thing?' Lucy broke off a corner of her cake and a sultana fell onto the cloth. 'Sorry, I'm making a fool of myself, aren't I?' She finished her cake and rubbed her fingers together.

'No, not really, Bertie is a great guy and, in case you are wondering, I told him about the baby.'

The men set off at a pace down the lane trying to keep up with a very excited Rex. His nose was in and out of every clump of grass and hedgerow. He startled a bird and made to run after it but quickly gave up. They watched his antics for a while, neither speaking to the other.

'How did you get on last night, with Molly I mean?' At first, Bertie wanted to punch him on the nose, partly because Molly was pregnant and he didn't seem to care and partly because he felt that Alistair should not be asking him such a question, it made him furious.

'Great. Molly is an amazing woman. She has hidden talents and a great career move planned.'

'What! Has she? I didn't know that. What is she planning to do?' asked a startled Alistair.

'Not for me to say, mate. I'm sure she will tell you when she is good and ready.' Bertie stole a sideways glance at Alistair and felt pleased to see him looking guilty for once. He hadn't contacted Molly, she had left him a text and he had ignored it and Bertie delighted in making him suffer even a little bit. The two men continued on down the lane and Bertie enquired about Alice and news of Alistair's progress in finding a bolthole. The two men chatted and laughed at Rex who dashed across a field chasing a rabbit; he sauntered back to them, head down and his tongue hanging out. Alistair filled Bertie in with news of Lucy's purchase of a house in Wareham before finally the conversation inevitably turned to work and Alistair, on much safer ground, issued some instructions to Bertie for the coming week.

'I will be back down again next weekend anyway,' Bertie said as he threw a stick for Rex.

'You're full of surprises today. Where are you going to stay, may I ask?' Alistair raised his eyebrows and glared at him.

'With Molly,' he smirked.

'In the cottage again, I presume?' queried Alistair.

'You presume wrong, mate, at the farm. Rex, come here boy, time to go home.' Bertie whistled for Rex, who came running, waiting patiently as Bertie hooked his lead onto his collar. Alistair did not probe any further

'You're quiet, anything I need to know?'

'No...I was just giving myself a mental note to call Molly and I didn't mean to pry by the way.'

Molly had the table spread with cakes and the kettle whistling on the hob when they finally arrived back at the farm.

'Good walk?' asked Molly.

'Great,' replied Bertie with a grin. Alistair took his muddy shoes off and padded across the cold flagstone floor. They sat at the kitchen table, no one spoke. They just ate the delicious cake. It was Molly who braved the silence.

'I sent you a text the other night, Alistair. Did you not get it?' Alistair began to choke on a crumb of cake.

'Yes. Sorry, Molly, I meant to call you but with Mum and everything, I forgot.'

'It doesn't matter now, anyway,' she said glibly.

'How long are you staying this time? Only I promised Alice that I would visit her and I won't if you two are fussing over her.'

Alistair stared at Molly, Bertie and Lucy stared at each other and then back to Molly and Alistair, his cheeks flushed put his cake down and fidgeted with his cup.

'Actually, I might go on Tuesday as Dad has everything under control and I could do with getting back to London myself.'

'I can manage if you want to stay longer,' butted in Bertie. Alistair gulped some tea.

'I give in. I'm in the way down here. Dad wants Mum to himself for a bit, so I will make myself scarce. I know Bertie is coming back next weekend and I'll be back probably the week after next, so please visit Mum, she loves to see you. Perhaps, I can call you?' Molly shrugged.

'If you like, I am busy next week and Mum has the Macmillan nurse coming but you can try.' Alistair harrumphed.

'I…I didn't know you would be down again next week…and staying with Molly?' she asked tentatively.

'Molly only wants my body', he grinned, 'to dig the garden, I mean.' They all giggled stiltedly.

'We must be going,' Alistair said to Lucy. 'Mum is expecting us.' Lucy stood up, kissed Molly and brushed her cheek with Bertie and they left.

'I must be going too, Molly. I don't want to get caught up in the traffic. Thank you for all my aches and pains. I'll see you on Friday.'

Molly waved to him as he drove down the road and turning towards the allotment with Rex padding behind her. She stood evaluating the work that Bertie had put in and heaved a sigh.

'Okay,' Molly said looking at Rex, 'he has one more chance and then that's it.' Rex cocked his head on one side, lifting his ears. She ruffled his head and he flopped down onto the ground with a snuffle. Molly pulled out her cell and sent a text to Alistair.

Chapter 19

The following week flew by for Molly. She saw Lucy once or twice but they kept the conversation away from both Bertie and Alistair. She had telephoned Stella who was not sympathetic to her situation at all; in fact, she advised forgetting all about him.

'He'll get over it or not, who cares? He's hardly the caring type, is he?' Molly knew she was probably right but no one understood how she felt about him and she had tried not to care. Alistair had gone back to London without seeing her but promising lunch the next time he was down. She accepted that whatever ideas she may have had about her future with Alistair, they were now almost certainly on the rocks, consigned to the scrap heap of her broken dreams. She had become firm friends with Alice visiting her whenever she could, helping her to return to a normal life. George would pop his head around the door to remind his wife not to overdo it. 'You must rest, my dear,' was his favourite mantra. George had had the fright of his life, he had suddenly become more visible around the house making, the bed, stacking the dishwasher; he had even mastered the art of hoovering, delighting Alice but the question of the garden still clearly hung heavy over George. So far, Molly had not been able to find a gardener for him and George had drafted a card asking Molly to place in the window of the local shop. Molly had been baking cakes again and delivering a few fresh vegetables from her allotment.

'The strawberries will soon be ready,' she told Alice. 'We just need a few more warm and sunny days, and then I will bring you some.'

'You are good, my dear,' Alice squeezed her arm. 'I don't know what I would do without you. If I had a daughter, I would hope she would be like you.' Molly felt embarrassed and gently rubbed her now tiny swell of a tummy.

'Are you alright, Molly dear? I didn't mean to embarrass you. I'm sure that Alistair does his best but he does have his business to deal with and he said that he would be down again next week. I don't think he knows how to help actually.'

'You're probably right. He has changed recently, I don't know why. I've been trying to figure it out, any ideas?' Molly tried to change the subject as she picked at her cake.

'Sorry, can't help on this occasion. Alistair always seems to have other things on his mind.'

'Has Lucy been up to see you?' she asked, already knowing the answer.

'Yes, she is a lovely girl. She made us a fruit cake. I shall be putting weight on. Speaking of food, I hear that Bertie is coming tomorrow to help you with the allotment again. Are you and he more than friends?' Alice was always straight, she didn't believe in anything else, it saved a lot of misunderstanding. Molly gave a laugh.

'Food and Bertie in the same sentence. Alice, you must think that he needs feeding up, he is a bit thin, I must admit, and no, we are just friends. Actually, he is a good mate, a very good mate. Someone you can trust in a crisis.'

'Really, my dear, is there a crisis then?' Alice probed.

'No,' Molly gave her a grin, 'you are fishing Mrs Warren. All I mean is that if there was a crisis, Bertie is the sort of person that you could turn to and he wouldn't let you down.'

'Oh, I see. He's a very nice young man. One day, he will make some lucky woman a very good husband, don't you think?' Alice was nodding to herself with a faraway look in her eyes. Molly wondered if she was thinking about Alistair and his suitability as husband material.

Molly steered the conversation away from the boys. She had had a couple of texts from Bertie but had missed a couple of attempts by Alistair to get in touch wondering if she should give him one last chance. She began to look forward to seeing Bertie again and had already planned the few days of help for the allotment; she had even enrolled Lucy to help. Molly brought her thoughts back to her and Alice. She looked around the cosy snug; *one day, I would love a room like this,* she thought.

'Penny for them, my dear,' Alice broke into her dreaming, she shook her thoughts away.

'Apologies, Alice, I was thinking about Bertie actually and the gardening I have planned for him,'

'Good idea, keep the men busy. I have always tried to keep George busy but it didn't work.' They both grinned and Molly jumped up.

'Speaking of George, I must be going before he tells us off again.'

'Thank you, my dear, and do bring Bertie along if you have time.'

'Will do,' she bent to kiss Alice on the cheek, still shocked at how frail she had suddenly become.

Friday came quickly with Bertie ready to test out his ideas on Molly that evening; they were planning dinner at home so that they could get an early start the next morning. The weather forecast predicting sunshine, summer was finally on its way and Bertie was actually looking forward to being up with the larks. He had carefully kept out of Alistair's way all week; conversation had been strictly business; he knew better than to risk a confrontation. Bertie drove down the motorway and with every mile, his mood got lighter, the lines smoothed on his forehead, his breathing slower and deeper. His whole body changed, relaxed, stress melting away.

'Who would want to live anywhere else?' he yelled up at the sky. London is looking duller and dirtier, it was hard work and a basement flat, the bright lights were for the tourists. He wound his way to Purbeck, realising just how much he relaxed and smiled just by driving over the bridge at Wareham. Driving across the water meadows lifted his mood and immediately helped him to feel safe like going 'home'.

The ducks quacked and the hens flew into the air clucking at him as he drove into the farmyard, the sight cheered him, he was the luckiest man alive. Just a few months ago, for him to enjoy the countryside was unthinkable. He pulled up by the barn and looked around for Molly. Rex bounded over, his tail wagging furiously, ever hopeful for a walk.

'Good boy, Rex, where's Molly then?' he patted his back and Rex nuzzled him for more attention.

'I'm here,' said Molly appearing at the barn door carrying a sack.

'Give me that,' Bertie called out as he rushed over to take the sack from Molly, 'you shouldn't be carrying anything heavy, even I know that.' He smiled at her, kissed her cheek and took the sack.

'Thank you, Bertie, but I have to carry on as normal. My parents are indoors and they don't know yet, so please try not to fuss me too much, alright.' Bertie raked through his hair beaming at her.

'Sorry, can't help it. Where do you want this anyway?'

'Over here and then we can go in for a cup of tea unless you want something stronger.'

'No, tea is fine. The beer can wait, we…I have work to do.' Over tea and carrot cake, Molly filled him in on the plans for the next day.

'I've asked Lucy if she would like to join us tomorrow. You don't mind, do you?'

'No, not at all. Is she good at digging then?' he grinned.

'No, probably not, but she can make the coffee and plant seedlings. I have plenty in mind for Lucy to do.' Bertie finished his cake and patted his stomach. He stretched his legs gazing around the room before settling his gaze on Molly.

'I was wondering, about tonight, hoping to talk to you. Perhaps, we could go for a walk or something,' he ventured.

'Sounds serious, you're not worrying about me, are you?' Molly gently stroked his arm.

'I can't help it,' he swallowed hard. 'I do care...' he trailed. Molly jumped in.

'Right, get your bags. Let me show you your room, then you can freshen up if you want to before I make dinner.' Bertie duly followed her up the stairs along the landing with its sloping ceiling and creaky floorboards; he had to bend his head to get through the door into the tiny bedroom that was his for the weekend.

'Thanks,' he said pressing the mattress. He caught sight of Molly watching him and his little ritual.

'It used to be my bed when I was younger, but the mattress is new and comfortable, not at all lumpy or as old as the house,' she smirked looking around the room. 'Oops, I can see a cobweb hanging from the beams in that corner, sorry about that.'

'Don't be sorry, it's just that everything about this place is amazing. I love it.'

'I'll leave you to it. Don't fall asleep, will you? Come down when you're ready. The bathroom is the last door on the left.' Molly left him alone and Bertie flopped onto the bed with a sigh, he could not have predicted this...ever.

Molly wondered what Bertie wanted to talk to her about. Whatever it is, it is clearly important to him, she mused, making a mental note to get busy with a feather duster too. She pulled out pots and pans, collected vegetables and began to prepare for dinner just the two of them as her parents had gotten into the habit of eating at lunch time in Spain. Her mind wandered as she jumped from relief to regret and back again about confiding in Bertie. Stella knew, of course, but she couldn't bring herself to tell her mum and dad or Alice…at least, not yet.

Bertie bounced into the kitchen and Rex leapt from his basket in expectation. Bertie obliged him with a ruffle and turned to Molly.

'Anything I can do?' he enquired.

'Yes, you can peel the potatoes. I'm making homity pie.'

'Sounds great. I was wondering what you will do when…well, you know.'

'When I have the baby?' she tilted her head to look at him wiping her floured hands on a tea towel.

'Yes. I mean have you thought about your career and…and everything?' he shrugged.

'Bertie, I've thought of nothing else, including how to tell my parents, George and Alice, as well as my clients. I have no answers for you if that's what you mean,' slightly exasperated as if she wouldn't have turned all these things over and over in her mind getting nowhere.

'Sorry, I didn't mean to sound insensitive, forgive me?' Molly grinned and hugged him.

'I love you, Bertie. You're so funny.'

'Do you, love me I mean?' He returned her hug and held her close.

'Yes, but I should have said I love the funny things you say and do,' she pulled away from him and placed the pie into the oven. Quiet for a moment, Molly pondered the awkward situation that she had unwittingly placed them in and turning to

Bertie, rubbing her face with the back of her hand leaving a trace of flour across her cheek. 'I shouldn't have told you. It's placed us both in a difficult position,' her face crinkling into tears.

'Hey, hey come here,' he gently wiped the flour from her face and wrapped his arms around her once more, gently caressing her hair. 'It's going to be alright,' he said. 'I promise.'

'How can you say that?' she pulled away slightly but not too far. It was good to feel love and care from another human being. He placed one hand on the back of her head and gently pulled her to him kissing her; she kissed him back with longing, then pulled away. 'I'm sorry,' she said, 'I'm so sorry, I shouldn't have done that. You are too nice, Bertie. I, I just can't do this.'

'Yes, you can,' he put his hand out to her and she took it. Bertie took a deep breath. 'I wish that baby was mine, we could get married...and then,' Molly was shocked, her eyes flashed wildly around his face...

'Is this a joke?' she gasped grabbing a tissue. Bertie pulled her to him once more dabbing at the tears trickling down her face smearing her mascara. 'You don't know what you are saying, Bertie. I'm pregnant with another man's child, why would you ask me to marry you? I'm totally confused.'

'It's not a joke. I've thought about it long and hard and I think that it is the perfect solution. We can say the baby is mine if you want to, no one need know; I have been thinking about a change of career, in fact, a complete change of my whole life if I'm honest. I know it's a shock,' he exclaimed, 'but I think it can work,' he paused. 'Do you think I could have a beer? I feel parched and a bit shaky.' Molly turned and grinned at him.

'Help yourself, they are in the fridge. I'm feeling shaky too but I had better have water or maybe just a very small glass of wine. I must check on the dinner.' Bertie helped himself to a beer turning just as Molly was lifting the homity pie out of the oven.

'That smells good,' he enthused, 'can I do anything?'

'Yes, sit at the table. I'll just get the veg and then we can discuss this…this proposal properly.'

'Alright,' he said sitting down. 'I suppose I do owe you an explanation.'

'You had better start at the beginning give me chance to think, I'm so confused right now.'

'You're a very good cook, Molly.'

'So that's it. You want to marry me for my cooking,' she managed a grin.

'No, no,' startled, he shot a look at her, only to see her smiling.

'Just teasing,' she said.

'This is the biggest thing in my life, you know. I rent a basement flat in London, I go to work, I run and I watch F1, go bowling with my mates on a Friday night and that's it, my life in a sentence.' He looked closely at Molly but she gave no reaction. Molly sat quietly waiting for him to continue without giving anything away, her mind churning the information wildly. 'I think that we could open a small organic café, serving coffee and cakes, that sort of thing. I can cook too, as well as working on the allotment.' Molly looked at him startled yet again with his plans. 'I can buy a place or we can live above the shop so to speak.'

'Hold on a minute, Bertie,' Molly grabbed his arm, 'you really have been thinking about this, haven't you? You have got it all worked out but you are forgetting one thing.'

'What's that?' he looked at her his eyes searching her face.

'I…I love Alistair and I couldn't marry you, expecting you to bring up a child that isn't yours. I don't think that you have considered me at all,' she got up lifting the kettle onto the hob and pushing a wisp of hair behind her ear. 'The thing is I love

186

my career. Your idea about a café is a good one but it's your dream, not mine. I appreciate you thinking about me, I really do, but this is mega,' she paused for breath.

'Well, will you think about it please, just think about it.'

'Okay, but I won't change my mind.' The kettle began to whistle and Molly made a pot of tea. 'Did you know, by the way, that Lucy turned Alistair down?'

Chapter 20

Before dawn the next morning, Bertie went for a long run; he hadn't been able to sleep, his head still reeling from the night before. He should have known better than to barge in with his own ideas. He was baffled. He ran harder trying to put his thoughts and feelings into some kind of order but to no avail, they chased him faster than he could run. He turned the corner back into the farm yard; Lucy's car was sitting beside his own, he stopped dead in his tracks. He felt a sudden ache in his chest, a grip that almost strangled him; he shook his head and sat on top of the stone wall and began to breathe deeply to calm himself.

'Bugger, bugger, bugger…' he gasped out loud as he drew in a deep breath.

'Are you alright, Bertie?' Lucy was walking across the farm yard with Rex lolloping along beside her, the sun shining through her hair, with a look of concern on her face.

'Hi, yes I'm fine. Just having a rest,' Rex nuzzled up to him and Bertie dutifully patted his head.

'Molly is cooking breakfast. She says that we can't go digging without food inside us.'

'I agree. I'll just grab a quick shower and I'll be there.'

Lucy returned to the kitchen and caught Molly rubbing her stomach.

'You alright Molly? You look pale.'

'No, no, I'm fine. I think I ate too much last night and I'm not as hungry as I thought.'

'Oh, right. I know the feeling. Some fresh air will do us good. Are you sure you are alright?'

'Honestly, yes, I'm fine. Where's Bertie? His breakfast is ready,' Molly looked across at Lucy waving a plate piled high with sausages, eggs and black pudding.

'He's having a quick shower. Actually, he looked exhausted after his run, what were you two up to last night?' Molly hesitated and Lucy felt a cold shiver down her spine but then Molly just smiled.

'We just had a late night. We sat talking till a ridiculous time, that's all.' Lucy had to accept this explanation and turning to sit at the table, she noticed the drift wood and shell sculpture.

'I like that, Molly. Where did you get it?'

'Bertie made it, isn't he clever?' She called up the stairs to Bertie to hurry up. Lucy twisted and turned the little sculpture scrutinising every detail.

'I like it. I didn't know that he had such talent. A real man of surprises,' she turned it around before placing it back onto the table.

'As well as digging, do you mean?' Molly grinned and placed scrambled eggs in front of Lucy.

Bertie came running down the stairs and stopped when he heard Lucy's voice.

'Thanks. No, I just meant that he is a really nice guy, I like him a lot. He has hidden talents.' Bertie sat on the stairs, his face turning from smiles to fear, assuming she meant Alistair. He pushed open the door bounding into the kitchen with an awkward grin attached to his face.

'Sorry, Lucy. I couldn't help but overhear you but you have got it wrong, you know. Alistair is very keen on you, he is just afraid that the moment is wrong what with Alice and everything.' Molly stood still, spatula in hand, her face ashen. Lucy stared at Bertie.

'What?' he raised his arms. 'What have I said? Did I say something wrong? You both look like you've seen a ghost,' he tried a chuckle pulling out a chair and sitting down. Molly placed his breakfast in front of him and shoved the ketchup towards him.

'Thanks for the info. I'll bear that in mind,' Lucy glanced at Molly before returning to her scrambled eggs. Molly turned back to the stove. Bertie tucked into his breakfast still wondering what had just happened, he could see Molly was stretching her head and circling her shoulders and whatever it was, he had got it wrong. Lucy shuffled her eggs about her plate. Bertie decided to carry on and began to ask Molly about the day ahead.

'Actually, I have some news,' Lucy piped up looking from one to the other.

'We have something to tell you too,' said Molly as she patted Bertie's hand. Lucy's mouth dropped open and her eyes widened, a little smile appeared on her lips but not her eyes.

'You go first, mine can wait.' she mumbled. Bertie watched as a crest fallen, Lucy looked up at her friend. He wanted to hug them both. Turning to Molly, he offered a weak smile.

'No, come on, you go first please. We want to hear what your news is,' Molly cleared away the plates and brought the coffee pot to the table together with toast, butter and honey.

'It's not news really. Well, I suppose it is, I have exchanged contracts on my house and will be getting the key soon, and I wanted to ask you both to join me for a glass of champagne to celebrate, that's all.'

'That's great news,' said Molly, 'we're very pleased for you, aren't we, Bertie?' glancing across at him. Bertie gently removed his hand away from Molly under the pretext of ruffling Rex's head.

'Yes, that's great news and I will be happy to help you decorate or knock a wall down or whatever you want,' he collected some mugs and poured out the coffee.

'So, come on then, what is your news?' Lucy folded her arms and Bertie could see that she was steeling herself for what was to come.

'Come on, Bertie, you tell her,' Molly grinned as she scooped a spoonful of honey onto her toast.

'I hardly know where to start,' he said once more giving his attention to Rex, 'however, I've given it a lot of thought and I would like to move down here, start an organic café...with Molly's help, of course,' he looked across at her and her face beamed, the smile radiating from her eyes.

'Oh...sorry, sorry. I'm obviously very pleased for you. It's just a shock, that's all. I can see that you are both very happy about it. Am I missing something else here? Only you look as if there is more to tell?' Lucy wrung her hands and rubbed them together under the table in an effort to remain calm. 'I think that I had better go,' her face twisted, tears stinging her eyes. She pushed her chair back scraping it across the stone flagged floor and made to leave but Molly grabbed her arm.

'What's the matter, Lucy, please sit down. Listen, you don't know the whole story.'

'What more do I need to know, how could I have been so stupid?' She grabbed her jacket. 'I've got to go,' she made to run out of the kitchen, but Bertie jumped up and pulled her into his arms. Lucy tried to pull away but he held on firmly until she stopped squirming.

'Hey, come and sit down,' he smoothed her hair and lifted her chin so that she had to look at him, he led her back to her chair. Molly grabbed the kettle and placed it onto the Aga for another pot of coffee. 'I think that you have misunderstood what's happening here. Molly and I are friends and she has agreed to let me cultivate the allotment and use the veggies in

191

my café. I really want to make a fresh start, get away from London and here is as good a place as any.' Lucy stared into his eyes, her face slowly relaxing, the crinkled lines disappearing.

'I thought…I thought, well, it doesn't matter what I thought,' she turned to Molly. 'Sorry, I'm sorry. Do you forgive me?' Lucy and Molly hugged.

'Nothing to forgive, we had better get started though on that garden. It's getting late,' she glanced at her watch. 'You two go and I'll catch up in a minute, it's gone eight.' Lucy and Bertie both laughed as they looked at each other and Molly shooed them out of the door, Rex following at their heels.

Molly loaded the dishwasher and filled the flasks with tea; she picked up her basket to pack in some treats as the door to the hall opened.

'Mum! You made me jump, you are up early,' her mother padded into the kitchen, her pink dressing gown flowing around her ankles, the pompoms flopping about on her tartan slippers.

'Sorry, love, your dad had a restless night and so did I. Is there a coffee in that pot?' Molly took down a mug and filled it. She pushed it in front of her mother and slid into the chair opposite. Her mother took a deep gulp.

'Your dad and I have been talking and as we are back now and well, our lives are so different to yours, what with young men staying over…'

'But, Mum!' Molly interjected. Her Mum held up her hand.

'Let me finish. We thought that you could move into the cottage in a few weeks' time, just until you can get something more permanent sorted out. We can't cope with all this coming and going, it's better for all of us. Right, that's settled. I'll take your dad a coffee up.'

'But, Mum, you gave me this house, it's mine! You can't do this to me and what are you talking about by young men? If you mean Bertie, he is a friend,' she gasped her head reeling.

192

'That's not quite true, Molly. We only gave it to you to live in in exchange for looking after the cottage, as you know. Anyway, I'm not here to argue, your dad is too ill,' she turned away leaving Molly open mouthed and tears welling up. Molly stared after her in utter disbelief. *What on earth am I going to do now?* She thought.

Chapter 21

Bertie rode the bus to work on Monday morning unaware that Alistair knew anything. He practised over and over in his head as to what he would say to him and how he would bring the subject up. He had told him that there was nothing going on between him and Molly and that had been the truth. He climbed the stairs thinking that honesty is probably the best way to go, that way you didn't have to remember who you had lied to or what the lie was.

'Morning,' he called out to Alistair as he entered the office and lolloped over to his desk. He dropped his bag onto the floor, stretched his back as it was aching from all the digging and walked towards the coffee machine. The smell of that first pot of coffee on a Monday morning always helped him to relax and plan the week ahead. 'Coffee?' he called out to Alistair.

'Yes, and bring yours in here with you,' came the reply. Bertie stopped short, he had never heard that tone before and he knew instinctively that Alistair knew. Had Molly telephoned and filled him in on the truth or did he hear it from Lucy? However, it was, he decided to let Alistair speak first. Bertie sat on the expensive leather and chrome chair that Alistair had allowed himself to indulge in and began to sip his coffee.

'Good weekend?' asked Alistair, 'Anything to tell me?' He sat staring coldly at him, giving nothing away.

'It seems to me that you already know about my weekend. Perhaps, you could fill me in on what you think you know.'

Bertie, doing his best not to upset Alistair, didn't want to tell him something that he might not already know.

'Judas…I would sack you here and now, if I could, tell you to get out of here.' Bertie jumped spilling his coffee, it was very hot and burnt his leg. He rubbed at it, moaning of all things that Alistair could have said, he had not expected that.

'Hang on a minute, for one thing. I've done nothing wrong to deserve being sacked and you just can't go around sacking someone because…'

'Because what, Bertie, because you lied to me? You swore to me that there was nothing between you and Molly and now you're talking about going into business with her, opening a café of all things. I think that I have every right to sack you if I want to. How could you do this to me and right under my nose? I can't believe it.'

'Now come on, Alistair, that's not fair,' his voice was rising along with his temper but he cleared his throat, reduced the throttle and tried to be rational about the situation. But Alistair cut him off.

'Not fair! Fairness doesn't come into it. Were you being "fair" when you stole Molly away from me? And…' he gulped hard, '…and she is pregnant with my baby, let's not forget that.' He jumped up pacing up and down his office, smacking one fist against his other flat palm. He looked out of the window, silence reigned over the two of them for a moment.

'Look,' Bertie said at last, 'you dumped Molly, did you think that she would become a nun?' Still Alistair said nothing. Bertie sipped at his coffee and wondered if he should get the whisky out but thought better of it. The phones would start ringing soon and he had to say something but what. In the end, he said, 'Have you spoken to Molly about it?'

'No, I don't need to, Lucy told me everything.'

'Clearly not everything, why don't you call her, find out the story from her?' desperately trying to be rational and keeping his job at the same time. Alistair flopped into his chair once more and picked up his pen clicking it on and off. Bertie watched with fascination, it was clear to him how much Alistair loved Molly but for some reason, he was denying it or couldn't see it or didn't want to.

'I've made up my mind, there's no point in speaking to Molly. What good would it do…and I still want to sack you.'

'But…don't you want to know the truth? You've got this whole thing so wrong…'

'No buts, I don't want to hear it. However, we will call it redundancy, I'll give you three months' pay and you can leave today. Start your new life,' he spat. Bertie stared his mouth wide open, leaping to his feet, they eye balled each other. Bertie gritted his teeth breathing heavily.

'After ten years loyal service, I think I deserve more than three months' pay. Come on, Alistair, you can do better than that. I might just sue, I would have every right.' He clenched his fists and leant onto the desk. Alistair, looked like he was going to thump him then as if he had thought better of it, gave a wry smile.

'Alright, I was thinking of transferring to Dorchester anyway. This, this situation, we'll call it, has just hastened my decision, that's all, so in recognition for your "loyal" service, I will be generous and give you six months' pay.'

'Fine, and a sweetener, shall we say ten grand?' Bertie squared his shoulders and thrust out his hand but Alistair didn't move.

'Ten grand it is.' Bertie dropped his hand.

'Have it your way, I'll get my things and I'll be gone in five minutes.' He left the office slamming the door behind him. He was seething with rage as he opened his desk drawer and began to pull out his scarf, a tube of mints with bits of fluff and hair stuck to them that he threw into the bin, a pack of tissues, a penknife, a photograph of his sister and family cuddling a koala and his faithful bottle of whisky. He stuffed them into his bag, the telephone rang and he instinctively put his hand out to answer it and pulled back. 'No, that's not my job anymore,' he muttered. It continued to ring as Bertie walked across the office, turned and looked at Alistair's closed door, he heard him answer the phone and Bertie left.

Bertie slammed the front door and jumped the steps two at a time. He turned and looked up at the office window wondering how on earth things had come to this, he just couldn't understand Alistair. It began to drizzle, Bertie turned up his collar as he made his way to the bus stop, dropping his bag onto the floor. His phone vibrated, he pulled it from his pocket. Alistair, he flipped it shut again, *whatever he wants, I don't care,* he thought shrugging his shoulders and shivering as the cold began to seep into his body. He kicked a coke can into the gutter, an old woman with a headscarf pulled tight under her wobbling jowls scowled at him. He picked up the offending can and put it into the nearest bin. He flipped his phone to call Molly but then decided to wait till he was home. *Home, the flat,* he suddenly thought, *I must pull out my lease and see when I can leave.* 'Then I can make some sense of my life,' he muttered. The old woman turned to look at him but said nothing; instead, she heaved her enormous backside off the seat and shuffled to the edge of the pavement just as the bus stopped. The journey proved to be tedious. There were hold-ups everywhere. Bertie drew patterns in the misted-up window staring blankly at the brightly lit shops, watching the crowds dashing in and out. He looked at his watch and sighed for the umpteenth time. What just happened? He asked himself for the fifth time. He began to work out how much money he had plus the six months' pay and Alistair's ten grand. He wondered how easy it would be to get a mortgage and decided to have that de-clutter he had been promising himself and...he must Skype his sister. But first things first, he would call Molly and let her know what had happened. He pushed open his flat door dropping his bag onto the tiled floor, it clunked. *Whisky*, Bertie grinned. He pulled out the bottle and unscrewed the top and screwed it back up again.

'No, I've too much to do and I don't need to drown my sorrows. Alistair has just opened the door for me to have a much better life and he doesn't even know it.' He made a coffee instead, sat down with a chocolate hobnob and pressed the number for Molly.

'Hi, Bertie,' she puffed, 'I'm in the middle of delivering a calf. Can I call you back?'

'Yes, talk later and Molly…'

'Yes.'

'Don't overdo it…promise?'

Bertie turned off the grill. He picked up a mug of tea and his cheese on toast clearing a space at the kitchen table, grabbing the brown sauce bottle, he shook the last dregs out all over the cheese.

'Mm…heaven,' he licked his lips, 'does it for me every time.' He had made good progress. He had found his lease and contacted the agent, the news was good; he could leave the flat at the end of August in six weeks. He worked out a timetable of things to do in London; he had a longer list for Dorset, where to live for one thing and more importantly right now, he needed a job. He took a slurp of tea only to spit it out again, it was cold. He pushed back his chair, rinsed his mug and switched the kettle on again. Plans vied for position in his head, he realised that he didn't even know when Molly's baby was due and he had never thought to ask her. His cell buzzed, he glanced at it.

'Molly! Are you alright?' He removed the tea bag from his mug, added far too much sugar and sat at the table.

'Yes, I'm fine but you're not. I'm so sorry, Bertie. Alistair has just told me what happened.'

198

'Did he tell you that he sacked me because you're pregnant? Not because I am thinking of a different career in Dorset. I don't know what's the matter with him, he wouldn't listen,' fury welling up inside him, this is not what he had planned and he tried to breathe more slowly.

'No...not exactly. He was very busy, said he would call me tonight.' Bertie burst out laughing.

'Sorry, Molly, but that was funny, I needed a laugh. We need a long talk, a very long talk. I'll call you tonight and I'm thinking that I might come down again next week for a few days, if that is alright with you?'

'Of course, it is. But there's something you don't know,' she cleared her throat. 'Mum and Dad want me to leave the house, find somewhere else to live.' Bertie was stunned.

'But I thought the farm was yours now.'

'So did I, but it's a long story and I don't have time right now. Look, let me call you later. I've got a few things to sort out, okay? Bye.'

Bertie closed his cell. He looked around at his flat, the dominating feature was his rowing machine. This small space had been 'home' for a long time and as he contemplated his move, he began to wonder if he was making a mistake. He sipped his tea and rummaged in the cupboard and found a packet of chocolate mini rolls. He ate one and then another, he glimpsed a photo poking out from behind a canister on the worktop and pulled it out. It was a picture of him when he was about 6 or 7 years old with his sister, her arm protectively draped around his shoulder. He pushed it back deciding to get started on his de-clutter immediately, no point in putting it off any longer, he had nothing else to do. He opened the wardrobe door and a heap of items fell onto the floor. *This is going to take longer than I thought,* he stood staring at the jumbled mess of pullovers for a minute before picking them up and dropping them onto the bed, *and I wonder what time it is in Australia.*

Chapter 22

Molly sat on the bench by the allotment sipping peppermint tea; she had discovered a liking for it now that normal tea tasted horrible. This bench had become her sanctuary. Rex pushed his nose onto her lap and she stroked his ears, he looked up at her as if he understood.

'Bertie is right,' she told him, 'I can't carry on much longer like this.' Her dungarees were beginning to feel a bit tight, she undid the zip a little and flipped open her phone. Appointment made with the doctor for the next day, Molly looked at the ever so small tummy that she had developed.

'Hello,' she said, 'I'm your mum.'

Next on the list; her parents, how they would take it, she wasn't sure, especially now and then there's George and Alice but before she could tackle that problem, she decided to call Alistair. Molly rolled her eyes at Rex, smiled and took a deep breath.

'Hi, sorry about this morning,' she paused and waited.

'Hello,' he said rather frostily, 'I can't believe what you two are planning. You've only known Bertie two minutes and you're pregnant. Why didn't you tell me that you two were seeing each other?' Molly let out a gasp, she jumped up stepping on poor Rex's tail, he yelped in pain. She stalked up and down the path.

'Well, how are you, Mr Alistair Warren, no pleasantries? And anyway, why do you care? You made it quite clear to me that you wanted some "space" and you haven't exactly kept it a secret that you fancied the pants off Lucy. What did you expect me to do? Wait until you had had a fling and see if you wanted me back? I don't think so,' she panted rapidly as she stomped around her arm flaying in the air.

'Sorry, it's just that it has all been such a shock. I never imagined that Bertie would sneak in and take you from me.'

'He didn't.'

'What do you mean, he didn't?'

'Bertie is a really nice guy. You have no idea and you sacked him for what, may I ask?' Molly could hear him breathing but Alistair said nothing, 'Well?'

'I didn't really sack him, we reached an agreement. I was just so annoyed that I had heard from Lucy about your plans with Bertie...I suppose I was jealous and stupid and well, you're pregnant.' Molly heard the catch in his voice but ignored it.

'It was your idea to keep our affair secret. You made it quite clear that marriage and children were not your idea of fun,' she said scathingly. 'So...' she sat down again, out of breath, 'so I have to get on with my life and don't worry, I won't tell George and Alice that the baby is yours.'

'I'm sorry, Molly. I don't know what to say, I suppose there was a time when I wouldn't have been pleased, but now...well,' he paused.

'Exactly,' she sniffed and smudged the stupid tear on her cheek.

'Bertie...he, err, knows all about us,' he almost whispered.

'Of course, he does, you were good mates. Look, I haven't rung to argue with you. If you've nothing else to say, I've got things to do, and for your information, Lucy knows everything,' Molly abruptly closed her phone, not giving Alistair another chance to say anything. She mooched around the allotment, hands in pockets, unable to concentrate. The vegetables were growing well and the rabbits had missed a few lettuces, it was a lovely evening with the sun still high in the sky. 'It could have been you,' she said to the imaginary Alistair as she stared at the blank phone, 'we could have been so happy but now I have to move on.'

She put on a bright face and called Bertie, feeling better hearing his concerned voice. He had lost his job and his life was being turned up-side-down because of her, she wouldn't let him down, they would make a good team together.

'That reminds me,' he said, 'I suddenly realised this morning that I don't know when your baby is due, do you know yet?'

'Sometime in December, I think. I'll know more tomorrow, I'll let you know. I will have to go for a scan...sorry, I'm sure that you don't want to know about such things.'

'I do want to know, honest...what have you told Alistair?'

'Nothing...he doesn't care anyway, for me or the baby so, no, I'm not going to tell him,' Molly gulped and looked up at the sky just as a blackbird flew down and landed near her feet. He began to toss leaves around searching for bugs and worms, she smiled as she watched his antics.

'I think that he does care, he just doesn't know how to show it or he's too afraid.'

'Well, I just can't risk anymore heartbreak and that's that. I'll ring you tomorrow after I have been to the doctor's. I must ring Lucy and then Alice...' Molly flopped down onto the bench and shivered; she found her friend's number and pressed it.

'Hi, Molly, how are you?'

'I'm alright, just worried about you. All that gardening, I thought you might have back ache or at least callouses on your hands.'

'I'm not that incapable,' she giggled. 'What's wrong?'

202

'Can we meet tomorrow afternoon? I have a doctor's appointment in the morning and I really do need to see you. There's so much I want to tell you.'

'Okay, text me…and Molly, get some rest. You sound all done in.'

Molly clicked off her phone and struggled to her feet. Rex gave a snort and shook himself, wagging his tail. Molly had one more call to make, this time to Alice; she arranged to have coffee with her later in the week. Appointment made, Molly sat pondering her call to Alice. Alice had given nothing away, she either didn't know or she was waiting for Molly to tell her. *There will be more to tell by Thursday and I can't face telling Mum and Dad tonight,* she thought as she wandered back to the house. Molly filled the bath tub and poured in some wild rose bubble bath; she swished her hands in the water before climbing in and sliding down into the depths of its relaxing balm. She closed her eyes. Her biggest worry was still Bertie but right now, there was nothing she could do.

Molly walked out of the doctor's with a bundle of papers, appointments to be made, a scan to organise and much more. She had also had a ticking off for not visiting him sooner.

'Having a first baby at your age can be tricky,' he had said, 'and there could be complications.' She didn't think that being over 30 constituted being an older mother. Still, she felt happier and more content with her expanding waistline and tender breasts. She looked at the card that she had been given and there was the expected date of birth, the 14th of December. She drove home on a high wondering who to telephone first, then decided that she would savour the moment all to herself, she would be seeing Lucy later. It had become all too clear that plans needed to be made. She would make a special meal at the weekend as Bertie was coming down, maybe the roasted Mediterranean veg, he liked so much, with couscous. She sipped her coffee surveying the allotment, trowel in hand. This was a whole new experience for her. She opened her phone scrolling down to Bertie's number.

'Hi,' he said, 'everything alright? I wasn't expecting you to call till tonight, but I am pleased just the same.' She relayed her appointment with the doctor to Bertie and they both laughed at the idea of her being an aged mum.

'Actually, I've been thinking, we have to make a lot of plans and I can't do it by myself so I was wondering as you are not working, would you like to come down earlier than planned so that we can get our heads together?' Molly traced a pattern in the soil with her foot and Rex looked from her face to her feet and back again.

'No problem, how does Thursday sound?'

'Great, drive carefully,' said Molly as she closed her phone. She stood up walking back to the farm to make lunch before her allotted time to meet Lucy. Deciding that now was the time to break the news to her mum and dad.

Arriving at their favourite coffee shop, Molly saw Lucy's car and with a heavy heart, she climbed down from the Land Rover and headed inside. Lucy already had a large cappuccino in front of her and she was pulling marshmallows out of a heavenly looking 'rocky road'.

'So, first things first, would you like the same?' she asked waving her hand towards the waitress and pointing to her drink and cake, 'Then you tell me what the doctor said.' Molly nodded and recounted her visit to the doctor including her telling off. Lucy laughed, she wasn't at all surprised.

'And when is your baby due?' Lucy asked placing the last crumbs into her mouth.

'December, the 14th.'

'That's wonderful, a possible Christmas baby, how romantic. What did your mum and dad say?

'They were really annoyed as if I've done it on purpose to spite them or something and they were even more annoyed when I wouldn't tell them who the father is. They think I don't know, can you believe it?' Her voice was creeping up a pitch, her face flushed. She looked Lucy in the eye, 'I don't know what I am going to do.'

'Look, one thing at a time,' she squeezed her friend's hand. 'Let's get two more coffees and go over your options.'

'I'm sorry,' blurted Molly an hour later having filled in all the gaps. 'I shouldn't be burdening you, you've got your own problems. How's everything going? With the house, I mean.'

'Oh, that's going okay. I can't wait to get my hands on that key and stop trying to change the subject,' they both smiled as Lucy said. 'Look, come on, we've been here long enough. Come back to mine for a bit. Mum and Dad are both out and we can look at your options.' Both chairs scraped along the stone floor as they moved and the woman at the next table looked across with a pinched look on her face.

Once ensconced in Honeysuckle Cottage with a packet of crisps and a glass of cola, the conversation returned once more to Molly's dilemma.

'Bertie has been brilliant, he has really supported me these last few weeks,' she scrunched the empty crisp packet and aimed it at the fireplace. 'I don't know what I would have done without him. It's such a mess really, but what choice do I have?'

'Lots of choices actually,' she drained her glass of cola, 'you could be a single mum like lots of other people or have a termination or put the baby up for adoption,' she eyed Molly for a moment and continued, '…but you're right about Bertie though, he's such a caring person and I hope that you are not just using him to get to Alistair?' Molly spluttered her cola coughing as it caught in her throat.

'No…no not at all,' she pulled a tissue from her bag and dabbed her mouth. 'You can't believe that I would do such a thing, do you?'

'Lucky for you, I was just teasing.' Lucy sat back and kicked off her shoes tucking her feet under her. 'But seriously, come on, what are you going to do?'

'I really don't know, for the first time ever, I really, really don't know except that I am keeping my baby.' Molly's thoughts drifted away from her, her face impassive. Lucy snapped her fingers.

'Hey, come on, that's a start and I am proud of you.'

Molly left Lucy and walked down the road, her head now in a whirl of fog. She trudged a few hundred yards kicking one or two stones and stopped by the mill pond. The ducks swam over quacking and squabbling, vying for the best position in front of her in order to catch the few crumbs that Molly threw in. She lifted her head and watched the birds. 'Alice,' she said to herself, 'now I have to face Alice. What on earth am I going to say to her and George?' She turned back up the lane to her Land Rover and got in. It should have been her happiest moment, telling Alice and George about the baby, instead she felt anything but happy. She turned on the engine and rested her head on her hands. *I just might tell them the truth, better than even more lies,* she thought. She drove slowly down the lane praying for an answer to pop into her head but nothing came. The crunching of the wheels in the gravel sounded louder than usual, it would be impossible to pretend that they weren't in and go away again, she laughed to herself and anyway, she couldn't do that to them. The front door opened.

'Molly, my dear, do come in. It's lovely to see you.' Alice held out her arms to hug her and kissed her cheek, making Molly feel worse. George hovered in the background, smiling.

'How are you, my dear?' he enquired.

'I'm fine,' she said handing him her jacket.

'Come and sit in the snug. We are just about to have our earl grey and cherry cake.' Molly smiled to herself, what a pity that people like George and Alice don't exist anymore. She obediently followed them into the snug, it was warm and cosy with the afternoon sun streaming in through the French doors. She relaxed.

'I think that you have something to tell us, don't you dear?' Alice smiled as she patted her hand.

'You've heard then?' Molly looked anxiously from one to the other.

'We would rather hear it from you dear, wouldn't we, George?' George nodded and picked up another chair to join them by the coffee table. He began to pour the tea and offered one to Molly.

'I thought that you looked peaky the other week when you said that you were tired but obviously there was more to it than that.' He removed his glasses and began to polish them with his handkerchief looking more like the old doctor from her childhood.

'It's hard to know where to start,' she managed, 'and I'm sure that you don't want the whole story so it is quite simple really. I am going to have a baby.'

'Congratulations, my dear,' said Alice warmly, 'you will make a wonderful mother.'

'Thank you,' said Molly.

'… And when is this happy event due?' Alice took a bite from her cherry cake carefully putting the crumbs onto the edge of her plate.

'Well, the baby is due in December and Bertie is coming down again on Thursday, as he's not working anymore and we have a lot to discuss.' No sooner had the words left her mouth, Molly knew that she had made a mistake; both George and

Alice looked at her aghast but it was George, who got there first.

'What do you mean "not working anymore"? Why isn't he working for Alistair?' Molly tried desperately to think of a plausible reason but nothing was forthcoming.

'Alistair sacked him,' she almost whispered in reply.

'Alistair sacked him,' they chorused, 'but why?'

'I have only spoken to him briefly. It would be better to hear it from him.'

George and Alice looked at each other and back at Molly, eyes wide. George got up and walked around the snug, hands behind his back.

'But this makes no sense, no sense at all,' he huffed loudly. 'I will speak to him, get to the bottom of this.'

'Please don't distress yourself, dear,' pleaded Alice putting her cup down, seeing the obvious stress engulfing Molly. 'I'm sure that there is a reasonable explanation for what has happened.' She turned to Molly.

'So what is he going to do now? Bertie I mean?'

'We have a few ideas but nothing decided yet. I think that we will both have a better idea after this weekend.' Molly tried to be vague.

'Well, we are very surprised, my dear, about Bertie but I'm sure that things will work out for the best. Now drink up and I will pour you another cup of tea.' Molly felt the sting of tears; she grabbed a tissue and sniffed endeavouring to make them disappear. George excused himself and left the girls talking about babies and the merits of breast feeding; disappearing into the hall, he picked up the phone.

'Alistair, you alright, my boy? Only I hear that you have sacked Bertie, now what is going on?' Molly heard him say and her heart sank down to her toes. She strained to hear George, not wanting Alice to realise what she was doing.

'I suppose so, but your mother and I are very concerned, and we want to know what's happening so please make sure that you do call. I don't want to cause your mother anymore upset than is necessary.' Molly heard him say. A moment later, George reappeared in the snug. He walked over to Alice gently resting his hand on her shoulder; she looked up and smiled at him instinctively. Molly surveyed the scene unfolding before her and felt very envious of the obvious love they had for one another.

'Now, my dear, I have an idea,' said George as he settled himself once more beside his wife, 'something that may just help all of us.'

'Oh, what's that, George?' Molly could feel the love of friendship emanating from them as she smiled at this lovely couple.

'Well, you know that I have been looking for a gardener, to no avail. I'm afraid, as young Bertie is between jobs, perhaps, he would be willing to come and work for us, and we will see if he is as good at digging as you say he is; keep him in the family, so to speak.' Molly placed her cup on to the table, her eyes wide, she beamed at them.

'What a wonderful idea. I'm sure that he will be very pleased, he won't let you down.' She jumped up and hugged them both. 'Thank you, thank you so much.'

'It's nothing, Molly, you have been so good to us. It's a small way in which we can repay you.' Molly wanted so much to blurt out the truth, but she couldn't; she would have to continue with the charade and make the best of the situation that she now found herself in.

'George, dear, that is such a good idea', Alice clapped her hands, 'and then perhaps, Bertie can tell us what is going on.'

Chapter 23

'Something's not right,' said Alice as she reached for the marmalade. 'Molly does not exude the sort of radiance that one expects from someone expecting their first baby. No, something is wrong, something just does not add up,' she bit into her toast and reached for the coffee pot. 'This little puzzle will take some investigation and I know just the person who can help me.'

'Don't you think that it is none of our business, my dear? I'm sure that we will find out in time and I don't want you over exerting yourself.' He shook out the newspaper and disappeared behind it but Alice was undeterred.

'Well, I don't like to see anyone upset and Molly was clearly upset and she side stepped the question of, "who the father is?" I wonder if it is Bertie or someone else.' She crunched that last bit of toast and cradled her cup of coffee.

'I'm going out today into town, my dear. Can I get you anything?' George folded his newspaper and placed it onto his side plate giving her his full attention.

'I don't think so, but if you are going anywhere near the farm shop, you could get some fresh bread and maybe some strawberries and goats' cheese.'

'I think that I could manage that. Now promise me that you will sit down and not attempt any housework.'

'Oh, George, don't fuss so much. I can manage a bit of dusting and anyway, I get very bored just sitting, doing nothing.'

'Make sure that that is all you do. I won't be long.' He bent and kissed her forehead.

'What are you doing in town, dear? Maybe I could come with you.' George hugged her.

'I'm not happy either, my dear. I feel very disconcerted at this turn of events. I have a feeling that Alistair is not telling us the truth at all.' He pulled Alice to him placing a gentle kiss on her lips. '...So, I am going to make an appointment with old Barrington. I want to sort out one or two things. Nothing for you to worry about, I promise.'

Alice took off her reading glasses and closed her book when she heard George banging the front door shut. A moment later, he opened the door to the snug.

'There you are darling, would you like an earl grey?' He grinned at her sheepishly.

'Please, then you can tell me all about your morning.' George disappeared humming to himself.

'Here we are.' George was carrying a large tray with tea and crumpets.

'What have you been up to?' asked Alice. George didn't often take to humming and his grin rather made Alice feel that he was planning something.

'Nothing my dear,' he bent to kiss her and although this show of affection was much more than usual, Alice didn't object.

'I know that look,' she teased, 'and I know that you are up to something.'

'All in good time, my dear, all in good time.' He picked up the pot of tea and began to pour it for her. Alice knew that sooner or later, George would reveal all; he never could keep a secret for long.

Alice sat dozing in a deck chair, soaking up the late afternoon sunshine. A bee came buzzing along the terrace, bobbing in and out of the geraniums. It was all very well, this relaxing, but Alice was getting rather bored. She heard a commotion in the hall and to her delight, there was a visitor.

'Lucy, my dear, how lovely to see you. Please, come in.' George ushered her into the snug and relieved her of yet another cake. 'You girls must think that we are starving,' he teased. 'Molly came yesterday and brought us a cake, too. Now, you sit down and talk to Alice and I will make the tea.'

'Lovely, thank you.' She turned to Alice and held out a bunch of flowers. 'How are you getting on, Alice? I see that George still has you confined to barracks.' They both chuckled.

'He has but not for too much longer. How are you, Lucy my dear? What news have you for us? I feel completely left out of things at the moment.'

Lucy launched into her story about the house and the renovation work. She was busy at the garden centre, although the pollen was making her suffer with hay fever; and as for her other job at the care home, it was not as easy as she had imagined. She regaled them with funny stories and incidents but the good news was that she was now on the books of an agency that supplied staff to hospitals.

'It's a start,' she told Alice, 'although, I much prefer babies.'

'I'm sure that you will find something more permanent soon,' she said positively, '...and speaking of babies, what do you think about the news from Molly?'

'What did she tell you?' queried Lucy as she looked at Alice over the top of her cup. Alice let out a laugh, she had tried to trick her but Lucy had seen straight through her.

'You girls do stick together, I admire that. I am referring to the news about Molly expecting a little one in December.' Alice saw Lucy's hand tremble. 'Are you alright, my dear? You are very pale.'

'Yes, yes, I'm fine. It's still rather a shock to me, too.'

'I'm sure it is, Lucy dear. We are thrilled, of course and wonder when Alistair will take the plunge; there's no fun for an older father, they don't have the energy, you know,' she sighed and looked downcast.

'I'm sure that he would like to be a father one day,' ventured Lucy.

'Yes, I'm sure you're right. I just wish that he would hurry up.' They both laughed just as George was returning with the tea tray.

'Can I join in the joke?' asked George.

'No joke, my dear. We were just talking about the lovely news from Molly and Bertie, of course, changing his life.'

'Oh, I see and I imagine that you were discussing Alistair and when it might be his turn, no doubt.'

'Spot on, darling, you know how desperate I am to be a Grandma, but I shall have to be patient.' They settled down to tea and cake, Lucy was very quiet.

'Penny for them?' smiled Alice.

'It's nothing really. I suppose I am a bit envious, but I've only just escaped from one relationship and I need some time on my own, you know sort myself out a bit before going out again.'

'Quite right, my dear, no sense to hurry into these things,' smiled Alice.

'I have been thinking that when I am up to it, we would love to have you all to visit and have dinner with us, wouldn't we, George?' Alice clasped hands with George and he gave a reassuring squeeze.

'Not yet, you know doctor's orders,' he grinned, 'but we will see in a week or two.'

'That's very kind of you, Alice, but the only way we could accept would be if you let us do all the work. You can be the supervisor and that's it.' George nodded in full agreement.

'That's settled then. The next time that Alistair is down, we will see what we can do. Although, he is struggling at the moment without Bertie, it's such a pity that things haven't quite worked out for Alistair; it may be some time before he can get away.' Lucy looked up, her eyebrows raised at Alice.

'It serves him right. He shouldn't have sacked Bertie just because...' she stopped in mid-sentence and gaped blankly for a few seconds.

'...Because of what Lucy?' George put his plate down and folded his napkin.

'Sorry, me and my big mouth, it's nothing to do with me. I am not the one who should be telling you anything.'

Alice placed her cup and saucer back onto the coffee table.

'Telling us what exactly? Is there something that we don't know?' She looked intently at Lucy who floundered under her gaze.

'Sorry, Alice, I really cannot tell you, it's not my place. You will have to talk to Alistair about it.'

'You're quite right, we shouldn't have pushed you. Now tell us about your prospects with this agency.' Everyone relaxed and Lucy talked about the shortage of staff and resources and the advantages of working for an agency.

After Lucy had left, George and Alice sat down once more and looked at each other.

'I wonder what is going on with our son?' she asked.

'I really don't know, my dear. I have tried to talk to him about it all and he simply says that he didn't sack Bertie, he is adamant that it was agreed that as Bertie would be moving anyway that he might as well leave immediately in order to make all the preparations for his move.'

'It does seem odd though. Alistair was never one to confide in us but something like this...and I'm surprised that Bertie would leave him in the lurch, after all these years; it doesn't make sense to me at all.'

214

'We shall just have to be patient.' He sipped his tea. 'Actually, I have something for you.' George walked over to his desk and brought back an armful of glossy brochures and placed them onto the coffee table. 'There you are. I got these in town, this morning. That should keep you sat down and happy for a while. Choose a holiday,' he declared.

'A holiday!' she beamed up at George. '...Thank you, darling. When are we going?'

'Well, I would suggest not for a week or two. I want to be sure that you are up to it. We don't want a repeat performance of the other day, do we?' he teased.

Alice sat back contentedly riffling through the brochures, alighting on one headed 'cruises', she pulled it out and looked closely at George.

'Cruises...?' She asked raising her eyebrows at him.

'Whatever you like; we can go on a cruise if you wish.'

'Oh George, you know how I have always longed to go on a cruise, but I thought that you didn't like them?'

'Big tin boxes floating on the water; doesn't seem natural to me but then neither did flying and I think that I would prefer a ship to a plane.' He got up once more and cleared the tea things away to give her more room. He smiled as Alice opened the first brochure.

'A holiday,' she said again, 'now I know you're up to something.'

Chapter 24

Thursday morning dawned and with it, Bertie. Rex alerted by the noise of an engine began to bark and Molly opened the bottom half of the barn door to let him out. He dashed across the yard skidding up to Bertie, his tail whizzing round and round.

'Hey, you must have been up very early to get here at this time. What's wrong? Can't you sleep?' she called as she leant against the door frame, coffee in hand. Bertie grinned at her.

'Something like that…I have really tried but everything just keeps churning round and round in my head. Am I too early?' He knelt to make a fuss of Rex who was not going to be ignored.

'No, of course not. I'll make you some breakfast. Eggs, bacon and beans, do you?'

'Yes, please. I'm sorry Molly for being a bit of a grouch but lack of sleep, too much whisky and not enough food takes its toll.'

'That's not like you, sit down. I'll make a pot of coffee and we can talk.' Bertie pulled her to him and embraced her in a bear hug. He pushed a wayward curl away from her face.

'I've missed you.'

'I've missed you, too.' *At least that was truthful,* she thought to herself. 'Now come on, sit down. I want to know why you can't sleep.' Bertie pulled out a chair and crashed down into it resting his arms on the kitchen table. Rex crept up by his side and gently nuzzled him. Bertie ruffled his head, Rex

216

shook himself, flopped down and settled himself by Bertie's feet with a snuffle. 'You haven't changed your mind, have you?' Molly turned to look at him just as Bertie screwed his face and twitched his nose.

'No, and yes.'

'What do you mean? Which is it?' She slid the plate down in front of him with a crash. Bertie jumped.

'The thing is I probably didn't think it through properly. For one thing, I've lost my job, I'm packing up to go who knows where and then there's Lucy…'

'Lucy?' Molly searched his face but all she could see was a very lovely but troubled man. She collected two mugs and poured them both a coffee. Bertie stopped eating, his fork in mid-air.

'Boy, I needed that,' he grinned at her. 'I don't know any more, it seemed so simple but now it is so bloody complicated. And Lucy, I just don't know what is going on with her and Alistair if anything, do you?' Bertie scooped up the last of his breakfast, mopping up the egg with a piece of toast.

'Not really, sorry. But if you've changed your mind, I understand. I'm sorry about you losing your job; I never intended anything like that to happen.' Bertie put sugar in his coffee, swilling it around.

'I know you didn't. Alistair was furious, accused me of all sorts of things; he was not in a mood to listen. Anyway, I've put my notice in on the flat and started to get rid of the clutter. I'm glad in a way. I stayed with him for far too long. I need something different to stretch me, you know a new challenge,' Molly listened unconvinced but nodded. 'I suppose we just need to sort out the details, get ourselves organised, more importantly you need somewhere to live.' He looked up for the first time from his coffee and gave a weak smile.

'No, sorry Bertie, you haven't answered my question yet. Have you changed your mind?' Bertie reached across to her and took hold of her hand.

'Let me ask you something first, it's just that it is becoming so real and I want to be clear about everything.' He caressed her hand and kissed her fingertips. 'You know, when we first met, I thought that Alistair was the biggest fool in the world, still do actually; how he could keep you a secret, I do not know. I would want to show you off to the whole world...but this is massive. I want to move to Dorset and I need to know if you are up for this business venture? I know things are complicated with the baby but you know I'll help the best I can, don't you?' He traced a pattern around her knuckles still gently holding her hand. Molly placed her hand on top of his and lifted his chin so that she could see into his eyes.

'Look, I'll be honest. I fell for Alistair big time and the thing is I do like you. I like you a lot actually. You are the most wonderful person but I've accepted that things are not going to work out with Alistair, even though I still love him. I've tried not to. So, what I am saying is that I love your plan, we can make it work...somehow.' She let go of him and picked up the kettle placing it onto the Aga. Bertie jumped up and grabbed her off her feet swinging her around saying, 'I do love you but...'

'No, please,' she said breathlessly. 'I think that your mind is really on Lucy, isn't it? And it's because of some stupid loyalty to Alistair that you have kept quiet,' she paused. '...And I know that she really likes you, too. So, here's my idea.' Bertie put her down, a grin stretching across his whole face.

'What's that? I'm all ears but you have to let me take you out to dinner tonight.'

'Oh, I was thinking that we could stay in, maybe cook together and then you can show me your business plan, it sounds really good.'

'Even better...you sure?'

'Yes, I'm sure.' Molly began to clear away the plates just as the kettle whistled so she made another pot of coffee. 'Oh, I nearly forgot. I visited Alice and George the other day and George wants to know if you would be willing to do some gardening for him; he'll pay you, of course.'

'Wow, great. I think that I will go and see them, see what they want done. I am so fed up with decluttering and the charity shop has more of my things than I have!' he smirked.

'That's settled then. You can tell them this afternoon about your plans for the future.'

'Alright,' he said, 'good idea.'

That afternoon, Bertie jogged up the drive to see George busy with the secateurs in the front garden. George pulled off his gloves and held out his hand to Bertie.

'Bertie...we weren't expecting you today but welcome, nonetheless. I'm sure that Alice will have lots of questions for you later but how can I help you?' George put the clippings he was holding into the trug, placing his hands on to his hips.

'Thanks. Actually, I came to see how I can help you. I understand from Molly that you may have some gardening work for me to do?'

'Yes indeed. Let's go in and I will make a cup of tea, then we can sit down and discuss it.' Bertie followed him into the kitchen. It instantly felt homely and welcoming, not what he had expected; after all, their son had just sacked him. He wondered what Alistair had told them, not very much, he guessed; Alistair was not usually one for saying much. He took his shoes off and followed George into the snug. How strange, he thought, that lovely sitting room and they spend all their time in here. Alice looked up as the door opened and immediately smiled at Bertie.

'Oh, how lovely to see you,' she beamed. 'Come over here and sit down. I'm dying to hear all about your news.' Bertie bent and kissed her cheek, he sat down and began to fidget.

'Where to start,' he said folding his arms. 'I'm sure that Molly has told you anyway.'

'Yes, of course, she has but I would still like to hear it from you,' smiled Alice with a twinkle. *She's a cunning old bird, she's checking our stories and I don't blame her. I probably would too,* thought Bertie with a grin.

'Well...the only update I have for you is that I am going to go and see my sister, spend a month in Oz later in the year. Molly and I are going to sit down tonight and go over my plans and see how we can help each other.'

'Very sensible,' nodded Alice, 'and how do you feel about that?' George pushed open the door and came in carrying a tray piled high with china cups and saucers and a fruit cake. Bertie came to his rescue helping him with the tray.

'Oh, it is fine by me, whatever Molly wants. You know these women, sorry no offence.' He took a sip of his tea and a slice of cake taking refuge in his appreciation of every mouthful.

'How did you and Molly meet?' Bertie nearly choked, he took another mouthful of cake and smiled at the memory of it, how they had walked into the Kings Arms and he had been dazzled by the beauty of both, Molly and Lucy.

'It was here when Alistair brought me down to visit for the first time.'

'Oh yes, just after Alistair had startled poor Lucy's horse and she fell and broke her wrist, I remember.' She picked up the plate and offered Bertie another slice of cake.

'No thanks, Mrs W. I came to see what gardening it is that you want me to do and I won't be able to work if I eat too much.'

'Ah yes, now the garden,' butted in George, 'there is a lot to do as I am afraid that I have rather neglected it recently, so I wondered how you might feel about working every day for the next week or so and help me get it up together and then perhaps, a regular few hours once a week. How does that sound?' Bertie was surprised thinking that he would only be needed for the odd hour or two.

'That would be great, George. Are you sure? I mean I don't know anything about plants. I might pull out the flowers and leave the weeds.'

'I will supervise,' interjected Alice. 'I'm much better and now that the weather is so lovely, I shall enjoy sitting in the garden and watching you.'

'Right, that's settled then', said George, 'and I will pay you, of course.'

'Oh no, I couldn't accept payment. You have been so kind to me and it's one way that I can repay you.'

'Nonsense, my boy, you are out of work now. I couldn't possibly let you work for me without payment, now that's the end of it,' he said decisively. Bertie accepted George's offer as he did need the money.

'What are your plans now for work since you left Alistair. We were rather surprised that you left so suddenly,' Alice peered at him, her head on one side as she picked up her cup and saucer. Bertie realised that Alistair had not told them the truth and he couldn't do that for him so instead he swallowed and coughed. 'Would you like another cup of tea?' Alice raised the teapot.

'Yes please, sorry,' he said wishing that he could change the subject. Bertie cleared his throat.

'Actually, that's what Molly and I are discussing tonight. We have one or two ideas, the veterinary practise is doing well and my venture wouldn't interfere at all.'

'That's a good idea. What would you do together?' she paused looking straight at him. 'And then there's the baby, of course.'

'Well, I'm not sure if she would want me to tell you at the moment as nothing is sorted yet, but knowing Molly, you will find out soon enough,' he smirked.

'I'm sure you're right,' said Alice patting his arm, 'but don't worry, everything will work out for you both.' If only you knew, thought Bertie; he gave her a weak smile and gulped down the rest of his tea.

'I must be going. What time do you want me in the morning, George?'

'Not too early, my boy, I…I mean we don't get up too early these days so how about half past nine?'

'That's fine by me, see you tomorrow.'

Escaping, he felt quite pleased with himself that he had managed not to tell them any lies and successfully negotiate the traps that had been laid in front of him. He jogged back to the farm in a better frame of mind; the future started to look promising, he would work for George, give up his flat, go to Oz, move to Dorset and then hopefully start the organic café he wanted. As he arrived back at the farm, Molly was out by the allotment; she waved to him to come over.

'You look better. Have you sorted something out with George…about the garden I mean?'

'Yes,' he said breathlessly. 'I start tomorrow morning. Actually, George would like me to work every day over the next couple of weeks and then a steady one or two days a week, what do you think?'

Molly put her trowel down, pushing a wisp of hair from her face.

'If you want to Bertie, it sounds like a good idea. You can stay here with me for now, in the cottage, although I am going to have to find somewhere else to live soon.'

Bertie plunged his hands into his pockets, Molly looked lost and lonely for a moment, they had made some tough decisions and it would be even tougher for her. He put his arms around her and held her close; she snuggled into his shoulder. They stood still for a few moments, then Molly straightened herself up to her full height, stretching, picking up her gloves and retrieving her trowel.

'Right, okay then, there's work to do here today. Especially, now we are considering an organic café…and I've been thinking, there are farmers' markets and home producers too to consider.'

'Hold on, what do you want me to do now, today?' Bertie pushed his hair back and rolled up his sleeves as a smile crept across his face.

Chapter 25

George finished pottering in the garden, put the tools away and walked slowly round to the boot room door. Satisfied with his efforts, he pulled his boots off, the twinge in his back reminding him of his age. He let the boots drop to the floor in an untidy heap promising himself a soak in the bath later. He glanced at his watch, relieved to see that it was time for a sherry; he would take a tray into the snug and see if Alice had woken up. He had felt troubled all afternoon turning over in his mind their conversation with Bertie. He had been extremely agitated, not like him at all. Something wasn't right but he could not quite see what it was. He padded into the kitchen pulling his loafers on and opened the cupboard for the sherry; he poured the amber nectar with an appreciative smile looking forward to the moment when he could relish that first sip. He dutifully carried the tray, plus the bottle on this occasion into the snug. Alice was awake.

'George, how lovely, you read my mind.' Their evening ritual began, they sat opposite each other in their wing chairs, sipping sherry.

'Something's not right,' Alice declared with a quizzical look.

'I know,' he sighed closing his tired eyes for a second, 'but it's none of our business.'

'But I think it is. That poor boy, he deserves better and I am so surprised at Molly.'

'It's not the first time that things like this have happened, my dear. We will just have to go along with it.'

'Well, I'm not happy about it and why won't Alistair come and see us? We still have not had a satisfactory explanation about all this. It is very worrying.' George put his glass down, the last thing he wanted was for Alice to start upsetting herself. He took her hands and gently stroked them.

'We must let the young people sort it out for themselves, my dear. It really is nothing to do with us.'

'But…it's not right, there must be something we can do?' She looked at him widening her big blue eyes.

'The best thing that we could do would be to support each of them and hope that things really will sort themselves out.' George topped up their glasses. 'I will speak to Alistair again this evening and see if I can at least get a commitment out of him about when he is coming down to see us. In the meantime, Bertie will do this wretched garden for us and I am sure that the girls will be over to see you, whether it will be together remains to be seen.' He sat back again in his chair trying to put an end to the conversation and catch forty winks.

'Darling, I am so sorry about the garden. I had no idea that you disliked it so much. I will do my best to do some pruning, I'm sure that I could manage that.' George nearly spilled his drink and spluttered rather crossly.

'You will do no such thing. It is me that should be sorry. It's my back that's playing me up and I love our garden, it's just all this,' he waved his arm about, 'nonsense that's going on. Please don't worry about it. Bertie will be here tomorrow and I can have a rest.' Alice looked sheepish as she settled back to sip sherry when the telephone rang. George groaned as he rubbed his back, hobbling out of the room. He marched back into the snug a moment later sporting a big smile on his face,

'My dear, that was Alistair and he has agreed to come for the weekend in two weeks' time; maybe then we can get somewhere.' He breathed in deeply, he could smell the perfume of some flowers and spotted some old fashioned pink roses by the window and smiled in appreciation.

'Thank goodness, I'm so relieved. It will be lovely to see him either way.' She settled back in her chair picking up the crossword. George too felt relieved, his bigger concern being the welfare of his wife, his son could take care of himself.

'If you like,' said George tapping his steepled fingers, 'we can go to the garden centre tomorrow and pick up some bedding plants; have a coffee too. What do you say?'

'Oh, George, yes please, I would love that. I am feeling so much better and the fresh air will do me good.' George circled his shoulders in an attempt to release the knots, his head fell to one side and he was very tired and sleepy assuring himself that it was the hard work and nothing to do with two glasses of sherry. Sometime later, he woke with a start, it was the telephone once more and Alice was missing. He dashed into the hall just as Alice picked up the telephone. He watched his wife with loving concern.

'Yes, of course, my dear, it will be lovely to see you both. Alright, about 12 o'clock would be fine. Bye, Molly dear.'

George slipped an arm around her waist and nuzzled her neck, he breathed deeply.

'You have a lovely smell, my dear and I do love you so much.' They stood still enjoying a precious moment together. 'Now what have you been up to? I think I dozed off for a minute or two?' George said innocently.

Alice hugged him again and pulling away, she said, 'I think that it might have been more like half an hour, but I am pleased, it will do you good.' George knew a reprimand when he heard it but had no energy to argue. '…And I have made tea.'

'Made tea,' he exclaimed, 'but you shouldn't be doing that.'

'It's only beans on toast, nothing special.'

'My favourite,' he grinned, 'gourmet food at last.' They walked into the dining room where Alice had laid out the best china, linen napkins, a bottle of wine and lighted candles. George looked appreciatively around the room.

'...For beans on toast?' He looked at Alice with raised eyebrows.

'No,' she said, 'for us.'

They sat down to a feast, with a coffee cake taking pride of place in the middle of the table that Lucy had delivered that morning.

'I take it that Molly will be visiting us tomorrow, judging by your comments on the telephone earlier,' he said between mouthfuls of beans smothered in brown sauce.

'Oh yes, I nearly forgot. She said that she would make a quiche and bring it over for lunch rather than give Bertie sandwiches and I said that I would make some salad and new potatoes.'

'Good but I don't want you over doing it.'

'You have to let me do something, George and besides we are going to the garden centre first, I know that is because you think that I will be outside trying to supervise Bertie.'

George knew that she was right and conceded the point saying, 'Alright, but after lunch, you leave the clearing away to me and you can sit and chat to Molly.'

Bertie arrived and was soon put to work in the garden. Alice had a vegetable patch that had been started earlier in the year, now overgrown, the strawberry plants were choked and other vegetables, indistinguishable from the weeds, were struggling to grow. He scratched his head wondering where to start when he spotted the rhubarb. He picked a good armful of the lovely long pink stems, discarding the caterpillar eaten leaves to the compost bin and delivered them to the kitchen door where Alice had made his first coffee of the day.

227

'Oh, Bertie, rhubarb. We can have that for dessert.' She offered him a biscuit and he took a couple of custard creams before retreating outside once again. He watched them disappearing down the drive in George's old Morris Minor and settled down into a comfortable routine clearing weeds. The sky was clear blue and he was already feeling hot, he pulled off his sweat shirt determined to master his new occupation. His phone buzzed, it was Molly.

'Just making sure that you are alright,' she said and Bertie assured her that he was fine, already getting hungry and it was only 10 o'clock. He picked up the spade leaning on it for a moment as a blackbird had started pecking amongst the soil that he had just dug; he stood watching this hive of activity when his phone buzzed again. He flipped it open without thinking, expecting it to be Molly once more.

'Bertie, at last,' said Alistair. The hairs on his neck began to prickle and he considered closing it without speaking but conceded that maybe, they should be at least on speaking terms; after all things were about to change dramatically.

'What do you want?' he said rather curtly.

'I don't know where to start really, you left so abruptly.'

'And whose fault is that?' He snapped.

'Sorry, sorry. I wasn't trying to attach any blame. I just wanted to say that I am sorry for my outburst and I shouldn't have let it end as it did. I wanted to apologise and ask you to come back to work.'

'Too late, Alistair. I've moved on and I am enjoying myself, thank you very much,' not even attempting to hide his sarcasm.

'Oh, well, can we at least be civil to each other? I'm coming down for the weekend in a fortnight and I don't want mother to be upset or find out what has really happened.'

'I bet you don't, and anyway, I am working for them doing the garden for the next couple of weeks and they are fine. I'll stay out of your way when you are here. Going to see Lucy?' He just couldn't help himself but he had to be sure. There was a pause.

'No, I won't be seeing Lucy. I took her out to apologise, we are just friends,' he paused again, '...but I had hoped that we might have a drink in the pub.' Bertie held back, *lost them both,* he thought to himself. He glanced around at the garden and the sky feeling a pang of regret too, they had been good friends for ten years. Was he going to let it all end like this?

'Maybe,' he said, 'now I must go as I have promised to clear this patch of ground before lunch. Molly is coming over with a quiche I think and we are having lunch with your mum and dad.' He couldn't help twisting the knife and closed his phone.

Bertie returned to his task grinning at the thought of Alistair having lost both women, probably, and comforted himself with the knowledge that he at least could claim to have them both as friends. He stopped his digging and sat on the low wall surrounding the vegetable garden and opened the box that Molly had given to him that morning. Inside, he found a packet of crisps, a chunk of bread and cheese as well as a slice of cake and a flask of coffee. He watched the birds swooping and singing their hearts out. He let the sun warm his face. 'How could I have been stuck behind a computer all these years when this is out here,' he asked the robin who was hopping nearby. 'No more desk jobs for me, this is just perfect.' He relaxed against the wall, enjoying the moment when a voice broke into his meditation.

'Hello, Bertie, I didn't know that you were working here?' He sat up with a start as if he had been caught out playing truant.

'Lucy,' he exclaimed, 'how lovely to see you.' He patted the stone wall next to him, 'Come and sit down. I've drunk all the coffee, I'm afraid.'

Lucy sat down obediently.

'I came to see Alice and George,' she said by way of explanation.

'They've gone out. George thought that Alice could manage a wander around the garden centre and a coffee. They won't be long, I'm sure.'

'Oh, that's alright. I don't mind sitting here in the sun and waiting.'

There was an awkward silence for a moment or two and then Lucy ventured, 'There is something that I don't understand, Bertie. Please tell me to mind my own business if you want to but what is it between you and Molly? Alistair knows the baby is his and yet, you seem to be the one looking after her. I suppose what I am trying to ask is if there is more to it.'

Bertie shuffled his feet then turning to Lucy, her eyes pleading, searching his. He fell into them with a passion and in one quick moment, his lips found hers, she responded eagerly and urgently. They kissed deeply and longingly unaware of everything and anyone around them. Lucy pulled away from Bertie, her eyes darting around his face.

'Please, Bertie, I understand even less now. What is happening?' He gently lifted her hand and kissed her finger tips each one in turn. 'I love you,' he said at last, 'that is what is happening.'

'But…'

'Shush,' he said as he tilted her chin and kissed her once more.

'We'll sort something out, do you love me?' Worry dropped from his mind and love swooped in to take its place. Lucy was looking anxious, her eyes racing around his face.

'Yes…yes, I think I do.'

Bertie put both arms around her and hugged her to him, she felt wonderful, she smelt wonderful; his life was wonderful. His life, but he didn't care what anyone else thought. He held on to her stroking her hair.

'I don't know is the answer, but I am so happy that you love me too. I thought that you were in love with Alistair and I was going to try and stand by Molly, you know help her out if I could even, though it broke my heart to think of you with Alistair.' Lucy smiled up at him with such love in her eyes.

'And I thought that the baby was yours and that I had lost you forever.' He hugged her again,

'You will never lose me.' They sat in silence for a moment.

'I should go. When will I see you?' Lucy stood up to leave and Bertie pulled her back.

'I'm not sure but please don't worry. Everything will be okay.'

'Okay. It doesn't stop me worrying though.' They stood up and Bertie put his arms around her pulling her close, kissing her once more.

'I'll call you,' he said. He watched her walk down the drive and wondered how he could return to work feeling so incredibly elated, happier than in a long, long time, no in forever. Lucy turned and waved to him, he was still watching her; he returned her wave and picked up his spade.

Chapter 26

Alistair edged his way down the lane as he could see someone walking slowly, head down. A gentle toot and he could see that it was Lucy, she appeared to be lost in her own world. He slowed to a stop beside her and lowered the window.

'Hello, Lucy, you look happy. Been to see Mum and Dad?' Lucy looked surprised to see him.

'Alistair! Err no, well I mean yes. Actually, no one was in. I saw Bertie, he's doing the garden for them. What are you doing here? Sorry, I mean that it's just that I never expected to see you mid-week.' A little smile crossed her lips and Alistair scanned her face puzzled.

'Are you alright?'

'I'm fine, isn't it a wonderful day?' Alistair stuck his head out of the car window and looked up at the sky.

'I suppose so. Look, I'm only here for the day. I have to get back to London tonight, but I'm glad to have bumped into you. I have arranged to come down for the weekend the week after next, would you have dinner with me?'

'I'm not sure, can I get back to you on that?'

'…Of course.' He smiled.

'See you then,' she waved at him as she walked up the lane leaving Alistair staring after her.

George opened the boot and popped in two trays of geraniums, two trays of petunias and two trays of primulas; he banged the lid shut shaking his head and tutting.

'What's the matter, George?'

'Just a little concerned, my dear, with all these plants.' He started the engine and let it idle. 'It's such a beautiful morning, my dear, pity to go home just yet. I thought that we might drive over the top of the Purbecks. It's so lovely up there and we could have a little walk if you feel like it?'

'Darling, what a wonderful thought. I would like that very much.' She squeezed his arm and George drove off down the road. It was, indeed, a beautiful day. They meandered over the top of the hills and stopped to admire the view before George turned the car in the direction of home.

'I think that's Lucy coming up the lane, George, pull over, will you?'

'Hello, my dear,' said George, 'how are you? Were you coming to see us?'

'Hello, yes. I've been down to the house and I saw Bertie. He said that you had gone to the garden centre.'

'Jump in, my dear, and I will put the kettle on,' encouraged George.

'Yes, please do,' said Alice, 'we can have a chat. I have a few questions to ask you.' Sensing danger, George turned to his wife.

'Come now dear, we don't want to be troubling Lucy with your questions; she's come to see you. It can wait, can't it?' Lucy glanced over at the house.

'Actually, thank you for your kind offer but Alistair has just driven down the lane, he is talking to Bertie,' she pointed in the general direction of the house. 'I will see you another day if you don't mind.'

'Alistair,' exclaimed Alice, 'I wonder what's wrong? Sorry, my dear, of course, we would love to see you perhaps tomorrow.' Lucy agreed and waved to them as George drove down the road. 'I hope that nothing is wrong, George. I'm

233

feeling quite worried now. Alistair never turns up without making arrangements first and never mid-week.'

'Please, Alice, don't upset yourself, we will find out soon enough. Perhaps, he just wanted to surprise us.' George could think of lots of reasons why Alistair would turn up like this but none of them were to surprise his mum. George gave a toot and both men turned to look. Bertie lifted his arm in greeting but Alistair did not look happy.

'Oh, dear George, something is wrong, very wrong, just look at Alistair.' George slowed to a stop and lowered the window.

'Alistair! What a lovely surprise.'

'Hello Mum, Dad, it's too nice a day to be cooped up in the office and I had some business to attend to, so I thought that I would stop by on my way to Dorchester.'

'That's wonderful, are you staying for lunch? Please say you'll stay.' Alice begged.

'Now, now dear leave him alone. Come on in, Son, and have a coffee with us. I'll just put the car away.' George dropped his wife by the front door before turning his car towards the garage. Excited about seeing Alistair so unexpectedly, Alice disappeared off to the kitchen. George noticed the look that passed between the two men and caught a snippet of conversation.

'This isn't over, Bertie,' he heard his son say as he watched them through his rear screen. Bertie shrugged, 'Suit yourself but I am not the one with the problem.' George returned to the house making straight for the terrace where Alistair was sitting with his coffee.

'Now that your mother is out of the way for a minute, are you going to tell me the real reason that you are here?' He hadn't a minute to lose. Alistair looked away across the garden and back at his father.

'I told you, I have business in Dorchester and thought that I would drop by.'

'Alistair, I'm your father,' he huffed, 'however, I respect your decision and trust that there isn't something that we should know. Now, are you staying to lunch, for your mother's sake?'

'Sorry, Dad, not this time.'

George conceded and turned his attention to a crowd of bluetits squabbling over the peanuts that he had put out that morning. He changed the subject when he saw his wife.

'Bertie is really getting on with the work in the garden, he's a Godsend; I don't know how we would have coped without him,'

'Oh yes, he is.' Turning to Alistair with obvious joy, she said, 'I have plenty of new potatoes to add to the salad, so please say you'll stay to lunch.' But as Alistair opened his mouth to reply, George jumped in to answer for him.

'Alistair is busy, my dear. We are lucky to see him at all. He will be back soon enough.'

'Ooh,' sighed Alice despondently, 'are you going straight back to London today?'

'I'm afraid so, Mum,' he smiled.

Alistair drove to Dorchester in no better mood than he had arrived, even more despondent if anything. His confrontation with Bertie, his own fault, had not gone well and he was at a loss as to what to do next. He did not have an appointment in Dorchester but decided to look at some property and have lunch at a very good pub, he had found up at Poundbury. He parked on the main street opposite an estate agent and walked across the road. Glancing not very purposefully in the window, he saw an office for rent with living accommodation above. He stared at it wondering if he should consider the move he had been promising himself. It wasn't exactly what he wanted. He had thought of investing in a little cottage to let out to holiday makers but maybe this would be a better investment. He ventured inside and sat down. The agent offered to take him there immediately, Alistair held back. Instead, he collected the details and continued to wander up the street looking in more agents' windows. The smell of fresh coffee enticed him into a little café and he sat in the window reading and re-reading the details of the office.

'What the hell…' he muttered and flipped open his phone. He arranged to meet the agent in half an hour giving him time to drink his coffee and drive up to Poundbury. He found the property and sitting outside, he perused a double fronted newly constructed property looking just like a Georgian town house. The front door led straight onto the street and there were two tubs with bay trees in them sitting either side of the door. He got out of his car and wandered around. Behind the house was a gate, unfortunately locked, and a separate garage; it looked very nice indeed, he could see himself here. The agent screeched to a halt in a cloud of dust apologising for being late. Alistair couldn't help but smile at this dishevelled youngster, his tie askew and with a dribble of his lunch on his jacket.

'Right,' he said, 'let's go in.' He unlocked the front door and indicated for Alistair to help himself to a look round and the young man began texting. Alistair opened cupboards and doors, looked upstairs at the accommodation and found himself standing by the window looking out at the view across Poundbury to the hills beyond. *What a lovely place, could I make it as successfully here?* He let his thoughts wander to his club in London, the theatre and finally Molly.

'What have I done? I will call her,' he half smiled to himself forgetting all about the young lad.

'Pardon?' asked the still scruffy young man with his phone firmly in his palm.

'Attached to your body, is it?'

'Sorry…' he replied. Alistair smiled.

236

'I would like to find out more about the lease.'

'I've brought a full copy with me,' proudly handing Alistair the lease and redeeming himself a little.

'Great. Do you mind if I go and have my lunch and read this through, and meet me here again in say two hours, that will give me time to speak to my solicitor.'

'No, not at all. I have someone else looking later today anyway.' Appointment made, Alistair retreated to the pub for a pint of ale, a ploughman's lunch and some reading. Lunch over, he spoke to his accountant, his solicitor and finally, the agent for his property in London; making lots of notes and writing down unanswered questions to tackle the agent with later.

He returned to the property, left his car and walked around the streets nearby. There were other business premises and a sign announcing a new supermarket, it all looked very busy. He looked for evidence of any other financial services company but couldn't find any, at least he wouldn't have any competition and judging by the cost of property in the area, people would have money to invest. Everything appeared to be going well, at least on the business front. He made his way back to his car and found the agent waiting. His tie straight this time and all evidence of his lunch had been removed. They went into the property with the agent conducting him around, selling the merits of the premises. Altogether different this time, now that he thought Alistair might be a real customer. Alistair didn't need any convincing but he asked questions and put a proposal to him offering less than the asking price and placing some restrictions of his own. The poor young lad was at a loss and said that he would have to discuss it with his manager and the landlord; they would be back in touch as soon as possible. The agent made to drive away and Alistair paused.

'I thought that you were showing someone else around today?'

'Ooh,' he replied, 'they cancelled.' And drove off.

'…Thought so,' smiled Alistair. He set off to London feeling more confident and relaxed, getting his life back on track. He leaned over to put on a CD; losing control, he swerved and skidded off the road and into a ditch.

Chapter 27

Molly arrived with lunch. She slowed to a stop beside Bertie waving to him.

'How is it going?'

'My back aches,' he stretched putting both hands on the small of his back. '…But not bad. Alistair turned up this morning, he gave me a real verbal going over,' Bertie leaned onto his spade gazing at her.

'What! What did he say? Why would he turn up like that? What did he want?'

'Slow down,' Bertie grinned. 'He doesn't know anything. I rather think that he was plain, old-fashioned jealous that I am working in the garden for his parents and that we are having lunch with them, with probably a good dose of guilt, too.'

'You're probably right, that sounds like Alistair; he always wants to be the one making the decisions and he hates anything happening without his knowledge.'

'He loves you, you know. Otherwise, he wouldn't be so angry.'

Molly made no reply, she found it hard to believe if he loved her. Why had he never said so? And why had he been so off-hand about the baby? Acting as if he couldn't care less what she did or with whom. None of it made sense.

'I'll see you up at the house. Give us ten minutes and then lunch will be ready.' She set off again and parked in the bay to the side of the house, retrieving her basket from the car just as George opened the front door.

'Let me carry that for you. It's far too heavy for someone in your condition.'

'Thanks,' she said, 'how's Alice?'

'Come on in and find out for yourself. She's in the kitchen waiting for you.'

Molly found Alice busy with a bowl of salad and a large pan of baby new potatoes. She kissed her on the cheek.

'You are looking so much better, Alice. How are you feeling?'

'Marvellous, my dear and I am looking forward to a chat over lunch. Did George tell you that Alistair popped by this morning on his way to Dorchester and some business meeting?'

'No, but Bertie did.' Quickly realising that they did not know about the confrontation between Alistair and Bertie, she casually asked, 'Is everything alright with Alistair?'

'Yes, I think so. You know him, he never gives much away.'

'That's true. Do you want to warm the quiche? I only made it this morning but you might want to pop it into the oven for ten minutes.'

'No, I don't think so. Everything is ready, we only need Bertie to come in and we can eat.' The door to the boot room opened behind her. 'Right on time,' beamed Alice. Over lunch, they chatted about the garden and the weather keeping off the subject of Alistair. Inevitably, Molly knew that Alice would have to ask.

'You're looking very well,' ventured Alice. 'How are things with the baby?'

'Fine, I'm doing just fine. I have my first scan next week and then I will feel a lot better.'

'We didn't have scans in my day, I wish they had; it is marvellous to see a new life inside you. Don't you think so, Bertie?' He coughed and shot a look at Molly.

'Err yes, I suppose so. I must be getting back to the garden though…' he pushed his chair back as if to leave.

'You can't start work just yet, on a full stomach,' George interrupted, 'come out and sit on the terrace with me. We can have a cup of tea before you start work again.' Soon enough, the girls arrived with Alice carrying in a plate of biscuits followed by Molly with the tea tray; both men jumped up to take the tray from Molly but George got there first.

'Now you two, I thought that I might take this opportunity to ask you something.'

Molly felt an instant panic, she began to feel a prickle all over looking worriedly in the direction of Bertie.

'I'll help if I can,' he cleared his throat.

'Good. Now I want to know the truth about this whole business.' Bertie sat squarer in his seat.

'You really ought to ask Alistair.'

'No, I'm asking you and please, I want the truth.' Bertie took a deep breath glancing quickly at Molly.

'I left because Alistair sacked me.'

'Well, I gathered that much and not from Alistair, but I want to know why after all these years? What happened?' Molly gulped as she stared at Bertie.

'…Well, firstly, he knew that I would have to leave soon as I am moving down here to work with Molly,' he paused but George made no comment and continued, '…and to be fair, Alistair did ask me back but then we decided that he would make me redundant as he is planning a possible move himself.'

'Mm…that does sound more likely but I don't understand why there is such a secret being made of it all, and I want to know what that was all about this morning.'

'He'll tell us soon enough, George, and I'm sure that Bertie wouldn't want to break a confidence,' smiled Alice.

'No, that's right. You know how Alistair likes to surprise people.' Molly was grateful for a change in the conversation.

241

Bertie hadn't lied even if he hadn't told the whole truth either. Alice launched once more onto her favourite subject of babies asking Bertie his opinion on breast feeding and nappy changing, sharing the role as she put it.

'Whoa, out of my depth here, Alice. Must get back to the garden.'

'...And I will take care of the washing up, dear. You talk to Molly.'

'Did you know that Lucy dropped by this morning when we were out?' She smiled sweetly at Molly.

'No, is she alright? I must give her a call later.' Molly sipped her tea and picked up a chocolate biscuit.

'Then Alistair turning up out of the blue. What a pity, everyone couldn't have stayed for lunch, don't you think?' *She is a canny old bird, she is trying every which way she can think of to provoke me into opening up but it is not going to work, no sir.* Alice waited politely sipping her tea.

'Bertie told me that Alistair had made a quick visit, but if you are going to ask me about his mystery trip to Dorchester, I'm sorry but I have no idea.' Molly gave a short and forced laugh as she had been wondering the same thing.

'...And Lucy?' queried Alice.

'To be honest, I don't think that Lucy will know either, but you could ask her; she wants Bertie to help her with some decorating and he has offered to help after he has done your garden, of course.' They both sat quietly before Alice appeared to remember something.

'By the way, Molly dear, Alistair is coming for the weekend soon and I mentioned to Lucy about her and you and Bertie, of course, joining us for a meal one night. She seemed to think that it was a good idea but suggested that you two girls do the catering, everyone thinks that I am helpless, I could do it myself but George won't hear of it.' Molly swallowed hard, it

242

was sweet of Alice but she had no idea how awkward it would be for everyone.

'I agree with Lucy, but why don't we have a day out on the beach? We could have a picnic. We can use Mum's beach hut down at Studland.'

'What a lovely idea, Molly. That would be marvellous.'

Molly returned to the farm, determined to do some gardening herself but as she drove along the lane, she decided to visit Lucy. She pulled over and opened her phone,

'Hi, are you busy?'

'Actually, I'm at the house doing some cleaning as I've finished work for the day, but you are welcome to come and see my new abode.'

'Great, I'll pick up some coffee and cakes. See you in about 20 minutes, is that alright?'

'Sure, see you later.' Molly soon arrived with the refreshments and they wandered outside where Lucy had placed two folding chairs and set up a box as a makeshift table with a duster over the top onto the patio. She surveyed the garden, it was overgrown with brambles, nettles and with some sort of tree in the middle covered in pink blossom. It could be an apple or a cherry.

'This looks lovely and at least you will have plenty of blackberries this year if nothing else,' she mused. Lucy was grinning way too much for Molly.

'Is there anything I should know?'

'...Definitely not,' she fussed with the chairs, turning them towards the sun. 'I saw Alistair this morning on my way back from the Warrens,' Molly changed the subject.

'I've brought your favourite coffee. You look as if you need it.'

'Thanks, come and sit down, I need a break.' They talked about gardens and laughed at all the pies and crumbles that

Lucy would be able to make from the blackberries and learned that the tree was probably an apple. The subject turned to Bertie with Molly suggesting that as Bertie would not be at the Warrens' on Saturday, perhaps, he could help Lucy with some of the heavier work with Molly promising to make dinner back at the farm afterwards.

'Thank you, there is so much that I can't manage on my own. If you're not busy one day next week, maybe you could come with me to choose some paint and wallpaper?'

'I would love to. Oh, and by the way, I spoke to Alice about this meal that you mentioned. However, we are going to have a picnic down at Studland instead.' She paused and reflected on the old days when it was her and Alistair having secret meetings, riding out together and making love in the fields surrounded by buttercups and song thrushes. Lucy snapped her fingers.

'Hey, Molly…where have you gone?'

'Sorry, I was remembering the many good times that I had with Alistair, but it's over now.' She chewed her lip and Lucy squeezed her hand saying nothing.

Molly reluctantly returned to her office and sat staring at the heap of paperwork in front of her; VAT returns not her strong point. She shuffled them once more and prepared to make a final check. She pushed her chair back and headed for the kitchen, weariness flooding over her, she scooped her hair back into a pony tail and made a cup of camomile tea, coffee tasted odd these days. She inspected her one overnight patient, a rabbit with long floppy ears and returned to her desk. An urgent sounding knock startled her. She glanced at the clock, it was way past closing time; but never able to resist an injured animal, she opened the door.

'Alistair! What are you doing here?' He was leaning on the door jamb holding his head. There was a streak of blood on the back of his hand. 'What happened to you? Come in and let me take a look at you.'

'Thank God you were here, Molly,' he leaned on her shoulder as she led him to a chair. Molly collected swabs, scissors and dressings and listened to Alistair as he recounted his incident with a deer on the road and how he had swerved, ending up in a ditch.

'Well, no real damage done, just a dent in your ego,' she mused. 'How about the deer? Was he okay?'

'I think so. He just leapt over the hedge and disappeared.'

'I'll make you a cup of tea. You look a bit shaken and then you can tell me about your trip to Dorchester,' her voice trailed off as she disappeared. With a mug of hot, sweet tea in his hand, Alistair looked at Molly with big hound dog eyes but Molly strengthened her resolve and turned to look at the unfinished paperwork still sitting on her desk. 'You don't have to tell me, force of habit to ask, that's all.'

'Molly, look...I'm so sorry,' he picked up her hand and gently stroked her fingers. 'I've always been honest with you about things, keeping my life secret from mother. She just pushes and pushes wanting me to "settle down" and...Molly...I miss you.' Desire raced through her body like red hot molten iron; she tried hard to move her hand but it stubbornly refused to budge even an inch from beneath his touch. She let him talk. 'I am such an idiot, I thought that you and Bertie, well you know and then, I sacked him. I should never have done that, it was more than stupid but I couldn't bear the thought of you and him,' he glanced up at her face. Molly let her eyes speak for her. She pulled the band from her hair letting her curls tumble around her face. Alistair was on his feet. They pulled at each other's clothes as their lips melded into one, paper and pens flew onto the floor as the need overtook them. When he finally entered her, Molly's body was screaming with desire and love. 'You always did look sexy in that uniform,' he grinned at her as he enveloped her closely to him. Her phone beeped and Molly groaned.

'That's my reminder to go home, Mum will be wondering where I am. I was supposed to do my VAT tonight.'

'Come on, I'll help you,' he slid his hand around the back of her neck gently pulling her to him, kissing her forehead, her nose and her fingertips.

'Stop before I can't,' she bit her lip, holding back on saying more.

'Okay, if you're sure, I have to get back to London tonight, too. Can I call you tomorrow?'

'Sure…' Alistair disappeared leaving Molly wondering yet again what turn her life was taking. She locked the door and turned to leave when an idea struck her. There was an old barn attached to the surgery that she had planned to turn into an extended practise one day. It was single storey with a pitched roof, the beams were solid and she could see the sky where some of the tiles had slipped off the roof. She patted her tummy.

'I think that we have just found our new home, little one,' she grinned to herself.

Chapter 28

Bertie tapped gently on the door of Lucy's new home; she opened it in a flash and he forced himself to resist the temptation to sweep her up there and then on the doorstep.

'Hi,' she beamed. Bertie was lolloping on the door frame grinning at her stupidly.

'Hi' was all he could manage to say. He had been waiting for this very moment all week and it felt as though it would never come. Lucy closed the door behind them and Bertie turned to look at her, his arms swooping around her, their lips finding each other hungrily. There was no need to say a word. He scooped her up and carried her upstairs, kissing her eyes, her lips, her hair. He laid her gently onto her bed and unbuttoned her shirt, caressed her curves with his tongue; she pulled him to her, feeling his need as much as she felt her own. They entwined in a move of such love and power fulfilling their desire for each other.

It was the phone buzzing that disturbed them from satiated slumber. Lucy picked it up, suddenly wide awake, she turned and stared at Bertie.

'It's Molly. I will have to answer it.' She grinned tracing his jaw line with her finger. He jumped out of bed.

'Of course, you go ahead.' He leant over and kissed her forehead as she flipped it open. Lucy grinned at him, desperately trying to stifle a giggle as Bertie stood before her revealing his manhood in all its glory.

'Great,' she managed to say as she waved at Bertie to leave the room, throwing a pillow at him still trying to smother another fit of the giggles.

'Sorry, Molly,' she said finally, 'yes, we are getting on very well. What are you doing today?' Bertie knelt on the bed and massaged her shoulders, mesmerised at the way goose bumps slowly covered her body. 'No problem, Molly…and thanks,' she flipped her cell shut. 'Molly will be here in half an hour. She's bringing sandwiches and we haven't done anything yet.'

'Oh, I don't know,' said Bertie twiddling her hair. She gave him a gentle nudge and jumped off the bed.

Bertie and Lucy set into the task of demolishing the stud wall with renewed vigour, nothing could spoil the high that they were feeling; it came crashing down, covering them with dust. As the dust cleared, Bertie began shovelling debris into a wheelbarrow and out to the skip. Lucy opened all the windows to help clear the air before Molly arrived; she dusted some garden chairs and created a makeshift table just in time as Molly knocked on the front door.

'You have been busy,' she exclaimed, 'things are looking good.'

'Yes, they are looking very good,' Bertie turned to Lucy catching her eye. She began to explain to Molly her plans about the new kitchen with bi-fold doors onto the garden. The bathroom was serviceable till she could afford to change it to white from avocado and she was planning to move in as soon as the decorating and kitchen were finished.

'How long do you think that will take?' asked Molly as she opened her basket pulling out crisps, vegetable sticks and hummus.

'Well, it depends on my job interview next week. I need to get back into full time work as soon as possible. The house is becoming a money pit,' she grinned. 'The hardest job was this wall and thanks to Bertie, things are moving. I shall soon be able to get the plasterer and fitter in.' Turning to Bertie, 'if you could help me again, especially with the decorating, that would speed things up,' her eyes twinkled with mischief.

'Oh, I think that I could manage that.'

Molly moved across to Bertie pulling out a tissue, 'You've got dust in your eyes,' she said and gently wiped his face with a tenderness that surprised him; his face contorted for a second as he saw Lucy clench her fists before turning to look into the picnic basket.

'That's better,' she smiled at him, 'now let's eat.' Bertie glanced over at Lucy only to see the back of her head and her shoulders shake. He wished that he could scoop her up again and hold her close, smooth her hair and tell her that everything would be alright.

'I'm ravenous after all that work, what have you got in there, Molly?' he asked over his shoulder whilst pulling out a slice of quiche and tucking into it. Lucy washed up three mugs and made the tea.

'This is a lovely spot, Lucy,' Molly ventured, 'very handy for the shops and you could walk to the station at a push.'

'Yes. I'm very pleased with it actually and to get parking is great.' They chatted about trivia in a slightly awkward fashion and Bertie continued his exploration of the food basket.

'You're quiet,' said Molly. Bertie had just taken another mouthful of carrot cake and pointed to his mouth indicating that he couldn't speak and tried to grin.

'Sorry,' he spluttered, 'I'm enjoying this food and thinking about how much I can achieve this afternoon. What have you got in mind for us to do?' he said to Lucy looking at her with affection. She flushed pink coughing slightly.

'Well, I was hoping to clear out all this rubbish and make a start on removing the old units.'

'I think that we could manage that,' he replied, 'what time is dinner, Molly?' he asked turning to look at Molly only to find her looking rather downcast. She straightened up with a fixed smile.

'If you could be back by six, I'll have dinner ready for seven. How does that sound? I need to call Alistair and then maybe we can have a chat.'

'Good idea.'

'That was a delicious lunch. Thanks, Molly.' Lucy began to repack the basket with the detritus and collected the empty mugs. 'See you later.'

Molly collected her things and as she walked back to her Land Rover, Bertie was sure that he detected tears in her eyes. Bertie and Lucy sat looking at each other with silly grins plastered on their faces. They had today. Bertie stood up opening his arms, gesturing to Lucy who needed no excuse. She leapt up and snuggled up to him, they kissed that was all that was needed. They began working again in earnest, determination pushing them on; once Lucy could move in and away from her parents' home, they could be together undisturbed. Bertie could see Lucy looking him over from the corner of her eye, scanning his body, tracing the shape of him. He felt desire spreading through him like fire but pushed it back. Later, Lucy carried two mugs of steaming tea into what would become her sitting room.

'Tea up,' she announced. Bertie placed his hands onto the small of his back stretching, he moaned.

'It's really taking shape. What are you thinking of doing about this old fireplace?' He took a dark chocolate biscuit and began munching and pointing at the tiled 1950s hearth in a hideous shade of silvery blue.

'I was thinking of ripping it out and putting a wood burner in, what do you think?'

'Great idea, it will heat this place up a treat. I'll make a start on that in a minute, might as well do it now and fill up that skip.' Lucy spotted a biscuit crumb on the corner of his mouth and with her finger, knocked it away smearing the chocolate. She stood on her tiptoes and licked it away.

'Mm, that was good.' Bertie could resist no longer; he lifted her up and kissed her over and over again, his lips urgently seeking hers. She took his hand and led him upstairs.

''I'm filthy,' he said. 'I will make your bed dirty.'

'Who cares?' she replied lifting off her top once more.

Six o'clock arrived and Bertie forced himself to leave Lucy and return to the farm. Molly was waiting for him with a can of ice cold beer; he slid onto a chair and gulped it down. His mind wandered to Lucy and what she might be doing right now…he was becoming aroused.

'What are you thinking about, Bertie? Bertie!' she teased.

'What? Err, can I have another beer?' he shook the can and tossed it into the rubbish bin.

'Sure. I was just saying that I couldn't get hold of Alistair today and I wanted to tell you something.' She passed him another can nudging his arm and Bertie dragged himself back form far away in Lucy's bed.

'What? Sorry, missed that bit. I'm so tired and I need a shower; see you in a bit, then we can talk properly.' He got up from the table and dragged himself upstairs still feeling aroused, simultaneously happy and anxious. Crunch time was coming and not soon enough for him, why did everything have to be so complicated? Feeling clean and refreshed, he returned to the kitchen with all hope of talking to Molly gone; Lucy was sitting at the table looking gorgeous, sipping a white wine, he felt aroused again. He stuffed his hands into his pockets scrunching his shoulders around in circles.

'Hi, I used to think that I worked hard in London but today…now that was hard work.' He continued to circle his shoulders fighting the urge to touch her. Lucy smiled.

'Thanks for today,' she winked, wrinkling her cute little nose; she was alive with electricity and buzzing with energy. Bertie could feel it from across the room, he tore his eyes away.

'No problem. I'm exhausted and starving.' He rubbed his hands together. Both girls laughed.

'Men,' said Molly, 'they are all the same. Actually, I've been thinking, Bertie, that you should have a day off tomorrow. I have something that I want to show you, maybe have lunch out, what do you think?' Bertie's mouth dropped open for a second, stunned. He could feel Lucy's eyes boring into the back of his head.

'Err, I suppose so,' he stumbled. 'I, err, hadn't really thought about it.'

'Well, we've got to make a start as these things don't happen very quickly and the sooner you get premises, the sooner you can get your venture off the ground.'

'Yes, okay, you're right. Only I planned to do that after Oz.'

'Oz?' squeaked Lucy spinning her head in his direction, 'I didn't know that you were thinking of going over there so soon…and for a month,' shock registering on her face.

'It's all happened so quickly. I wasn't expecting to be sacked and well, it seemed like the best option at the time, and I do need to get earning and soon.'

'What about the money from George?' asked Molly glancing at him as she picked up a wooden spoon to stir the sauce.

'It's not very much to be honest—better than nothing—I know and I appreciate it, of course, but if I don't go soon, it could be years before I get another chance,' he paused looking down at his hands and tapping his fingers together.

'I can pay you a little for the work that you are doing for me,' Lucy ventured. Bertie turned and beamed at her, he reached over and squeezed her hand.

'I couldn't take money from you and anyway, the pleasure was all mine. I will do what I can for you in the next few weeks but then well, I'll have to see how things pan out.' He caressed the back of her hand with his thumb.

'Perhaps Alistair will help, too,' suggested Molly. 'I'm sure that he would love to.' Lucy pulled her hand away and walked over to the stove.

'Molly, that smells delicious. Can I do anything to help?'

'Nearly ready, you could get the green salad out of the fridge for me if you like and the cream.' Lucy retrieved the salad and placed the bowl onto the table; Bertie followed her to the fridge, helping himself to another cold beer. Her eyes looked pleadingly at him, he so wanted to touch her. They sat down together to a companionable meal, chatting about the progress on the house and Molly telling tales about piglets and the dog who had swallowed a sock. The conversation steered towards Alistair.

'I hope that you are not going to too much trouble for our picnic with the Warrens',' enquired Lucy. Molly began to reel off one or two ideas.

'Everything sounds good to me,' said Bertie as he tucked into another piece of pie, 'it's a lot of work though, why not just keep it simple?'

'I want to make something special for Alis...' Molly broke off glancing at the other two.

'That's alright, Molly,' said Lucy, 'we both know how much you love him. Don't you think it's time you two either got together or break it off...? This is not doing you any good.' They fell quiet. Bertie stopped breathing, for one second, he thought that Lucy was going to blurt it out about them. Molly looked from one to the other, the strain clearly showing.

'Actually, I tried to call him earlier. He must be in a meeting or something, it went straight to voicemail.'

'Why not try again now? Bertie and I will wash up,' turning to Bertie, 'won't we?'

'…of course. Come on, Molly, I think that you are wrong about Alistair. You should clear the air, get some things sorted out.' Bertie could see her distress and gave her a hug, kissing the top of her head.

'Okay. You're right, here goes,' she went upstairs to her room and closed the door.

The evening sunshine was streaming into the kitchen through the open, stable door cutting into the atmosphere that had built up within. Bertie grabbed hold of Lucy around the waist pulling her to him, smothering her in kisses. She pushed him away gently and began collecting plates. Bertie groaned and stretched, his back aching, but to no avail, washing up duty beckoned. He ambled to the sink rolling up his sleeves, memo to self to buy a dishwasher, he grinned. He was soon immersed in suds up to his elbows flicking bubbles at Lucy. She picked up a dish, dried it and as she passed him, she tweaked his bum. Bertie jumped in surprise, a plate slid from his hand onto the stone flagged floor, smashing it to pieces. Rex shot out of the open door. Lucy didn't try to smother her amusement, just giggled. Bertie wanted to grab her and whisk her upstairs but settled for a grin mouthing, 'Ouch.'

Molly picked up her phone and called Stella looking for support.

'Good, you should have done that before,' said Stella. 'You might as well tell him everything, get it out in the open so that you know where you stand. Call me back later and tell me how it went.' There was silence. 'Molly?' Molly sniffed unable to hold her emotions in check. 'I'm sorry, luv, but no matter what happens, we are here to help. Now, go and call him.' She rang off.

Molly curled up on her bed in the foetal position sobbing, she felt so alone. *What is the worst that can happen?* She asked herself, *come on, this is not like you. What has happened to your 'I can do anything' attitude?* She picked up her phone just as it began to buzz. It was Alistair. Sometime later, Molly joined the others back in the kitchen. She had repaired her make-up and felt ready to face them.

'Let's take our dessert outside,' suggested Molly. 'It is such a lovely evening and I've made a strawberry cheesecake and there is a jug of cream too, then we can have a coffee.'

'Good idea.' They both looked at her and then at each other making Molly smile as she knew how desperate they were to know what happened. Bertie picked up the dishes and cut the cheesecake into three rather large slices.

'No, no, Bertie, that's too much. Here let me do it,' Lucy took the cake slice from him.

'I forgot, you two eat such small helpings, I didn't think.' He poured a good slug of cream into his dish, picked up a spoon and wandered outside. Molly tried over and over how to tell them about her conversation with Alistair but nothing sounded right. It was Bertie who asked first, he just waded in.

'So, come on then, what did he say?' Molly had a large juicy strawberry poised a drop of cream hung on the bottom of her spoon then splashed into her bowl.

'Not much actually, he wants to talk, wanted to know how much you two knew and I told him that you know everything.' She looked from one to the other but neither of them spoke, she took a deep breath and carried on, '...He's coming down tomorrow, he wants to talk about it face to face. I told him that he doesn't need to feel obligated as I can take care of myself.' She saw the look that passed between Bertie and Lucy. 'You don't have to worry about me either you know, I've been making some plans of my own.' Bertie wrapped his arms around her, she snuggled her head into his shoulder as she sobbed.

Chapter 29

The next day, Bertie, as good as his word, drove around looking for business premises for the café. They drove, passed one after another crossing some off and keeping a few on the 'possible' list. Molly had packed another picnic lunch with boxes of salad, fruit, an onion tart and the remains of the cheesecake from the night before. They stopped on the top of Ridgeway where the rolling hills gave way to the sea in the distance. Bertie put up a table and two chairs as Molly spread out the food and bottled water.

'We are like an old married couple,' declared Molly. Bertie nearly choked

'You should let me take you out to lunch. There's a perfectly good pub down the road and I haven't had chips for ages.' They both laughed. There was a gentle breeze blowing swirling Molly's curls around her face. A bee buzzed by and settled on some flowers delving from one to another, Bertie watched with fascination.

'That's Tyneham down there. Do you remember visiting it when you first came to Dorset?' Molly was pointing to a cluster of tumbling down cottages in the bottom of the valley.

'Yes, I do. It is a special place, the whole of Dorset, I mean.' He tried to relax and taking a deep breath thought that this was as good a time as he was going to get.

'Molly...'

'Yes.'

'Molly, I've been thinking and I want to tell you something.'

'What's that? It sounds serious whatever it is,' interjected Molly sitting upright in her chair.

'I know that Alistair will be here this afternoon and I thought that you should know before you see him that Lucy and I, what I mean is that I really like her and well, we...' Molly jumped in with a chuckle.

'I know, Bertie. I could see it yesterday in you both and I'm really pleased for you.'

'You are?' he stared back at her.

'Of course. I was wondering when you would say something.' Bertie scrunched up his empty packet of crisps and threw it at her. 'Lucy is my best friend and I couldn't be happier for you both. Whatever happens today, with Alistair I mean, will you come with me to explain it to George and Alice?'

'...Course I will. They will be fine, you'll see, even if Alistair is not.' Molly burst into tears, she grabbed a tissue and tried to stop the flow but it was no good. Bertie jumped up and put his arms around her, Molly sobbed and sobbed. She blew her nose and dried her eyes but made no effort to remove herself from his arms. Feeling safe and warm, protected, it felt good to be entwined within them. Bertie remained motionless holding her tight. She lifted her head, a broad smile spreading across her face, she grabbed his hand and placed it on her swelling bump.

'Feel that? The baby is starting to move, isn't it wonderful?' She looked up at him once more planting a kiss on his cheek. 'Thanks, Bertie.'

'...What for?'

'Just being you.'

They cleared up the table and headed back to the farm. Alistair was waiting.

The following day, Bertie returned to the Warrens and continued with his gardening. Alice, now well on the road to recovery, with George still keeping a close eye on her, limiting her exploits to coffee making and a supervisory role. George became more of a 'labourer' to Bertie constantly collecting weeds for the compost and stacking up the clippings from the shrubs in order to have a bonfire. Bertie was used to George's continuous praise and thanks for his efforts putting it down to that; that was their way of accepting help, albeit paid help, in the garden, as if it was some sort of admission of defeat on their part. The day passed quickly with thoughts of seeing Lucy and her waiting embrace; he desperately wanted to see her. He pulled onto her drive and the front door flew open. Lucy was smiling, looking radiantly happy.

'Come on in quickly,' she said and gently took hold of the front of his shirt and tugged him inside. He kicked the door shut behind him as Lucy threw herself into his arms. They hungrily kissed, desire sweeping over them. All other thoughts forgotten, they ran up the stairs disrobing as they went. They fell into bed and entwined with urgent deep fulfilling love, finally falling exhausted side by side. Bertie raised himself onto one elbow and traced a finger over her chin, her eyes, her ears; he pushed a strand of hair back from her face and kissed her deeply. His hands found her breasts and cupping each in turn, he kissed and licked her nipples, hard and pointed. He slowly moved down her body kissing her soft delicate skin, resting his eyes on her mound now lifting towards him, her back arched. She opened her legs ready to receive him and in one swift movement, they joined together in a joyous rhythm. Sitting now with a mug of tea, they sat up in bed gazing at each other.

'Come on, tell me how it went, I haven't heard from Molly today so tell me everything.' Bertie recounted the events of the previous day.

'What about when you told her about us?' said Lucy, her eyes wide in expectation.

'Well,' he paused and sipped his tea. 'She had already guessed, which is good and then I left her with Alistair.'

'What happened next?'

'When I got up this morning, the house was quiet. I took Rex for a walk and went to work. So, I don't know anymore.'

'So, what happens now?'

'Well…I have told her to tell Alistair that we are together. She asked me to leave it with her as she wasn't sure how things would go but yes, she would tell him.'

'I hope you're right. I can't keep our secret much longer. I want the whole world to know.'

'We will have to wait, just till Molly has…' Lucy turned on him, her face contorted, no tears, just anger.

'Let me get this straight, we have to carry on with this charade for how long…and because you feel sorry for her, what?' She was incredulous and Bertie knew she was right.

'No, that's not it at all,' he tried to explain but Lucy wasn't listening.

She screamed at him, 'You came here, made love to me as if you love me and all the time you are still, what? What are you still doing, Bertie? Tell me.' Lucy was now shouting.

'No darling, it's not like that. It's just until Alistair knows the truth. I do love you, I love you so much and I want to be with you but…'

'…But not enough. That's it, isn't it? You're just like other men. You think that you can have us both, is that it? Well, I'm sorry but it is just not going to happen.' She threw back the bedclothes and started to pull on her underwear. 'Get out,' she said without looking at him, 'get out, I never want to see you again.' Bertie put down his mug and leapt over the bed and tried to put his arms around her. She pushed him away.

'Please, Lucy, please stop. Listen to me, you've got it wrong.' She beat her fists onto his chest in frustration, tears now rolling down her cheeks, she struggled to free herself but he held on tight.

'No, let me go. I don't want to see you again. How could you do this to me?'

'I'm sorry, Lucy. Truly, I am and I love you, I love you,' he said again stroking back her hair. He became aware of his nakedness and the closeness of Lucy meant that he was becoming aroused, he couldn't help himself. Lucy relaxed a little in his arms and he kissed her, she returned his kisses, he kissed her tears licking them away.

She nuzzled up to him and let out a low moan, pulling away again, she said, 'No, go away.'

He held on to her, there was no way he was going to lose her now. He lifted her chin up to him, 'Look at me...please.' She lifted her eyes to his. 'I love you and only you. Please believe me, it won't be for much longer, I promise.'

Chapter 30

The last couple of weeks had flown by and Alistair was on his way. Molly had said nothing to Bertie or Lucy about the outcome of her visit from Alistair, all went on as usual. Tensions were high between Molly and Lucy; Molly hated keeping her friend in the dark and despite Lucy's attempts to find out what was happening, she had remained tight lipped. The sun was shining and the sky had that clear turquoise brightness about it without even a wisp of cloud to spoil it. It was indeed a glorious day for relaxing on the beach at Studland. She packed up the food and had arranged to meet Lucy down at the beach hut. Bertie continued to work in the garden with George and Molly had asked him to cut a few roses to bring down to the beach too.

'…For a picnic at a beach hut?' he asked his eyes popping out, making her laugh.

'Yes, please, they are Alice's favourite flowers and they will look nice.'

'Okay,' he had said with a shrug.

Up early, Alistair had calls to make; his life was taking a different, more exciting turn. His negotiations had gone well and the paperwork had arrived for him to peruse before he committed himself to giving up London and taking on a new challenge in Dorchester. He had sleepless nights, tossing and turning about making the right decisions for himself as well as Molly.

He pressed the button on his phone for Molly and quickly stopped it again, he had promised not to call this morning. He tried to stay calm and made a coffee resisting the urge to top it up with his usual whisky. He opened a bag and put in a few essentials; on top, he placed a small red leather box. Picking it up again, he opened it for the thousandth time, a smile playing on his lips. He felt like the happiest man alive, snapping it shut, placing it back once more. With a satisfied twitch on the corner of his mouth, he picked up the contract and sat down trying to spot anything he may have missed before. There were drawings of the development and a scale plan of the property that would soon be his. He read through the impressive list of other business enterprises at Poundbury, there was a definite need for his talents in Dorset, he would make a killing. He closed the file and wondered why he hadn't done it before, flashes of his brother, his parents and Molly flooded his brain and he knew why; but that was history, a new life awaited him. Alistair picked up his bag and headed for the door. Leaving London behind, his mood lightened and he decided to take the long way down to Purbeck, he had plenty of time. He drove through the wild Hampshire countryside driving carefully around the ponies that roamed free everywhere. Stopping at one of his favourite pubs for a sandwich, he wondered what was happening in Trentmouth but resisted the temptation to call. He absently sat twirling his pint round and round, watching the amber nectar with vacant eyes. From nowhere, his mind took him back to that awful night when he had knocked Lucy from her horse. *What a nightmare.*

'Another pint,' came the voice of the barman breaking into his thoughts, 'only you have been looking deep into that one for a long time, you alright?'

Alistair downed the last mouthful and looked around.

'I'm fine, thanks, just going. I was remembering my previous visits here, a long time ago, it seems.'

'I thought that I'd seen you before. How's your young lady?' Alistair took a step back in surprise.

'My young lady is, err,' he stammered, '...is getting married.'

'Sorry, mate, me and my big mouth.' He picked up a cloth wiping the non-existent drips from the bar.

'Don't worry about it,' he raised his hand to signal his departure. '...Thanks again.'

He stepped out into the fresh air and took a deep breath. 'Here goes,' he said as he looked up into the blue sky. He drove into the nearest town and made straight for a coffee shop, any would do, he just needed a shot of pure caffeine. Feeling better, he bought a huge bunch of flowers for Alice remembering the last time he had stood here when Bertie had bought flowers not only for Alice but Molly and Lucy too; he certainly knew how to get the girls...and it worked. He turned back into the shop and bought two bunches of red roses, two can play at that game, a smug grin threatening to take over his face.

With renewed energy, in part the caffeine, he set out once more to Trentmouth, even putting the top down on his car. *This is the life*, he thought and turned on the radio, relaxed, carefree. He turned into the lane that led down to his parent's house, stopping in the gateway to view the scene in the valley below. He sped on and tore up the drive, stones flying everywhere, he was happy. *I have always wanted to do that, announce my arrival so to speak,* he laughed aloud. As he leapt from his car, his mother opened the front door and ran to him with her arms open wide. He groaned inside but allowed her to smother him with a kiss and a hug.

'Alistair,' she exclaimed, 'I'm so happy to see you. How was the journey? Come on in, you're just in time.'

'Just a minute, Mother,' he disentangled himself from his mother's grip and pulled the flowers from the car.

'My favourites,' she beamed and rushed off to put them in water. He picked up the roses and set off to find the two most precious women that he wanted to keep in his life. The terrace was the obvious place and sure enough, they were sitting in the shade enjoying homemade lemonade, his mother's speciality. The girls stood up to greet him. Lucy planted a kiss on his cheek and accepted the roses. Alistair turned to Molly, she had put on weight and there was a distinct bump under her dress now. His throat closed up, constricted by the sight of her, seeing her in all her glory, mother to be and looking radiant. He speechlessly held out the flowers, he would have preferred to cover her in kisses.

'Hello, Alistair, thank you.' She held out her hand and took the flowers.

'Aren't you going to kiss me?' He flushed pink but leaned in kissing her lightly on the cheek, her scent took him straight back to the days and wonderful nights that they had spent together; he wanted to drink her in, touch her and caress her but he pulled himself back.

'How are you? Do you need to sit down?'

He didn't know what to say.

'I'm not an invalid,' smiled Molly, 'just going to have a baby.' She stroked her bump with pride, thinking, *say hello to daddy*, but instead she looked up at Alistair and said, 'I'm fine, doing very well actually. What about you?'

'Me! I'm a nervous wreck, to be honest.' He paused. '...Aren't we supposed to be going down to Studland?' he whispered.

Molly grinned. This Molly was different, the same but oh, so very different. George appeared on the terrace just as Molly retreated indoors.

'Alistair, my boy, how good to see you.' George marched up the steps onto the terrace, hand outstretched. They shook hands like business acquaintances. Bertie was close behind, following his father up onto the terrace, his smile faded but he lifted his hand and shook his.

'Bertie.'

'Alistair.' It was enough, for now, the two men eyed each other. Alistair blinked in the sunlight, he shaded his eyes.

'You alright?' asked Bertie.

'Yes, it's hot, that's all.' He removed his jacket and looked out over the once glorious garden, his mother's pride and joy.

'You're doing a good job; Mother has been telling me all about it.' He felt ridiculous engaging in small talk, but he did not know how to talk to his once long-term friend anymore. George came back with a glass of lemonade. Alistair saw the smirk on Bertie's face but ignored it.

'Sit down for five minutes here in the shade, my boy. The women are fussing in the kitchen but the cars are packed, ready when you are.' Bertie looked down at his dirty hands and disappeared indoors.

'Look, Alistair, now that no one else is around, I want to get to the bottom of this nonsense. Tell me what is going on?'

Alistair looked at his father taking a sip of lemonade. He smiled, 'Sorry, Dad, you will have to wait. All will be revealed later.'

'I don't like disharmony and I don't like your mother upset and another thing, I definitely do not want any trouble tonight. Your mother has gone to a lot of effort, she is looking forward to this evening and the last thing I want is for you to cause any more concern for her, so just remember, you are to be on your absolute best behaviour.'

Alistair felt like he was ten years old again but he took his ticking off and just smiled, he couldn't let George in on any of it just yet. George slapped his hands on his knees, got up and went indoors. Left alone, Alistair let his mind return to the glorious days of meeting Molly in secret, visiting the theatre together when she was able to get to London and horse riding over the hills, walking the horses through the surf on the beach and making love in the sand dunes. He leant back in his deck chair, eyes closed, smiling to himself.

'Hey, you had better wake up, Alistair.' A soft voice broke into his reverie, he opened his eyes to see Lucy standing in front of him. He sat up quickly dragging himself forward to this moment, he put out his hand and squeezed hers. Lucy looked fazed, a twitch played on his lips. She smoothed her hair and cleared her throat.

'Molly told me that you are going to be making some sort of announcement this evening,' her eyes searching his.

'Yes, that's right,' giving nothing away, 'I just thought that as we will all be together for once, it might be a good time. How's the house coming on? I'd love to see it sometime.' Molly strolled out through the French doors.

'Come on you two, everyone is waiting.'

'Oh right, sorry, we were just chatting.' They followed Molly to the kitchen. George and Bertie emerged from the boot room picking up the baskets that Alice had prepared, filled with all manner of goodies from pork pie to quiche, salads, fresh bread and cheeses, all covered with yellow gingham checked cloths.

'My, my,' said Alistair, 'this looks good.' They all trooped out to the cars and set off down to Studland. Alistair kept an eye on Molly's Land Rover, his father chatting beside him; he looked at his mother in the back of his car thinking perhaps I have made the right decision after all, this move will be good. I have missed all this and somehow, I have got to try and put things right with Bertie.

'Actually,' began George, 'I, I mean we have something to tell you, Alistair,' he paused glancing at Alice, '...and rather than tell you tonight and possibly steal your thunder, I thought that we should tell you this afternoon.' Alice beamed at him affectionately.

'Okay, Dad, what's the problem.'

'No problem, it's just that as your mother has been rather ill this year and well, the truth is that I have been very worried about her and thought that it was time for us to take a holiday.' Alistair breathed a sigh of relief.

'It's about time,' he muttered. 'So where are you going?' directing his gaze at Alice.

'Your father has finally agreed to go on a cruise; in fact, we are going next week for two weeks up to the Norwegian Fjords.'

'I thought that you said that you would never go on a boat,' said Alistair.

'It's what your mother has always wanted and life's too short, my boy, to be difficult and anyway, it will make your mother very happy, so why not?'

'Brilliant and I'll bet the girls will want to whisk you off to the shops for some new clothes and stuff.' He chuckled.

'I'm looking forward to it. There is a lovely boutique in Dorchester that I've always wanted to go into. It will be fun.'

They arrived at the car park and began unloading the baskets for the short walk down to the beach hut. Alice walked with Molly and Lucy, Alistair could hear the excited chatter as Alice was telling them all about their forthcoming cruise.

'Look at her,' George said to Alistair, 'when have you seen her happier?'

'I don't know,' replied Alistair. 'I've never really thought about it before.'

'...And of course, you haven't forgotten that it is our Ruby Wedding Anniversary coming up soon, have you?'

Alistair shot a look at his father and gave a quick glance over to his mother. 'Well, yes actually, I don't remember these things, what do I know about wedding anniversaries? Sorry, Dad, I'll think of something.' Alistair caught sight of Bertie and in that moment, he felt a real pang of regret, especially so seeing how happy the girls were together. He watched as Bertie took the basket from Molly, saying something to her, which had elicited a gentle nudge to his arm.

The beach huts were all painted in different candy floss colours, with lots of families sitting in deck chairs and children on the beach. There was a buzz of excitement, castles being built and boats launched into the bay. As they neared the hut, Alistair shaded his eyes to see if his other surprise had arrived and sure enough, there sat Molly's parents with a carer adjusting her father's oxygen bottle. Molly had spotted them too and she speeded up along the beach. Alistair felt contented as he watched the hugs and cries of laughter from them all. They unloaded the bags and baskets and the boys set about putting up chairs and tables. It was the best possible day, the sun shining out of a crystal blue sky and the only time ever that the two families had been together. Further down the beach was a small marquee with a white arbour entwined with flowers. A few people were gathered around looking to see what was going on; there were a few chairs in front of the marquee and the faint sound of music. Alistair looked at his watch. He opened a bottle of sparkling elderflower and poured out eight glasses.

'What's happening?' asked Alice as she looked at the commotion unfolding down the beach.

'The National Trust now has a license to conduct weddings on the beach, didn't you know?' Molly informed her.

'No, I didn't know, how lovely.' She stood on tiptoes trying to see what was happening.

Alistair picked up his glass taking a deep breath; he smiled at Molly holding out his hand; she took it, their fingers entwined.

'Mum, Dad…you're going to be grandparents.' He looked into Molly's eyes and they kissed ever so lightly.

'What!' exclaimed Alice, 'I can't believe it, George, George, did you hear that?' She put her arms around Alistair and Molly in turn, kissing them both. George shook hands with Alistair and kissed Molly. He hugged his wife saying, 'It's wonderful, my dear, just wonderful, but I am confused, what about Bertie? We thought that...well, we don't know what to think.' He shook his head looking baffled. There were hugs and kisses all round with Molly's mum giving her a gentle telling off for keeping them in the dark.

'George, Alice, it's a relief that you finally know and we can all stop pretending. I am just happy for Alistair and Molly. Congratulations to the two or should I say three of you.' Bertie raised a glass.

'When are you getting married?' asked Alice giddy with joy, '...or, or shouldn't I ask.'

'It's alright,' laughed Alistair. 'Right now, in fact'. Glass in hand, he waved towards the marquee on the beach.

'...Right now? You mean here...on the beach, now?'

'Yes, Mother, just as soon as you put a rose in your button hole. Bertie mate, will you do the honours and be my best man?' He took two rings from his pocket. Bertie stepped forward and shook his hand.

'Too right, mate, I'd be delighted.'

Lucy and Molly were laughing and hugging each other. Lucy tucked a rose into Molly's hair. George stood back and Molly caught his eye.

'George, I would be honoured if you would push Dad's chair down the aisle so that he can give me away,' she smiled touching his arm, Alistair choked back a smile.

'I would be delighted, my dear, the honour is all mine,' said George.

They all set off along the beach towards the marquee, the registrar standing and waiting. As they approached, the music began to play; Bertie slipped his arm around Lucy's waist pulling her to him and kissed her.

'Fancy a trip to Australia?' he asked.

'Yes, oh yes, please,' she replied.

The End